Michael B McLarnon

SOPHIA

by Michael Trelissic

I wish to dedicate this book to my family, to members of my writing group, past and present and to Paulene

Copyright© 2022 Michael Trelissic

*to my good friends
Mary and Bill
with Love,
Michael*

Michael B McLarnon

Love Story

PROLOGUE

It is very rare indeed for a love to be so present that everyone and everything that surrounds it fades into an irrelevance. Even the boundaries, set from your early years, collapse into nothingness as your very soul merges with that one other, that moment when a flower first senses the sun and opens, revealing its beauty and fragrance, to receive the worship it was created for, like a pure bride receiving her husband.

CHAPTER 1

The soft keys of Moonlight sonata flowed through the open doors of the conservatory, blessing the gardens as though led by a colourful, fragile butterfly.

Michael stopped by the flowering cherry tree and observed as he listened. He knew that Sophia was unaware of his presence, evident from the way she played. Should he back away and disappear the way he had come, across the lawns and over the walls of the estate? No, he had come this far and anyway he had nothing to lose. Yes, he was not of her class but this was 1963 for goodness sake. He wouldn't be horse whipped for having the temerity to approach and speak to her, even though technically he was trespassing.

Sensing rather than knowing that the tune was in its final stages he braced and approached the French Windows and showed himself as she raised her hands from the keys.

"Miss Sophia." he stammered.

One might have expected the young lady to shout out in alarm but she didn't

"Hello." she said in a in a calm feminine way as though she had been in casual conversation with a friend.

Michael expected more, like "What do you want or how did you get here?" but she just turned on the revolving stool and looked at him and smiled. She wore a summers dress of pastel flowers which flowed to just beneath her knees.

Had Michael been wearing a cap he would have removed it by now and would unconsciously have screwed it up in his sweating hands. But he wasn't, so he just nervously swept back his fair hair.

"Miss Sophia, I was wandering if you would like to come to a dance at the village hall next Saturday night?"

"With you, you mean?" she asked.

Michael couldn't believe he had got thus far without being ejected from the grounds but he still wasn't brave enough to just say yes, so he stammered.

"Well, a few of my friends are going and I just wondered if you would like to, to come with us?"

"I'd love to." she replied without hesitation and accompanied it with a beautiful, wide smile.

"O.K." said Michael, clearly surprised at her answer. And then turning to go Sophia called.

"Hold on."

Michael knew it was too good to be true, here comes the belated excuse.

But not so. "What's your name?"

"Oh." he said "It's Michael."

"How do you know my name?", she asked in a quiet undemanding way.

"Oh." he said.

"Yes, you called me Sophia."

"Ah, everyone knows your name. You're the girl from Hazelhurst Manor who goes to church every Sunday."

"Do you go also?"

"What me?" he laughed

"Why do you laugh?" she asked her expression changing not to a frown but to a curious expression.

"Well, its church isn't it." replied Michael cutting short his snigger when he saw Sophia's expression had turned into a frown.

"I tell you what Michael." she said considering how she was going to continue. "I'll come to the dance with you on Saturday if you promise to come to church with me on Sunday."

Sophia held her gaze as she waited for a reply

Michael was confused, didn't everyone their age snigger when church was mentioned? Perhaps it was everyone except Sophia.

"Well, if you don't want to find out more about me, that's fine." she said turning back to the piano.

"Oh, it's not that." protested Michael, "it's just that I don't know anything about church."

He was beginning to get the feeling that he was going to lose her when he had only just found her.

"Well Michael," she said turning to face him. "I don't know anything about your friends and the dance you've invited me to."

"Well, it's just a dance with a local band, they're called Jimmy's Rock and Roll Band."

"I've never heard of them." she replied flatly.

"You'll love them, they are talking about making a record."

"You'll love our new vicar, he's lovely." she retorted.

"Michael recognised the position he was in. There was no way he could get Sophia to come to the dance unless he agreed to go to church with her.

"Can we keep it secret?" he said at last.

"You mean, me coming to the dance with you?" she teased.

"No." he exclaimed, " the bit about me coming to church?"

"It's a deal." said Sophia with a huge smile, rising to shake hands.

Her hand was soft and clean, Michael thought, not like his poor mothers.

"Well then, I'll see you outside the hall at eight" he said.

"You're not coming to collect me then?" she asked, knowing full well that she was setting Michael another challenge.

"You mean at the front door?"

"Well, I don't expect you to climb over the wall." knowing that was probably the way he had come today.

"Do I have to, can't we just meet there, at the hall."

"We could but that would mean you had me at a disadvantage."

"How do you mean?"

"Well, I would have to approach the hall on my own, not knowing anyone and you would be stood outside with your friends looking."

"I see what you mean Miss Sophia. O.K. I'll come here and pick you up at a quarter to eight."

"Great, I'll see you on Saturday then. Oh, and Michael for goodness sake don't call me Miss Sophia, it's just Sophia."

Michael ran back across the lawns feeling a mixture of excitement and fear. He felt as though he could jump the seven-foot wall, but the excitement was too much and he stopped for a pee behind a great oak.

Hazelhurst Manor was situated on a hill that gave a view of the whole town. As Michael made his way home, he thought he could pick out his house set out on its own at the far end, next to farm land. It was far too big for just the two of them but it was taken on when his father was alive. Hearing the church bell strike five he started to run, his mother would be wondering where he was. Tea would be ready and she would have to leave for work soon.

"Hurry up love, sit down, your tea was ready five minutes ago, it's no good if it's cold."

"Sorry mum, I got held up."

"Alright love." she said retrieving his plate from the oven with a tea towel wrapped around her hand and placing it on the wooden table.

"I'd better be off. I'll be home by half past nine. Don't forget your homework."

"Oh mum, it's Friday night."

"Never mind that." she said as she opened the front door to leave. " It will mean you have the weekend free."

Michael turned to the plate of fish, chips and peas thinking she was right, it would leave the weekend free and also please his mother. She had been so proud when she received the letter from school saying that Michael was a talented lad and should stay on to take O levels. He found the homework easy but inevitably his thoughts drifted to tomorrow night and the lovely girl he had long admired from a distance. He guessed she was the same age as him but he couldn't tell for sure as she went to the grammar school and before that a private school in the city.

"Still at it?" asked his mother when she arrived home at a quarter to ten.

The old, tin, wind up alarm clock woke Michael at 7 a.m. as it was intended to. He had had a restless night thinking about his date with Sophia. Had he done the right thing? His mates would tease him mercilessly. How should he behave? Should he be a gentleman and pay for her to get in to the dance? and once inside would he have to sit with her and buy her drinks? It was two shillings at the door and his Saturday job wage wouldn't go much further than that, may be one drink.

And what about dancing? could she jive like the rest of us or would she want to do the waltz or something like that? Oh hell, it's going to be a nightmare, he would never live it down. And all this before going to church the very next morning. Oh God, what have I done?

"Michael. "called his mother from the bottom of the stairs. "You are going to be late for the shop."

He worked at the rear of the greengrocer's shop in the town breaking up the empty boxes. It was good money, ten bob no matter how many or few the boxes were.

"Coming mum." he said as he flew down the stairs, his hand sliding along the banister rail.

CHAPTER 2

The day went quickly and before he knew it Michael was in the bathroom getting ready for his date. He dressed himself more carefully than he normally did, choosing his red shirt with open neck and his new black trousers. He decided not to risk shaving, he didn't want to cut himself again like last month. After splashing himself with copious amounts of the after shave his aunty Lena had bought him last Christmas, he rushed downstairs and cleaned and polished his only pair of shoes, they were brown. Snapping the lace Michael threaded the longest piece back through half of the eyes and fastened them into a small bow.

Michael's mother appeared behind him in the hallway and smiled at him through the mirror.

"Got a date love?" she asked coughing from the effects of the aftershave.

"Not really mum. It's just a dare sort of thing." he said blushing a little.

Mum stared fondly at her son. He was growing up so fast. He was the image of his late father. Suppressing a tear, she brushed his shoulders nervously.

"What do you mean son? a dare."

"Well, a couple of the lads dared me to ask her out."

"Ask who out?" she asked firmly

Bowing his head, which is something he did when he wasn't sure, if what he was doing was the right thing, he replied.

"The girl from the manor house." he said quietly. "Miss Sophia."

Mum covered her mouth in shock or surprise. Michael wasn't sure which.

"And does the poor girl know you asked her out for a dare?"

"No mum." he replied lowering his head even further.

"Michael, this isn't like you. When she finds out, and she will, she will be so humiliated."

"I'm sorry mum, it started out as a dare but when I met her and asked her, I really liked her and anyway I'm going to be punished for it."

"How do you mean son." asked mum softening her stance.

"Well, when I asked her to come to the dance tonight, she said she would if I promised to go to church with her the next morning."

Mum laughed. "Oh, I like this girl, good for her."

"But mum."

"It'll do you good Michael, anyway it won't do you any harm."

As he turned to leave, mum asked.

"Aren't you a bit early?"

"I promised I'd call for her."

"At the big house?" mum asked incredulously.

Michael nodded and his mum started to giggle. Yes giggle, he thought later. It suited her pretty face. He loved her so much.

"Hello." called Michael timidly through the intercom at the tall metal gates.

"Yes?" came a firm reply eventually. The voice was cold and old like that of his headmaster.

"I've come to pick up Miss Sophia for the dance."
"And who shall I say is calling?"
"Michael."
"Michael who?" came back the austere enquiry
"Michael Flynn sir."

The brief formal exchange was followed by a good five-minute silence.

Michael was about to press the intercom once more when a sharp buzzing sound came from the locks on the side gate and it slowly opened. Proceeding through an avenue of poplar trees which took him a good fifteen minutes he eventually emerged onto a wide gravel road which surrounded the imposing four story Georgian manor house. There was a series of stone steps in the middle leading to the double door entrance. They were open. Standing there, twelve steps above him he recognised Miss Sophia with a middle-aged man who he guessed was her father. He was dressed in green trousers and tweed jacket whilst she wore a yellow dress with matching scarf tied loosely around her neck. She looked gorgeous.

"Good evening young man. I hear you are taking my daughter to a dance with a rock n roll band playing."

"Yes sir, is that alright sir?" he replied nervously stroking back his hair once more.

"I suppose it will have to be; my daughter is strong willed." he replied smiling back at his daughter.

"Oh daddy," she half shouted, "You are so embarrassing."

Michael looked up at father and daughter high above him and wondered if they thought how far below, he was. Perhaps she coming out with him was mildly amusing to his lordship and a way of connecting with his tenants in the town.

But then she ran down the steps and linked him as though he were a familiar old friend.

"I'm so excited about the dance." she cried tightening her grip on his arm.

"Good." was all he managed to reply leading her off across the gravel road.

"Hold on." she said "Daddy's taking us in the car.

"Oh, right." he thought. He had seen the jaguar pass through the town many times but never dreamed he would ever get to see and feel it from the inside.

The sleek bottle green car pulled up beside them and an elderly chauffer stepped out and held the door to allow Sophia's father to take the driver's seat. He guessed the chauffer was the man on the other end of the intercom.

"Come on " said Sophia pulling Michael towards the rear door.

The seats were made of dark green leather and the thick pile carpet contrasted with his brown shoes. The smell of the leather competed with the that of his aftershave and made him slightly nauseous. Sophia again linked his arm and confided she was a bit nervous.

"There's no need to worry." reassured Michael, "I'll look after you.

Lord Lympstone could hear the conversation in the back and felt reassured.

"This seemed a pleasant lad, even if there was no future their relationship."

Once clear of the gravel road the car sped along the tarmac down to the village and stopped by the church.

"Is this alright?" he said bringing the car to a halt

"Phew." thought Michael, thankful he hadn't stopped outside the hall. He noticed the clock on the magnificent dashboard said that it was just 8 p.m.

It was a warm June evening and still light as the couple walked around the corner towards the village hall. As soon as the jaguar was out of sight, he uncoupled the link Sophia had once more locked him in as he felt sure his mates would be outside waiting for his arrival. Stopping abruptly, he turned to Sophia.

"I have a confession to make." he said looking into her lovely face desperately hoping that she wouldn't instantly terminate their relationship.

Sophia looked back into his earnest young face, all at once no longer in charge and looking apprehensive.

"Go on then." she said softly, all of a sudden, looking apprehensive.

"I need to tell you something. I." Unable to finish he was desperately grateful for the distraction when it came.

"Michael." It was his mother's voice calling as she was approaching the church grounds.

On any other occasion he would have been sorely embarrassed, but not today.

"Oh mum." he cried in sheer joyous relief. "What are you doing here?

"I was just passing. Who is this delightful young lady?"

"Oh right." answered Michael "This is Sophia, a new friend."

"Pleased to meet you love, I'm Rachel Flynn, Michael's mother." she said holding out her hand.

"Pleased to meet you Mrs Flynn." said Sophia with a smile as she took her hand. Feeling the roughness of Rachel's skin against her soft manicured hand said a lot about both ladies. They instantly liked each other.

"I take it my son is taking you to the dance Sophia."

"Yes, I'm really excited." replied Sophia still holding onto to Rachel's hand.

"Well don't let his mates intimidate you. This is the first time Michael has taken anyone to the dance and you are sure to be the centre of attention and the object of a bit of teasing if I know them."

"Thank you, Mrs Flynn, I'll bear that in mind."

"I'm glad he has asked you out at last, I know he has wanted to for some time and in the end, I hear one of his friends had to dare him to ask you."

"Really" said Sophia turning to Michael. "Is that what you wanted to confess?"

"Sort of."

"Well, I'm glad you did." said Sophia taking his hand, glad that his mother had neutralised a situation that could have led to an abrupt end to their brief relationship.

"Well, its lovely to have met you Sophia." said Rachel as she started to leave. "And Oh, I'll make sure Michael is up bright and early tomorrow for church."

Turning the corner, the hall came into view and sure enough there were half a dozen lads stood outside. Seeing the couple approach the tallest called out,

looking not at him but at his female companion.

"Mike, you're late." followed rapidly with "You did it, is this Miss Sophia?"

"I'm sorry." said Sophia "My fault. You must be the lad who dared Michael here to ask me out. What's your name?"

"Tom." came the meek reply.

"Well thank you Tom." said Sophia her confidence leaving her audience dumb. "As a reward, you may have the first dance."

Taking his hand, she led Tom into the hall where the band was playing Jailhouse Rock.

Any worries Michael may have had about her ability to jive were immediately dispelled as he watched, together with the rest of the hall, Sophia danced around Tom, her skirt twirling almost constantly. He looked at her in awe, is there anything this girl can't do? The bar was empty as everyone was watching Sophia dancing so Michael pulled out the remaining coins from his pocket. After giving his mum four shillings housekeeping and paying the entrance fee, he had two bob left, enough to buy soft drinks. After the dance with Tom, Sophia searched for Michael in the crowded hall and eventually found him carrying drinks to a table at the back of the hall.

"Oh, I enjoyed that." she said breathlessly as she joined him.

"I got you a coke." he said "Is that alright?"

Not waiting for an answer, he asked "Where did you learn to dance like that?

"At my ballet lessons." she replied between sips.

"That wasn't ballet." laughed Michael.

"I know that silly." she laughed back. Our teacher thought it would be good for us to diversify so that the ballet didn't get too onerous."

Michael smiled back not really knowing what onerous meant.

"So, you jived with other girls?" he asked.

"Yes, and with the boys although there weren't as many of them as girls."

Michael coughed as his drink went down the wrong way. The thought of boys at ballet lessons had never occurred to him.

"Are you alright?" she asked.

"Yes, I'm fine." he said.

"Would you like to do Ballet Michael?"

She was serious, he thought as he looked at her face.

"I don't think so." he said

"You're smirking again. " said Sophia showing her serious face once more.

"I'm sorry, what I mean is that I'm not a very good dancer."

"Let's put that you the test then, you can't be worse than Tom."

"No one is worse than Tom." thought Michael as he allowed Sophia to lead him onto the dance floor. The band were playing Hello Mary Lou, his current favourite. She suited his style very well and the pair danced without any mistakes or misunderstandings. Michael suspected she adapted to his style very well and at the end a few couples applauded their performance.

Returning to the table he noticed that their glasses were almost empty. Once more he needn't have worried.

"Same again?" asked Sophia smiling.

The lighting at this end of the hall was dim compared to the bright lights on the small stage. Johnny and his rock n roll band were playing a ballad and the floor was almost empty. Looking across to the bar he could see Sophia in conversation with a couple of Teddy Boys who seemed to be pressurising her. Quickly rising he hurried over and asked if she were alright. He didn't recognise the older lads; they weren't from the town.

"It's alright Michael, I was just explaining to the boys here that I'm a bit tired and don't want to dance."

Michael stared at the taller of Teddy Boys as they looked at him smirking.

It seemed like an age but then Tom and half a dozen mates who had seen what was happening and lined up behind Michael.

"Just as well we prefer dancing with our mates." said the shorter of the two Teddy boys as he shouldered Michael as they turned away.

Sophia thanked Michael's friends as the couple returned to their table.

Sitting on his hands waiting for them to stop shaking he asked Sophia several times if she was alright but then noticing that a crowd was surrounding the dance floor, the pair approached.

The two Teddy Boys had been joined by another six and they were dancing in an exclusive circle to a fast tune, Jungle Rock. Each dancer wore a different coloured suit, red, yellow, blue, green, orange, purple, black and cream. All had different coloured psychedelic socks with beetle crusher shoes and Michael had to admit it they looked impressive. Sophia was dancing holding his hand and absolutely enjoying herself, all thoughts of the recent altercation forgotten. The time flew and when Sophia's watch told her it was 10 o'clock she was genuinely shocked.

"Michael, I've got to go, daddy will be waiting for me outside." she shouted over the music.

This was the first he had heard that her dad was picking her up and the disappointment showed on his face.

Sophia rushed to the exit and before he could say anything she was gone. Following her outside he was just in time to see the door of the jaguar slam shut and the car speed away. He was still staring into the distance when he joined by his best friend Tom.

"She was quite something." said Tom. "Shame she's left early."

"Yes." agreed Michael wondering if that was it, the end of a brief acquaintance.

"Are you seeing her again?" asked Tom.

"Not sure." he replied. "She wants me to go to church with her in the morning."

"And are you?" asked his friend without any hint of a snigger. "I would, she's a smasher."

"Yes, she is." sighed Tom.

CHAPTER 3

Michael woke early from a dreamless night wondering about this new feeling he was having. All he could think about was Sophia. Is this what was called love? he wondered. If it is, it was uncomfortable. Why did she leave the dance last night in such a panic? Was she afraid of her dad? He seemed alright; a bit posh but so was Sophia.

The sound of the church bells ringing reminded him that he was due to meet the object of his new feelings at ten o'clock. His mother answered his unspoken question by shouting up the stairs that it was half past nine and he needed to get ready for church. Looking in the bathroom mirror he decided that he didn't need a shave but a little aftershave wouldn't do any harm.

"Have a nice morning love." called his mother as he left the house in a rush.

Looking at her son's untouched breakfast, she hoped he wouldn't get hurt. If it were just the two of them it would be fine but it never is and the gulf between her family and his was great.

Michael struggled with his tie as he tried to straighten it against the collar of his new white shirt that had appeared in his wardrobe that morning.

"Thanks mum." he thought as he approached the gates leading to the church. " I wonder how much it had cost her."

The green jaguar approached. Feeling awkward Michael strode along the path towards the young vicar waiting outside the church.

It was a beautiful day and the setting was perfect, an ancient old church set in colourful gardens and aging gravestones. But hearing car doors slamming behind him Michael felt that he had walked into a trap, the vicar in front and Sophia's family behind.

"Hello young man." called the vicar. "I don't believe we have met." he said offering an outstretched hand.

Taking the hand Michael felt his heart thumping in his chest.

And then to his relief he recognised Sophia's voice behind him saying

"I see you two have met. Good morning reverend."

She was with her dad, whom he recognised and an elderly lady.

"Good morning, Michael " said dad in a formal voice "This is my mother; mother this is the young man who took her dancing last evening."

The old lady offered a stiff, gloved hand. "Young man." she said stiffly in a cool, upper-class accent.

Getting the impression that she had taken an instant dislike to him, Michael brushed back his hair, as he always did when nervous, He took her hand without shaking it.

Sophia approached Michael, straightening his tie before linking her grandmother, and proceeded to enter the church leaving her father and Michael to follow. The vicar led the party to their private pew with gate at the front of the church. Michael was the last to enter and sat between the gate and his Lordship. Looking down at his brown shoes, one of which was still tied with the broken lace he felt decidedly underdressed even though he was wearing his best black trousers, freshly pressed by his mum. In contrast Sophie's father was dressed in a light grey suit and looked immaculate.

As the organ started to play from the rear, Michael turned to look and saw Mrs Murray looking straight back at him from the pew behind. If things couldn't get any worse, news of him would be all over the village by lunch time. Surprisingly though, he was gripped by the sermon about the elderly lady quietly putting everything she had into the collection, whilst the Pharisees made a great show of putting in what they could easily spare. It made him think of his mother and what on earth he was doing in this company. As much as he liked Sophia, loved her, he was fooling himself if he thought it would go anywhere.

As the family chatted with the vicar at the end of the service, Michael mumbled that he had to be somewhere and then slipped away, turning to take a last longing look at the girl of his dreams. She wasn't looking.

Two weeks passed and although Michael thought about his lost love every day, he had resigned himself to never seeing her again, from close up anyway. Mum had noticed her son's sadness but decided not to mention it, it was probably for the best. It was Saturday morning and after sharing the breakfast table he set off for his job at the shop as usual. The morning was uneventful and Michael had decided to carry on with his homework when he got home. The front door was slightly open and he heard a conversation taking place in the living room. His mum was laughing with another voice he recognised, it was Sophia's. Heart pounding, he pushed the door open. His mum beamed at him.

"You've got a visitor love."

Sophia turned on the upright chair.

"Hello Michael." she said in a soft voice still smiling.

"I'll leave you two alone." said his mum rising from her chair. "There's tea in the pot." nodding towards the table. "I'll see you later love, I might have to work a bit late"

Taken by surprise Michael sat and looked at Sophia. As always, she was dressed beautifully, this time in a flowered dress and blue flat shoes.

"I've been thinking about you." she said. "You left rather abruptly after church and I haven't heard from you since.

"Did you want to, "he asked

"What do you mean Michael? Yes of course I wanted to." she said. "What was it? Did something upset you?"

"The truth is." he said lowering his head giving him a good view of his shoes which were now fastened with two broken laces. "I don't think I fit in."

"I don't understand." she said pulling her chair forward and taking his hand in hers and lifting his head with the other, so that the couple were looking directly into each other's faces.

Realising there was no way she was going to let him avoid her gaze, he looked straight into her eyes and spoke.

"I really like you Sophia, I like you so much I didn't want to cause any problems with your family.

"How do you mean?"

"Alright then, you are forcing me to say it. It's the class differences."

Sophia was an intelligent girl and immediately understood, but then asked.

"Did you mean it when you said that you really liked me?"

"Yes, I do but."

Before he could finish his sentence, Sophia leaned forward and kissed him full on the mouth for a full five seconds.

"And I really like you, Michael," she said breathlessly.

The kiss and the way she said his name made Michael tingle all over and he kissed her back causing them both to overbalance and end up on the linoleum floor, which even in summer, was cold, but it didn't stop either of them from laughing.

"I'll make another pot of tea." said Michael, climbing back to his feet and heading towards the kitchen.

Sophia followed, bringing the empty cups and saucers. Michael noticed that his mum had used her best china for her visitor.

"Does this mean we shall continue to see each other?" Michael asked in a quiet voice.

"What do you think?" she replied smiling. "Do you think I go around kissing everyone I have no intention of ever seeing again?"

"What about what I said about the differences in our families. "

"We'll deal with that as we go along."

"And your dad and his mother?"

"Well, gran was only here for the weekend rarely visits. As for my dad, well, as I said we'll deal with everything as we go along."

"I haven't met your mum, what's she like?"

"My nan says she was the loveliest person who ever lived." replied Sophia looking sad and lowering her head.

"I'm sorry." said Michael. "My dad, I am told was also a lovely man." he said, wanting to hold her, but suddenly felt afraid to.

It didn't matter as Sophia stepped up and held him saying. "That sort of makes us equals."

That quiet moment was only interrupted by the old kettle whistling.

The young couple spent the next two hours talking about their likes and dislikes in music as Michael showed off his modest collection of 45 rpm records and his pride and joy, his new Dansette record player. When it was time to go Sophia once again kissed him and then reaching into her bag said

"Oh, I nearly forgot, I've brought you this little gift."

She handed him a small brown paper bag.

"I've written my phone number on the bag. I'll expect a call in the week. "

she said, and then she was gone.

Sitting on the chair by the table Michael was in a daze. Today was the first time he had been kissed by a girl, and what a kiss. Dreaming, it was a full five minutes before he opened the bag, he smiled, it was a new pair of brown shoe laces.

Telephones were few and far between. They were usually owned by priests and doctors, there were very few in private homes and none at all in Church Street where Michael lived with his mother in their rented cottage.

"I'll expect a call in the week." she had said so this being Wednesday he checked the number of pennies in his pocket and then set off for the telephone box on the corner of the adjoining street. He had never made a phone call before apart from dialling the operator for a laugh with his mates. But this was serious and he was alone.

After a couple of failed attempts, he finally
heard the ringing tone at the other end. The call was eventually answered by a firm, posh male voice.

"Hazelhurst Manor."

It was the voice of the man who had given him such a hard time when he used the intercom at the main gate. Urgent pips hammered down the telephone as he hastily pressed the button with the large A and heard his four coins fall into the belly of the black box.

"Could I speak to Miss Sophia?" he asked timidly.

"Miss Sophia is unavailable." came the curt reply.

Disappointed and four pennies poorer Michael retreated, later feeling that he had been lied to by a person who had been instructed to do so.Never the less he tried ringing again on Thursday and Friday but he was again rejected in the same curt manner. Feeling frustrated and hurt, he mused that he was now down by twelve pennies, a whole shilling. But he was in love, so he wasn't about to give up without one final try so on Sunday he rose early intending to go to church. His plan, which he had turned over in his mind many times the day and long night before, was to confront Sophia to ask if she had really given instructions for his calls to be rejected. But it was raining hard, so he delayed his departure to the last minute before setting off at a run in his best trousers and only jacket. By the time he reached the church porch he was saturated and late. His plan had been to intercept Sophia on her way into church but that had not been possible because of the heavy rain. His shoes with the new brown laces leaked and as he entered the church, he squelched his way to the first empty pew under the distaining stare of Mrs Murray and most of the congregation. To make matters worse the vicar paused his address and spoke directly to Michael.

"It's good to see you, young man but perhaps you had better trot off home and dry off."

That sentence uttered by the vicar in front of the whole congregation was the reason Michael would never go to that church again. Before he squelched his way back down the aisle past the smirking Mrs Murray, Michael glanced at the pew Sophia and her family had occupied with him just two weeks ago, it was empty.

The following week Michael came down with a heavy cold and missed school. His mother dosed him with aspirin and cough mixture every morning before sending him back to bed and going to work. By the Thursday, she knew there was something more than just the cold that was bothering him and sitting on his bed said.

"What is it love, you're still not pining for that girl, are you?"

"No mum, it's just the way that man spoke to me, he made me feel really bad, like I was nothing."

Seeing the tears welling up in her son's eyes she hugged him saying, "We'll talk about it later." and left for work with a heavy heart. She herself had been snubbed many times by people who thought they were better than her but she was not going to stand for her son to be treated like that, not while she had breath in her body. The lord of the manner may own her house and most of the town but he did not own her and he definitely didn't own her son.

By Friday morning Rachel knew what she was going to do. Her plan was to confront his lordship next time he came to the Town Hall which he did on the final working day of each month at lunchtime. She chose that moment because she knew Michael would be at school.

Thursday 31st arrived and after seeing her son off to school, Rachel steeled herself for the day ahead. It had been a long time since she had worn her best dress, a plain maroon woollen piece that she had last worn for Michael's Christening. A string of soft while pearls adorned her neck and her black hair contrasted beautifully with her pale face and red lipstick. The image in the mirror pleased her, it was going to be a good day.

The day was bright and sunny. At eleven o'clock she slipped into her shiny black high heels and set off for the town hall. As she passed the church Mrs Murray who was leaving the graveyard stopped, stared and then muttered something under her breath which Rachel could not hear but knew it wouldn't have been complimentary.

"Sorry, I didn't catch that." said Rachel staring defiantly at her.

"I said some people have no shame."

Rachel stopped and looked intently at the woman in the drab grey coat and flat brown shoes whom she had known for many years and in fact had gone to school with.

"I quiet agree." she said "Who on earth but a complete hypocrite with a vicious tongue would be such a regular churchgoer."

Rachel arrived at the town hall at the same time as a green jaguar she had seen so many times before. As the chauffeur opened the rear door, she positioned herself between the grand entrance to the town hall and the car.

As his Lordship alighted, Rachel stepped forward.

"Lord Hazelhurst, my name is Rachel Flynn, Michael's mother. I wonder if you are aware that my son, at your daughter Sophia's invitation, rang her on three separate occasions, has been rebuffed by your butler, no doubt under instruction from a member of your household."

"I'm terribly sorry but I have a meeting to attend." he said as he hurriedly made his way up the steps. Before entering the building, he turned briefly to glance downwards at the angry woman, still staring defiantly at him.

"I don't know why I thought he might have behaved differently," said Rachel out loud. "Too much of a coward to tell me the truth, that he simply thought his daughter was too good for my son. Well, we'll see about that."

    The chauffer, who had witnessed the scene, sat upright in the driver's seat, a broad smile spreading across his rugged face as he gazed at the beautiful woman before him, her face flushed with anger.

CHAPTER 4

The summer holidays meant that Michael had more time on his hands. All his friends had now left school and had started work but he would return after the six weeks break to study for his G.C.E.'s, a decision his mother had strongly supported. But he felt guilty about allowing his mother to continue to support him and said as much. But Rachel would have none of it.

"Listen son you have an opportunity that neither I or your father ever had. He would have wanted you to grasp it with both hands. You didn't know it, but your dad passed the scholarship, but because his parents couldn't afford the cost of the school uniform for grammar school, he didn't go. That is not going to happen again. Your mates are going to have money in their pockets but their lives will be the same as their parents and nothing will change. I have my job and you have your little job at the weekend, so we will be fine."

So, Michael accepted that but it didn't stop him getting full time work during the holidays and he took a temporary job on the local farm where his best friend Tom had taken a job as a full-time labourer. Rising at six in the morning was a bit of a shock to his system and working until six in the afternoon doing hard physical labour was tiring but it had its compensations. He was working with his best friend and he was able to give his mum £6 a week for housekeeping. The long, mainly sunny days working in the fields had an effect. It turned him from a spindly boy into a physically strong bronzed young man that the girls noticed, especially at the village hall on Saturday evenings. He had walked a couple of girls home and kissed them goodnight but he couldn't forget Sophia, she was so special, and the girls noticed that when he kissed them, he wasn't really there, so no matter how much they tried to get him to go further, he never did.

September saw his return to school to the newly formed sixth form which was so different from previous years. There was only six of them, none of whom were close friends like Tom. Three of them wore glasses and one had asthma. He remembered him; he never got the cane because of it. The other one was Jake, an unusual name those days; he played rugby like him and they got on because of it. There were mornings when the weather was bad as he walked to school and this made him think of his friend Tom, having to rise early and work all day in all weathers but there was nothing he could do so he didn't dwell on it. The Christmas holidays came in a flash and Michael was pleased with his end of term report, he knew it would make his mum happy. As Christmas eve fell on a Saturday, Rachel could see that her son was itching to see his mates at the dance in the village hall so she gave him ten bob to go out and enjoy himself. It would be good to see his old friends, especially Tom who he hadn't seen since he started work full time at the end of the summer. It was a relief knowing that none of his new school mates would be going, except maybe Jake. The last time he went to the village hall he was with Sophia and he smiled as he remembered the huge impression she made. Looking around the hall he thought he saw her but he felt disappointed when it turned out not to be her. Of course, it wasn't her, what would she be doing here anyway? But then feeling a firm slap on his back he turned defensively but it was Tom, just what he needed to bring him back to reality. He seemed bigger, much bigger and stronger as he crushed him in an embrace.

"How you doing mate? Come and have a drink." he said dragging him to the bar. "Two pints of larger please."

Michael knew that Tom was only just 17 but he could get away with 20 and he soon thrust a pint into Michael's hand.

"I heard that posh bird of yours had packed you in Mike. Is that right?"

Michael didn't mind being called Mike, he quite liked it coming from his best mate but couldn't help looking down in the mouth as he replied.

"That's right Tom. I wouldn't have minded if she had told me to my face but she just cut me off without a word."

"Probably for the best Mike, people like that only mix with their own."

Just then a buxom lass snuggled up to Tom as she said hello to Michael."

"You remember Gillian Mike?"

"Hi Gillian, you two together?"

"We certainly are." she replied showing her left hand.

"Engaged." said Michael revealing the surprise he felt.

"Well, we're all grown up now." answered Tom. I'm earning good money and we've put our name down to rent a cottage in the village."

"Wow, that great", murmured Michael trying his best to sound really pleased.

Just then, the band started to play another song and then they were gone dancing by the stage.

"See you later Mike." Tom had said hurriedly as he was dragged away.

Michael stood by the bar taking in all that had just happened. It looked like he had lost his best friend who was now a man with a fiancé and he was still just a schoolboy who had lost the love of his life. But then Jake arrived.

"You drinking? he asked.

"No, I mean, my mate Tom bought it for me."

"I thought you might be in here, I'm on my way to the rugby club, want to come?"

"Why not." said Michael in a statement rather than a question. "I'm done here." and quickly finishing his drink he left with his new best friend.

CHAPTER 5

Three years later, Michael presented himself as a fresher at the reception of Liverpool University. His mother Rachel stood a few yards behind guarding his bags. She looked around in wonder, so many people, so many different accents, so many students from all over the country. She even spotted a number of black and Asian students. She hadn't noticed the man standing next to her.

"A proud day?" he ventured.

"Indeed, it is." said Rachel looking at the voice. He had a soft Scots accent and she guessed him to be a similar age to herself.

"Boy or girl?" he asked sweeping back his brown hair just like Michael always did.

"Boy", answered Rachel pointing "That's him, second from the front of the English queue.

"Good looking boy." said the Scotsman. "That's my girl Laura third from the back of the same queue, the one with the same colour hair as me.

"Lovely." said Rachel returning the compliment.

Seeing a mischievous glint in his eye she quickly added "Laura, I mean."

"Yes, I knew that." he said as they laughed.

"My name is Andrew, Andrew Stuart, pleased to meet you." he said holding out his hand, "and your boy's name?

"Michael, and my name is Rachel. Pleased to meet you also."

"A proud day for the family. Laura's mother would have been so proud"

"Yes." agreed Rachel. "Same here". Registering the fact that he was probable a widower but unwilling to reveal her marital status, not yet anyway.

Michael returned clutching a wad of papers and a couple of brochures and a key with a colourful fob. Lifting his bags Rachel said "Nice to have met you, Andrew.

"Same here Rachel, perhaps we'll bump into each other again."

Taking the heaviest bag from his mother, Michael led the way to the exit having registered the fact that his mum was on first name terms with a man, no doubt a parent of a fellow student.

"Who's Andrew?" he asked trying to make his tone casual.

"Oh, just someone I just met, his daughter Laura is reading English like you."

"This way" said Michael leading. He had noticed a new spring in his mother's step and a soft smile on her lips.

The Halls of residence were new and consisted of six floors served by a lift. He was on the third floor, room 6 C, which had a view of Liverpool Cathedral on the left and a large building site on the right which was to be The Metropolitan Cathedral of Christ the King. Several large ships could be seen below on the river Mersey, straight ahead, about a mile away.

As Michael looked through the window his mother was already unpacking, placing his clothes neatly on hangers and folding his underwear and pyjamas before placing them into the chest of drawers, just like she always had at home.

"Come on Michael, shape yourself, unpack your haversack. This desk is lovely."

Turning away from the window Michael said.

"This is so different mum from anything I've ever known. I'm going to make the most of it. Thank you," He said, a tear emerging in his eye.

Rachel stopped the unpacking and looked at her son before reaching up and clasping him in a most tender embrace.

Michael B McLarnon

"Now mum, I want you to live your life more for yourself. I'm going to be fine"

"Her son had a perception far beyond his years." thought Rachel. "Just like his father, but the love of her life was gone and her son was now a man."

She realised, of course, that he was right. There was no point in sitting at home waiting for a letter or next visit. She was 43 and now her son was away at university, she would forge a new life. Yes, she might well accept the next offer of a date, but her son would always come first.

CHAPTER 6

It was a big day, the day when the post office was coming to install a telephone. Yes, it was extravagant but she needed to be contactable now her son lived so far away in Liverpool. Anyway, she could afford it since she had a full-time job at the Town Hall in the planning department as an administrative assistant. They were a good employer and they didn't mind giving her the afternoon off. It was two days later in the evening when the telephone rang for the first time. It was her son; he had received her letter and was excited to hear his mother on the other end.

"Hello mum, it's Michael."

"Hello love." she shouted down the phone.

"No need to shout mum, I can hear you."

"Sorry love." she replied laughing. "I should know better; I answer the telephone all the time at work. Anyway, are you alright love?"

"Yes, I'm fine mum. Listen, remember Laura and her dad you met on registration day?"

"Yes."

"Well, I've got to know Laura. I see her at lectures and in the S.U. and her dad remembers you and asked for your number. Is that O.K. mum?"

As Rachel thought about it, the pips started, so she quickly answered.

"I suppose so." But before she could ask why he wanted it the call was ended and she wondered if Michael had heard her. She didn't have to wonder for very long. The next evening the phone rang again.

"Rachel?"

"Yes." she answered, feeling her heart rate quickening as she realised it was a man's voice.

"It's Andrew." he said in his soft and pleasant Scots' accent.

"Hello Andrew, how are you?"

"I'm grand, and yourself?"

"Yes, I'm fine, and you?" she continued in a slightly nervy voice.

"You've already asked me Rachel, I'm still grand."

Rachel laughed, "Yes, sorry, it's just that I'm still getting used to having a telephone."

"Yes, of course." Hesitating for a moment he continued. "I'm in London next weekend for a medical conference, terribly boring and I wondered if you like to meet up in the evening, for dinner perhaps?"

"Oh, I'm not sure."

"I'm sorry Rachel, I've taken you aback, I'm sorry. Tell you what, why don't you have a think about it? I'll ring you back on, let's say Wednesday evening. Is that O.K. with you?"

"Yes, I suppose so." Rachel replied hesitantly.

"That's grand, Speak to you then." And with that the line went dead.

Rachel stood still for a few moments, still holding the telephone, until a feeling of excitement spread throughout her entire body. How her life had changed over the past few weeks. She had moved on from just a widow with a son to support to a single woman whom a man had found attractive and wanted to take out to dinner. Standing in front of the only mirror in the house she fingered her hair and pouched her lips and closely examined her face for any early signs of a wrinkle.

The following days were like a blur.

"Calm down girl." she told herself over and over.

Her friend at the council office, Peggy, was almost as excited as Rachel was when she told her the news.

"Oh my," she said. "He sounds like a doctor."

"What do you mean Peggy?"

"Well, medical conference. They don't just send office boys to a conference do they girl?"

"No, I don't suppose they do."

"And not just any doctor. I mean all the way from Scotland. Maybe he's a professor."

"Don't be silly, he's not old enough."

"Professors aren't all old you know, especially not these days."

"Oh Peggy, don't get me more excited than I already am."

"Alright girl, he's probably coming just to carry the professor's brief case."

Both ladies burst out laughing, attracting the attention of the office manager.

"What's so amusing ladies?" he asked.

to which both replied in unison "Oh nothing Mr. Melcher, sorry."

Rachel had hoped Michael would ring again before Wednesday so she could ask her son what he thought about the invitation from Laura's father. Today was Tuesday, so would have to ring him. She had hoped not to have to do this, he might think it was an emergency. Knowing the telephone was situated near the stairwell on his floor it was probable that he would not answer it himself.

"Hello" she said as a female voice answered.

"I wonder if you mind knocking on room 6 and telling Michael his mother is on the telephone."

"Certainly." came the confident reply.

Young people were so confident these days, nothing seemed to bother them.

"I'm sorry," came the same voice. "He's not in. Can I give him a message?"

"Yes, thank you. Can you tell him his mother rang and would he call me back please?"

"Sure."

"And Oh, please tell him it's nothing urgent, I just want to,"

"Yes, I'll tell him."

"Thank you."

And that was it. The phone went dead.

Normally, Rachel would go to bed at 10p.m. but not tonight. She must wait for Michael to ring, but by 11.30 she decided that she must retire, she didn't want to oversleep in the morning.

Rachel couldn't wait to get to work to talk to her friend, she was happy, and passing Mrs Murray coming from the other direction, she even managed a smile and a good morning.

"Well, have you decided? "asked Peggy.

"Decided what?" replied Rachel with a mischievous smile on her face

"You know perfectly well girl." said the Londoner.

"Well, I was hoping Michael would ring so I could ask him what he thought."

"You don't need his permission, Rachel. He's a man now and anyway he would want you to be happy."

"Yes, I suppose so. Look out here comes Mr Melcher."

"Good luck." said Peggy as they left work that day.

The telephone rang at 6.30.

"Oh good, it will be Michael" thought Rachel as she lifted the receiver.

She was wrong."

"Hello Rachel, this is Andrew."

"Oh." she said taken aback.

"You sound disappointed." said Andrew in his low Scott's accent.

"Oh no Andrew, it's not that, I just thought it was Michael, I was expecting him to call."

"Oh sorry, shall I ring off to free up the line."

"No." she said in an unintended loud voice.

"No, I mean that's fine, it wasn't urgent or anything." In a tone that was now too low.

"Well." said Andrew in his rich heart melting brogue. "I just wondered if you've thought about my invitation to dinner."

Feeling all this excitement was building up to an unmanageable pitch she finally said. "Yes Andrew, I'd love to."

"There was an audible sound of relief as he continued. "I'll be staying at the Hilton opposite Hyde Park but I'd prefer not to dine there. I know a little place by the river that's really nice, it's called Arabian Nights. Can you get there by 8?"

This was too much information. Hilton Hotel, Arabian Nights, London. Her head was spinning but she didn't want to collapse altogether.

"Just be yourself," her friend Peggy had said. "When he rings, just act normal."

"I'm afraid I don't know London Andrew; it has been long time since I've been there. "replied Rachel eventually.

"I'll pick you up. You'll be coming up by train, I expect. Coming from Littlehampton, you'll be arriving at Victoria, right? What time does your train arrive?"

By this time Rachel was in a complete spin.

"Tell you what, I'll meet you by the big clock near platform 7." he said at last.

"O.K." said Rachel nearing exhaustion.

"Great, I'll get off the line in case Michael is trying to ring. See you on Saturday at say 7.30."

Rachel was still holding the receiver a full two minutes after the call had ended. "Saturday." she thought. "Thank goodness he mentioned the day. I would never have thought to ask."

"You're joking." screamed Peggy the next day. Are you sure he said Arabian Nights?"

"Yes, by the river."

"It must be the place I am thinking of then. Wow girl, he must really fancy you."

"Is it posh, then?"

"Posh doesn't cover it Rachel, It's positively exclusive. Princess Margaret goes there."

"You don't think she'll be there on Saturday, do you?"

"Who knows? We haven't spoken for a while, "laughed Peggy.

"Everything alright here ladies." Interrupted Mr Melcher in his stern voice.

Lunch was taken at their desks as always.

"I've no idea what to wear, "said Rachel for the second time.

"Not a problem girl, I've got a wardrobe full. Come back with me after work and we'll go through the lot."

Peggy lived in a large detached house not far from the council offices. Her husband was a surveyor and quite senior it would seem. They didn't have any children and she only worked because "she was bored at home all day"

"My goodness, you have quite a collection here Peggy." said Rachel as the wardrobe doors were opened.

"Yes, Ralph has to go to business dinners and he likes to show me off."

"You obviously like red." said Rachel moving the hangers along. "They go with your blond hair."

"They would contrast beautifully with your black. You will need at least two."

"No, I only need one evening dress."

"Are you sure about that? "asked Peggy with a twinkle in her eye.

"No, I haven't booked anywhere. "replied Rachel.
"It's my guess, you won't have to."
"Oh no, no, no. It's been so long."
"So long since what?"
"You know, since I've been with a man."
"You'll soon pick it up again, it will be like riding a bike, you never forget."
"Anyway, who says I'd want to?"
"I do." said Peggy and they both laughed.

CHAPTER 7

The train thundered into the station spreading steam across the platform. Rachel chose an empty second-class compartment. Settling down for the journey she carefully placed the ticket into her purse. It was a single to London Victoria. She was pretty certain that she would return the same evening but didn't want to risk wasting the return part of her ticket in case she did stay the night. The thought made her shiver with excitement. It had only been a few weeks since she had travelled by train with Michael on his way to Liverpool but this time, she was alone, on her way to meeting a man who could possibly change her life. But I'm getting too far ahead of myself, she thought. He might just be a gigolo, out to take advantage and then move on. Mind you, he might well think that when he sees my traveller. He'll know I'm expecting to stay the night.

"London Victoria next stop." shouted the ticket inspector as he moved along the outside corridor. Rachel quickly grabbed the handles of her traveller and removing the beautiful red dress loaned to her, she skipped along to the toilet and changed, leaving behind the skirt and blouse she had travelled in stuffed into her bag.

Alighting from the carriage she felt a drop of rain and quickly reached for her umbrella, but to her horror she realised she had left it on the train. Turning she realised there was no retreating as a wall of people moved her along. All she had to protect her from the rain, which was now pouring, was a light cotton jacket. As she walked to the platform gate, she felt her hair flattening and falling. She must get the next train back; this adventure was quickly turning into a nightmare. Heading at pace to the ticket office she was horrified to see Andrew approaching on an interception course. Lowering her head and wishing the ground would swallow her up, she kept on going but it was no good, he had spotted her.

"Rachel," he called. "Rachel."

It was no good, there was no escape.

"Oh Andrew. I didn't see you," she lied, trying to do something with her hair which was now saturated.

"My poor girl," he said. Placing his raincoat around her shoulders.

These words made her feel totally defeated and she gave up any pretence she might have contemplated and cried into his outstretched arms.

"It's such a mess, "she sobbed softly. "I wanted to look my best."

Andrew tried to reassure her "It's not too bad Rachel," he said as a feeling of great tenderness came over him. He led her to the taxi rank.

"The dress is ruined." was all she could say as Andrew asked the cab driver to "Take us to the Hilton Hotel, Hyde Park please"

Rachel enjoyed the comfort of the soft white bath robe she had wrapped around her body. Peggy's red dress lay crumpled and wet in the bath. This was luxury she wasn't used to. Nervously, she turned the door knob of the bedroom but hearing Andrew on the telephone she retreated but listened.

"I will be home on Tuesday evening and I'll call you then. My train leaves Euston about four. How's university?"

"Please don't mention me please," thought Rachel desperately, she's bound to mention it to Michael."

"Good, good. O.K. then, I'll speak to you on Tuesday. Bye darling."

Hearing the receiver being replaced, Rachel entered the main room.

"Feeling better?" he asked, rising from the armchair.

"Much better, thank you Andrew. I need to dry and press my friends." She paused and corrected, "my dress."

"Of course, I'll call room service."

"No need, I can do it. Does the room have an iron?" she insisted. All this attention was getting a bit too much, she wasn't used to it. "I need to get going." She muttered in an agitated voice.

Andrew seeing her distress didn't mention that she was too late to get the train back, he didn't want to panic her.

"What time is it?" she asked.

Looking at his wrist he replied "9.45"

"Oh goodness, I'll never make it," she said, more distressed.

"Don't worry Rachel, you can stay here."

Seeing the look on her face he quickly added. "I'll sleep on the couch; you can take the bed."

Reassured, Rachel relaxed, just a little. The whole debacle had taken its toll.

"If you don't mind Andrew, I'd like to go to bed now, I'm very tired."

"Of course, you must be exhausted. Sleep well. I'm free tomorrow, if you like, we'll do the sites."

The bed was enormous and Rachel fell asleep almost immediately in her bathrobe, even though her mind was racing. "If he says of course one more time, I'll scream," was her last thought before succumbing.

A soft knock on the bedroom door brought her out of her dream. Bright sunlight streamed through the window and she sat up with a start.

"Just a moment," she shouted as she manoeuvred out bed. Seeing her image in the dressing table mirror she opened the door only slightly. She didn't want anyone seeing the state of her appearance, looking like she had been dragged through a hedge backwards, as her mother used to say.

"You seemed to have slept well Rachel, it's 9 o'clock. Breakfast is being sent up. Is that, O.K.?" Andrew called in his deliciously soft Scots' accent.

"Yes, that's fine," replied Rachel casually, as though she was accustomed to staying in posh hotels with room service.

"I need the bathroom," she quickly added.

"It's the door to your right," replied Andrew.

Feeling embarrassment on top of embarrassment, she tried the door and was astonished by the on-suite luxury that confronted her. She just hoped she could master the shower.

CHAPTER 8

The morning air tasted sweet. It was Sunday and the London traffic was light. Park Lane looked different since the last time she had here. She had been with John on V.E. day when the whole city went wild. That had been the day Michael had been conceived in a cheap hotel in East London that had been badly bombed during the Blitz. It didn't matter that the area was bleak, she was the happiest she had ever been. She was with the man she loved and the future looked bright.

"Are you alright walking in those heals?" asked Andrew. He asked the question again which brought Rachel abruptly back to the present.

"I'm sorry Andrew, I was miles away." she answered. "Yes, I'm fine thank you. Mind you, I feel somewhat overdressed." she added, looking down on her friend Peggy's red dress.

"I managed to rebook our table at Arabian Nights. I booked an earlier time so you can catch the evening train back home."

"That's fine Andrew." This was a kind and thoughtful man. she thought, linking his arm as her confirmation that Yes, she liked him, this kind and generous man. The gesture was not lost on him and they smiled.

By the time they had strolled for a couple of hours through the park, they knew pretty much all about each other. Yes, he was a doctor, a surgeon in fact. That would account for him being addressed as Mr and not Doctor.

His wife, Margaret had also been a doctor before she was killed by a V2 rocket whilst working in a London hospital near the end of the war. He had had to bring Laura up with the help of Margaret's parents and his housekeeper.

Over the years, Rachel had learned how to be resourceful, she had to be. Although she felt out of place in this hotel, she was good at talking to people. The chamber maid was easy to talk to and after telling her of her predicament over what to wear for her dinner this evening she discovered the lost property department. She was amazed at some of the lovely things that had gone unclaimed over the past year.

"How about this?" said the girl holding up a beautiful dark green evening dress. "The label says Harrods and seems to be have left behind by a Russian diplomat's wife. I can't see her claiming it back any time soon, I heard her husband had been sent to Siberia."

"Thank you so much, I'll send it back in the next day or so."

"No need." said the girl. "I don't think they will be back. Anyway, I'm sure it will look so much better on you."

Andrew took a deep breath as Rachel appeared.

"Ready?" she asked with a new found confidence in her appearance and surroundings as she emerged from the bedroom. Her black hair contrasted perfectly with the green of her dress and bright red lipstick. Her brown Harrods carry bag containing her friends dress and her handbag didn't really match, but there was nothing she could do about that.

At the restaurant a Lawrence of Arabia figure welcomed the couple and held the door for them "Good evening," he offered; his eyes glued to the black-haired lady in the green dress. A shorter man in a suit and wearing a fez greeted Andrew with a bow and guided them across the richly carpeted floor to their table which had a view of the other tables, all of which had curtains draped three quarters of the way around them. A trio of musicians played a soft Arabian tune and a hundred tiny blue lights shone like stars from the ceiling. Rachel could not think of a more romantic setting. It was like having dinner on a warm evening in the desert.

Rachel allowed Andrew to guide her through the menu. "The sheep's eyes are good." he teased, before recommending the more familiar English dishes on the reverse side of the camel shaped menu.

A couple of tables were occupied by Arab couples dressed in national dress and another by a distinguished older black couple. Towards the end of their meal, aware that she had a train to catch, Rachel played with the dates that had been served on a palm leaf and was considering whether to have another when an English couple caught her eye. They were being shown to their table. Recognising them, it immediately changed her mood; it was Sophia and her father. Andrew couldn't help but notice, Rachel's face turned from sweetness to something resembling anger.

"What is it?" he asked.

"I'm ready to go." replied Rachel firmly, glancing once more at Lord Hazelhurst and his daughter. "What time is it please?"

"We've plenty of time," replied Andrew trying to calm his guest.

"I'd like to go now please." she replied flatly.

As Andrew indicated to the waiter that he would like the bill, Rachel stood and strode purposely over to his Lordships table. Seeing the expensive evening dress approaching he rose to welcome the lady he assumed must be an acquaintance. Rachel ignored him and addressed his daughter.

"Hello Sophia, I don't know if you remember me, I'm Michael's mother. I wonder if you knew that my son had telephoned you several times the week after we had welcomed you into our home but was told by your butler that you were not available. He even went to your church looking for you but in doing so was humiliated."

Lord Hazelhurst tried to intervene but was blocked by Rachel's firm upturned hand.

"I'm sorry Mrs Flynn, I had no idea. I wasn't told." said Sophia clearly shocked.

Glaring at her father she continued. "I assumed Michael didn't want to continue. It was after that I went to stay with my maternal grandmother in Scotland for the holidays."

"Well, Michael is now at university in Liverpool and happy. I believe you Sophia, when you say that you were not aware of your family's deception but please don't try to contact him, I don't want him upset anymore."

Andrew was waiting a few feet away holding Rachel's coat and carry bag.

"Sorry about that Andrew." offered Rachel, her voice trembling and whose facial features had started to lose the red heat in her cheeks. "I hope I did not embarrass you."

The taxi pulled up outside a relatively quiet Victoria railway station. Neither occupant had spoken during the short journey over the dimly lit London Bridge but their thoughts were running riot. Andrew was getting to know this woman very quickly and he liked what he saw. As they alighted, he was the first to speak.

"Rachel please remind me to never cross you." he said with a laugh.

"I'm so sorry Andrew, I hope my performance didn't spoil your evening."

"Well." he said pausing," It was certainly memorable." a smile crossing his handsome face.

"I'm sorry Andrew, it's been a wonderful weekend, one I'll never forget."

"Well, I was hoping I could see you again?"

"I'd like that Andrew, maybe you would like to come and visit."

Walking across the concourse, Rachel was now feeling excited and happy at the prospect of having a new relationship. She related the story that led up the confrontation with Lord Hazelhurst. They also exchanged stories of the challenges of bringing up a child without the support of a partner.

When it was time to board the train, Rachel turned to face Andrew, who was about to speak, when she stepped nearer and kissed him softly on the lips.

"Call me." she said, turning to head for the train.

CHAPTER 9

It was a Saturday and a big day; Michael was due home for the Christmas holiday. Rachel decorated the house as she always had, the Christmas Tree taking pride of place in the corner of the living room, adorned with borbels and mementos collected over the years, including two which Michael had made at school. Hearing the letter box snap she saw two envelopes on the mat. One was obviously a Christmas card. She looked at the envelope, the postmark was Edinburgh. Yes, it was from Andrew. His message was reserved, just like the man.

"Here's hoping you and Michael have a wonderful Christmas, kindest regards, Andrew."

Smiling, she kissed the card and placed it on the mantel piece, in the centre of half a dozen others. Puzzled, she opened the other letter, it looked official.

"Dear Mrs Flynn,

It is with regret that we must issue you with this Notice of Eviction and hereby give you four weeks' notice to quit these premises. This action is necessary due to plans, accepted by the Parish Council, to re-develop the land you currently occupy.

G. Jones, Estate Manager
  Hazelhurst Estate."

Stuffing the letter into her apron pocket she decided that his Lordship was not going to spoil Christmas; this was his revenge for her shaming him in front of his daughter. But he was not going to get his way, not this time, not ever again.

Michael looked every inch the university student. His college scarf, camel coloured duffle coat and old black shoes with brown laces marked him out as a young academic. He emerged from the steam of the train, like a character from a film. Carrying his bag with one hand he linked his mother with the other. She had so many questions. Beaming with pride they walked the short distance to their house. Michael breathed in the country air. Liverpool was so exiting but it was such a busy congested place, smoke and sounds ever present. But it was also the music capital of the world and he had seen The Beatles twice already. He had a part time job in the market and had been fully accepted by the friendly locals. No, he didn't have a special girlfriend but he had plenty of friends who were girls, including Laura.

"I hear you had dinner with her father in London. Was it nice?" he asked.

"So, he told his daughter." thought Rachel. "Good."

"Yes, it was lovely." replied his mother trying not to sound too enthusiastic. She wasn't sure how it would affect Michael; he was still her number 1 priority. "How do feel about that?" she asked tentatively.

"It's fine by me mum. Like I said when you took me to uni, I'm fine. It's now your time. Will you be seeing Laura's dad again?"

"Well, he said he would like to see me again." she replied still cautiously.

"Go for it them mum. You have my permission." he laughed, with a sidesway hug to her shoulder.

Having Michael home for Christmas made for a happy house, thought Rachel trying to put the letter of eviction from her mind. The phone rang several times during the evening, it was always for Michael, one or other of his new friends at university. This was a very different world she was now living in. The sound of a Beatles record, playing in Michael's room was constant.

"She was just seventeen, you know what I mean" evoked memories of her own youth, and she danced along to it in the Kitchen, remembering those happy carefree days.

Sunday was quiet, Michael was reading Pride and Prejudice, part of his course he explained. The open fire was roaring and the wireless was playing records requested by members of the forces overseas for their families and sweethearts here in the U.K. Rachel was washing the breakfast dishes when she saw the shadow of a slight figure pass the kitchen window. Few people passed that way without calling so Rachel made her way to the front door. There was no knock and the letter box remained undisturbed but she was curious and opened the door in time to see the figure of a young woman walking back the way she had come. It was snowing.

"Can I help you?" she called.

The figure stopped and turned; it was Sophia, her woolly hat caked in soft snow. She was holding an envelope.

"I've brought a Christmas Card."

Rachel could only stare. Sophia was stood in the dim light of the door with snow falling all around her with only blackness at her rear. She was a beautiful picture.

" You'd better come in."

Stepping inside Sophia said "I wasn't told, you know, about the phone calls."

"Michael's home, I don't want him upset, "whispered Rachel. "Please don't give him false hope, he's over you."

"I've really missed him." replied Sophia quietly.

"You've got ten minutes, I'll be upstairs. I haven't told him about London."

"Michael," shouted his mother, "You have a visitor."

Rachel's mind was in turmoil. She knew the power Sophia could wield over her son, she prayed she wouldn't use it. The next ten minutes were the longest of her life.

"Mum", called Michael nine minutes later. "Sophia is just leaving."

"It was nice seeing you again Mrs Flynn." Rachel looked at her son's face for a clue. He looked sad, but O.K.

"And you." responded Rachel. "Before you go, I have something for you. It arrived yesterday, presumably on your father's instructions. Please give this to him and tell him I intend to fight it."

Shutting the door against the snow filled wind, Rachel walked back into the living room.

"What was in the envelope?" asked Michael.

Anxious to find out what had gone on with Sophia, she replied. "Oh, nothing for you to worry about love, it was just a rent increase from the estate, their Christmas gift to their tenants." Quickly changing the subject, she asked about his meeting.

"O.K." he said looking up from his book. "She just wanted to explain why she hadn't been in touch. Apparently, her maternal grandmother was taken ill and had asked for her." She stayed with her until she recovered, three months in all. Apparently, she met someone whilst she was there, someone who is now at Oxford, same as her."

"I see." said Rachel, silently thanking her for this favour. It couldn't have been easy, remembering the look on her face when she arrived and the desolate look as she left. It was clear that she really liked Michael, maybe even loved him. Still, it would never have worked, Rachel told herself. as she busied herself in the kitchen.

The holiday passed quickly and before she knew it, Rachel was seeing her son off on the train. He had protested after his mother had pressed twenty pounds into his hand as he boarded, an amount he knew she could little afford, but short of dropping it onto the track, he could do nothing about it. He had insisted that his grant payments were plenty enough to keep him, and together with his earnings from his little job at the market he was well off.

Walking on to work, Rachel thoughts were crowded, chief amongst them, the eviction notice.

"I can put you up girl." Peggy had said, "At least until you find somewhere."

"That's good of you. but I need to provide a home for Michael, "said Rachel. "I'll see what I can do at the weekend."

Walking home, it was dark and raining. The last of the snow had been washed away but it was cold and the buildings seemed to close in on her, adding pressure as she thought of the bills she needed to pay, now that Christmas was over.

As she opened her front door, she noticed several brown envelopes on the mat.

"More bills." she thought placing them on the telephone table. The house was cold, she was cold. Wondering if she had done the right thing concerning Sophia, she set the fire with a few sticks and the last of the coal.

The telephone rang.

"This will be Michael saying he's back at uni." she thought.

"Hello Rachel, It's Andrew. How was Christmas?" he asked cheerfully.

Taken by surprise, Rachel replied sounding disappointed.

"Oh, I thought it was Michael. He went back today."

"Yes, I know." said Andrew, also sounding a little disappointed at her response.

"He's back safely, Laura rang me half an hour ago."

"Oh, thank you Andrew."

"Are you alright Rachel, you don't sound yourself."

"I'm sorry Andrew." she replied trying to lift her mood, "I'm just a bit sad seeing Michael off, you know?"

"Aye, I know lassie."

Rachel laughed at his choice of words.

"Oh Andrew, you sound so funny."

"Good to hear you laugh Rachel." He Laughed and then in a more serious tone, "I've missed you."

"And I you." she replied "But I can't really talk just now, I've just got in from work and I'm a bit wet. I need to get changed."

"You seem to make a habit of getting wet. I still have the image of you when we met at Victoria Station. I'll ring you tomorrow." And then trying to keep up his cheeky young boy impression he said. "Goodnight lassie, I'll ring you tomorrow. About 8?"

"I'd like that, Andrew." she said trying to sound enthusiastic. She didn't want to put him off, she really liked this feeling of being desired.

Later, having dried off and changing into her nightdress, she collected the mail and sat by the fire. She had been right, more bills, but this last envelope was marked Private and Confidential. It was from the estate office.

Dear Mrs Flynn,

After a further review of our development plans, we have decided that it is now not necessary to repossess that part of the land upon which the house you occupy stands.

We therefore withdraw the eviction notice issued to you last month. Furthermore, we are pleased to inform you that, as from next week, your rent will be reduced to the amount shown below.

G. Jones, Estate Manager,
Hazelhurst Estate

Rachel reread the letter twice more before setting it down and finally realising what must have happened and said aloud.

"Thank you, Sophia, bless you girl. Thank you."

CHAPTER 10

Two years passed. Rachel's relationship with Andrew had deepened but she is still cautious about taking the next step, she is from a cautious generation and anyway her first priority was still Michael, he would always come first. He would graduate this summer of 1968 and when he had found a good job, then she would allow herself more choices. But first, he must feel that he has a secure home with her. Things had been going well at work and she had a good friend in Peggy. Her finances had never been better; she was good at her job and had received annual merit increases in salary and cost of living. Also, her rent had not been increased for a second year, no doubt Sophia's doing. Also, Michael's university grant had been more than enough to cover his lodgings, and earnings from his part time job covered his train fares. This however did not stop Rachel secretly stuffing a few notes into his pockets each time he left. He would find them in different pockets after every visit. His first week back at college, he found a £5 note in a sock and another in his underpants, all washed and neatly ironed. This was his mum's latest effort to evade his last-minute checks.

Peggy always looked forward to Monday mornings when she would question Rachel on the latest chapter in her love life.

"Andrew has asked me to travel up to his home in Edinburgh." She revealed.

"When are you going?" asked Peggy eagerly.

"I haven't decided if I want too yet." replied Rachel quietly, "I'm not sure if I should."

"Now look here girl," said Peggy sharply. "You've kept him waiting for long enough. Do you want to lose him?"

"I know, but Michael."

Peggy cut her off sharply. "Michael will be fine. What do you think he's been up to at university for the last three years? This is the late 60's girl, just be thankful he's not on drugs. Anyway, hasn't he told you over and over that he's fine and you need to start living your life. You're a good-looking woman Rachel but your looks won't last forever."

Later that evening, recalling her friend's words she looked at her reflection in the bathroom mirror.

"I see what Peggy means, "she thought, feeling under her eyes. "Is that the start of a wrinkle?"

The telephone interrupted her self-examination.

"Hello lassie, this is Andrew. "he said in his lovely soft Scots' accent.

"I'd never have guested." she replied, secretly happy, that he continued to call her Lassie.

"I'm in London again this coming weekend. I thought we might meet up and travel back to Edinburgh for a few days, if you'd like to, of course. I'd love to show you my home and the sights."

"Oh, I don't know. It's a bit short notice to get time off." she hesitated. But then, remembering what Peggy had said, she quickly added. "But I'm sure it will be fine, I'd love to."

The next two evenings were spent at her friend house going through her wardrobe. Peggy loved showing off her beautiful collection of dresses and pressed Rachel to borrow far more than she could possibly get into a single suitcase. They giggled their way through a few happy hours, like a couple of teenagers talking about their first dates, those many years ago.

"Remember this one?" asked Peggy holding up the red dress Rachel had borrowed two years previously for her dinner date at the Arabian Nights.

"How could I forget." said Rachel who had never told her friend that the rain had nearly ruined it. Before leaving her bedroom, Peggy reached into her dressing table drawer and took out a strip of pink pills.

"You probably won't need these at your age." said Peggy with a cheeky smile. "Start taking them two days before you leave." And then finally, "Let's have a drink."

The trains were fewer on a Sunday but Rachel managed to get the 9a.m. to Victoria. She chose an empty compartment and settled to read Pride and Prejudice, left by Michael. She had been relieved that he had been fine when she had told him that she was travelling up to Andrew's place for a few days.

"Well done mum." he had said. "About time."

This started Rachel wondered once more about Michael. There had been no one special since Sophia. She hoped he would find his special partner, someone like Sophia but without the barriers that came with her."

At that moment Rachel noticed the shadow of a figure passing along the corridor. A few moments later the door of her compartment opened. It was Sophia.

"Hello Mrs Flynn, do you mind if I join you?"

Rachel's mind flooded with memories of her and her father. "No, please do." she said cautiously.

"I understand your reluctance. My family has not behaved well. I just wanted you to know that what happened what not of my choosing." said Sophia, looking sad but still so very young and beautiful."

"I guessed as much Sophia; I bare no ill will towards you. Please sit."

"Michael will be 21 this month, how is he?" asked Sophia eagerly.

"He's well, thank you. He will graduate this summer; he is predicted a 2.1. and has already started applying for jobs."

"That's wonderful Mrs Flynn. You must be so proud of him."

"Yes, I am." accepting what a sincere young lady Sophia was. She then added "Please call me Rachel."

"Thank you. When I saw you boarding the train, I was so pleased, I've wanted to talk to you for so long."

"And what about you Sophia, still at Oxford?"

"Just about." she replied, "Hanging on by my fingertips. I'm not as clever as Michael."

Rachel noticed that every time she mentioned her sons name, she did so with deep affection. She really liked this girl and was not surprised when she heard herself say.

"He's not found anyone else, since you, you know"

Sophia's countenance changed in an instant. "Do you think he would like to hear from me?" she asked in an almost begging tone."

"I don't know, he was so badly hurt the last time."

Sophia's face fell at hearing these words.

"Perhaps if you wait until he has graduated. I'll give you our telephone number, he should be home by early summer." Rachel added.

CHAPTER 11

Andrew was waiting at Kings Cross as Rachel emerged from the underground. A broad smile broke across his face as he rushed to meet her. As he went to kiss her cheek, she turned her face to meet his lips with hers.

It was difficult to tell if he was blushing, decided Rachel, as he had such a ruddy complexion. This was the breakthrough he had been hoping for but, never the less, it took him by surprise, and for a moment he was lost for words. This left Rachel in command.

"We need to get tickets." she said reaching for her bag.

"I have already done that." he said passing two of them to Rachel. "I've got you a return for Wednesday. Is that Alright?"

"Thank you, Andrew." she said, noticing that they were first class, before placing them carefully into her bag and suppressing her urge to ask how much she owed him. She had always been used to paying her own way but this was not the time or the place. He already knew enough about her to know that and Rachel knew enough about him to know he wouldn't expect her to repay him in cash or any other way, not out of gratitude anyway.

First class was nearer the front of the train and would be pulled by two engines, one of which she noticed was the Flying Scotsman. It bore a banner, announcing that today 1st May, was the 40th anniversary since it had first travelled non-stop to Edinburgh. Full of excitement, Rachel pulled Andrew along the platform for a closer look at this magnificent monster, stood there, gently belching steam.

"Wait until Michael hears about this; he'll be so envious." she cried over the sounds of the station.

Andrew was pleased to hear that she would or already told her son about her trip. It would make things easier, he thought.

As the mighty train pulled away, Rachel beamed like a little girl and gripped Andrew's arm. Thistripwas going to be a wonderful few days, she told herself.

"I can't wait to see Scotland." she had said. "The only view I've had was is black and white when I saw the film the 39 Steps."

Andrew had laughed, he loved the simplicity of this girl as well as her spirit, so unlike many of his colleagues at work, who were mostly a bit dour. He delighted in treating her to lunch and later a romantic dinner in the dining car, so much more interesting than what she had been used to, sandwiches wrapped in greaseproof paper and a flask of tea which had always gone cold.

Scotland viewed from the train was as beautiful as she had expected, its hills and rivers spoke of a romantic past. She almost cried with the pleasure of it all, what had she done to deserve all this?

"It must have been something good." she said.

"What must have?" asked Andrew.

"Oh nothing." she replied looking once more through the window.

The streets of Edinburgh were deserted as the taxi drew up outside Andrew's home in the dimly lit street. A half-moon shed a silvery light on the Victorian detached house which seemed to have an air of mystery about it. The front wall bordered a small garden which had seen better days, thought Rachel as she was escorted to the front door. Before Andrew could retrieve his keys from his pocket, a light came on behind the sky light of the huge door.

"Don't worry about Mrs Gray." said Andrew in a hushed tone. "She's very protective of me. She'll be fine once she gets to know you."

The profile of a stout shortish woman was illuminated at the top of the three steps to the entrance.

"You're very late doctor." she said abruptly in a strong Glaswegian accent.

"Yes, I decided to get a later train. This is the guest I told you about over the telephone. She'll be staying for a few days."

"I see. When you said you'd be bringing a guest I assumed it would be a man so I made up the room on the same floor as you sir."

"That's alright Mrs Gray, that will be grand."

"Very good sir, " she replied looking Rachel up and down with a disapproving look. "I'd better get on with making supper then." she continued.

Rachel had not yet spoken a word and wondered if the next few days were going to be as pleasant as she had hoped. Standing in the hallway she looked up at the stairs, the top of which she couldn't see as they were not lit. All romantic thoughts swiftly disappeared from her head and she concentrated on just surviving the next few days.

"Mrs Gray didn't even ask my name", thought Rachel.

Andrew reading her thoughts dropped the suitcases and ushered her into the living room. A small fire had been set in a very large fireplace but not lit. Only the sidelights had been lit, castings shadows over the walls supporting a high ceiling. There were two framed photographs on the fireplace, one of a young woman with long hair who she thought was probably his daughter Laura and the other was of an older woman, probably her mother, his late wife.

The back wall was lined with several large bookcases and the outside wall had long curtains hung by the sides of the windows. a grand piano was set a little way back. Rachel shivered; this was not how she hoped it would be.

"I'll get some matches for the fire." said Andrew disappearing.

Rachel stepped forwards and stared at the photograph of the lady she assumed was his wife.

"She was really beautiful." boomed a voice behind her, startling her.

"You made me jump." said Rachel, turning to face Mrs Gray.

Ignoring her and continuing to look at the photograph she said,

" She was a real lady, someone whom everyone loved and respected."

Rachel, feeling unwelcome was to about to respond when Andrew returned and crouched to light the fire.

"Supper is ready sir. I'll be off to bed now. Goodnight."

"Thank you." replied Andrew still tending the fire.

Rachel was horrified at the thought that this woman, who clearly disliked her, lived here and once more she shivered.

Andrew, misinterpreting said "It won't be long warming up darlin."

But the damage was done and Rachel continued to stand with her coat on but then, deciding to make the best of things remarked.

"I don't think Mrs Gray likes me very much."

"I'm afraid Mrs Gray doesn't like anybody much but she's been with us for so many years and hasn't any family of her own. She adores Laura though and has virtually brought her up ever since her mother died. And me working all hours, she has been invaluable, I don't know what we would have done without her."

"I see. "said Rachel feeling a little better, now she understood the situation.

"I think you are the first woman to stay over in this house since Margaret"

He paused, realising he had said her name. Recovering,

"Here, let me take your coat, "he said, trying to hide his sad expression.

Rachel allowed Andrew to take her coat even though she was still feeling the cold. She had a lot to process.

"He was still in love with his dead wife." she thought and this house and Mrs Gray were not about to allow him to move on. "There is no way I'll be getting into bed with Andrew on this trip."

The next few days passed slowly. Andrew was lovely, the perfect gentleman. Rachelhad wanted more but realised Andrew just wasn't in the right place mentally. How could he be, living in that mausoleum, with Mrs Gray watching his every move?

The castle and other sights in and around Edinburgh were interesting and the company pleasant but this trip had not been what she was expecting or indeed had hoped. The pretty, most revealing dress had laid undisturbed in the case. Mrs Gray would surely have had something to say had it not.

Andrew took her to the station on Wednesday morning and seemed to recognise Rachel's disappointment even though she had tried hard to hide it.

"I'm sorry." he said as he helped her onto the train. "It was a mistake to bring you into the house. I know that now, I have to move on."

Rachel kissed him on the cheek saying. "I know how hard it is Andrew, I've been there myself you know."

The guard's whistle allowed her to move into the carriage with her thoughts. She had a lot to think about. At least, he recognises that he needs to move on. Perhaps it's possible, I don't know.

The journey was long. First class is great when you are with someone, she thought but when you are alone, it can be very lonely.

CHAPTER 12

Peggy had, of course a lot to say. She had been expecting her friend I to return to work beaming with happiness and eager to tell her all about her trip. But the look on her face turned out to be more revealing, than the dress she had lent her.

"He needs to sort out that Mrs Gray," she said. "she sounds worse than that Mrs Danvers in the film, Rebecca."

"She was. "replied Rachel, laughing but unable to mask the sadness in her eyes.

Seeing this Peggy suggested, "Why don't you invite Andrew to stay with you?"

"Perhaps; but I think I'll leave it for a while."

"Alright, but don't leave it too long girl." said Peggy hurriedly, after seeing Mr. Melcher approaching.

A month passed without any word from Andrew.

"Perhaps, it's just as well." thought Rachel. Peggy did her best to cheer her friend up and had taken her out a few times. This had resulted in a few subtle enquiries from men as to her marital status but none of them compared to Andrew. Still, Peggy was good company and they had a lot of fun.

Michael rang to say he had been awarded a 2.1 and asked how many tickets she would like for the graduation ceremony. "Just the one." she had replied with a touch of sadness, thinking how proud Jack would have been of his son.

"Laura's dad will be there." he had said.

"Was this Michael's way of saying she would have company or did he know of her visit to Edinburgh?"

She thought it best not to add anything.

When Rachel told Peggy, she had an opinion; of course, she did.

"He knows alright." she said. "Laura would have told him. This is good news girl; it shows that Andrew wanted to know what she thought. I bet she told him to go for it, she would want her father to be happy."

"You think?" asked Rachel, her hopes rising.

"Well, you'll soon find out. When is the graduation?" she asked.

Later that evening Rachel rang her son to ask if he would mind if she brought her good friend Peggy along

"I'll get two tickets then." he had said cheerfully.

Rachel and Peggy hit the shops the following weekend. Rachel wanted something special for this occasion.

"Remember you need a drees that is appropriate for a graduate's mother but also something that will attract your man," her friend had said. "Whereas I just need something to attract a man."

"You're a married woman." Rachel scolded.

"I know, but it doesn't stop me dreaming." she retorted. "This is going to be a fun weekend."

The days passed quickly. It was getting dark as the train pulled into Lime Street Station.

"So, this is Liverpool." said Peggy, standing and swinging her hips. "The capital of rock and Roll."

Michael was there to meet them.

"I'll show you the sights tomorrow." he said after being introduced to Peggy.

"Can we go to the Cavern?" she asked excitedly.

"Sure." he smiled, "It's a bit dingy though."

"I like dingy." she replied instantly.

"Peggy was flirting already," thought Rachel.

"I know where your hotel is, I'll take you, it's not far, we won't need a taxi."

Peggy was impressed. As they emerged from the train station, Saint Georges Hall, guarded by two enormous stone lions met her gaze.

"It's like a roman city," she exclaimed.

"It was opened by Prince Albert in 1854," Michael explained with pride in his voice "he was said to have loved this city."

"This is an impressive young man." whispered Peggy to his mother.

Rachel quickened her step adjusting the hood of Michael's duffle coat.

"You need a new coat love." she said. "You've had this one since you started here."

"Yes mum, "he replied tolerantly, "here we are, the Station Hotel."

Carrying both ladies' cases, he backed into the doors and entered the lobby. There was a short queue at the reception desk. Several modest chandeliers lit the area and a uniformed youngster flitted between the desk and the lift.

"The ceremony starts at the cathedral at 11. I'll collect you outside at 9.30. You must be tired after your journey; I'll leave you rest."

Dinner was served in a massive room with a dozen huge chandeliers, the hotel information booklet explained that it was designed by a shipbuilder who had been involved in designing the Titanic. Peggy wanted to go out on the town but after Rachel promised to go with her on Saturday night she relented and settled for looking around at the various guests, guessing what they were up to, where they were from and whether the men were married or not. When Rachel retired, Peggy decided to sit at the bar, smoking a cigarette and imitating her favourite film star, Lauren Bacall.

Rachel fell asleep wondering if Andrew would be there tomorrow and if he would approach or keep it formal.

Both ladies chose the Full English at breakfast. Rachel asked with a cheeky smile,

"Did Humphrey Bogart show up sweetheart?" asked Rachel trying to imitate the actor's voice.

"Sadly not, but Sam did."

"Sam?"

"The pianist. But I left before he played the Messi an."

Peggy was a good friend, but Rachel wandered what would have happened if she had attracted a man. She wasn't sure. She had met her husband a few times and found him a quiet sort of man, nice, decent were the words that came to mind. Exciting, no. But she was sure Peggy was just enjoying herself, nothing more.

Michael arrived on time and walked them back along to Lime Street where they hired a taxi to take them to the cathedral. The short journey took them past the departmental store Lewis's which sported an explicit statue of a naked man outside the fourth floor, much to Peggy's amusement.

   "Oh, look at that girl." she had shouted as they passed.

   The taxi driver broke in with a broad scouse accent.

   "Yes love, he's been up there for years in all weathers. If someone from around here makes a show of themselves we say he's one of Lewis's."

   "You've got a nice day for it ladies." he said as he dropped them off on the broad pavement outside the cathedral. Peggy had insisted on paying.

   Michael handed two large tickets to his mother saying he had to go and collect his cap and gown." Just follow the signs," he said "I'll see you afterwards."

   The two ladies moved slowly along the queue to the entrance.

   "Can you see him?" asked Peggy.

   "No, "replied Rachel knowing full well who she was talking about. "Now Peggy please don't say anything if we do meet him, promise?"

   "I promise." she replied with a twinkle in her eye.

   " No really, I won't." she continued, sweeping a finger across her lips like a zip.

   The well of the cathedral was vast. Chairs were lined in rows and as tickets were checked, the guests were shown to their seats. Rachel and Peggy were directed to row H on the right of an isle at the near end. This gave them a clear view of the people directed to the front of both the right and left sections.

"Any sign of Andrew?" asked Peggy in a whisper.

"No." lied Rachel who had already spotted him in the left-hand section, at the end of row B. He appeared to be alone.

The chancellor of the university, dressed in his colourful robes of office started the ceremony. Behind him were seated the various heads of departments, all dressed in their appropriate gowns. And then a recorded fanfare announced

the arrival of the graduates who processed and lined the sides of the seated guests. When the chancellor had finished his welcome, he started to invite the graduates on stage to receive their rolled-up degrees, starting with those who had been awarded a first-class degree. As expected, they were few in number, the cream of the cohort. The last name to be called in this category was Laura McClain.

"Is that Andrew's daughter?" whispered Peggy. Rachel nodded smiling,

"She's a genius then, just like her dad.

Next there came those who had been awarded a 2.1 degree. Rachel tensed as she waited for her son's name to be called.

"Michael Flynn." called the chancellor over the microphone. Michael climbed the steps and shook hands and then took the scroll before confidently striding to the far end of the stage and descending the steps. Peggy had gripped Rachels arm from the moment the chancellor had announced Michael's name.

There were many other names called during the following hour and a half. Peggy was itching to get to the hall for a snack and a drink but had to wait patiently with her friend Rachel until the last of the graduates had been presented.

"Any sign of Andrew yet?" she asked, as at last, the chancellor closed the ceremony.

"That's him." she said following Rachel's gaze as they moved to go. "him in the tweed jacket near the front."

"Yes, but please don't say anything, I'll speak to him when we get to the reception."

The crowds moved along Hope Street, the street which connected the Church of England cathedral with the Catholic Metropolitan Cathedral at the other end.

Michael greeted his mother at the crowded reception hall.

"Mum, you remember Laura."

"Congratulations Laura." said Rachel meeting her eyes.

"Thank you," she replied scanning her from top to toe." I hear you visited dad in Edinburgh. I hope you didn't find Mrs Gray too scary, she is very protective, I'm afraid."

Rachel avoided giving an answer by introducing Peggy.

"Pleased to meet you dear," she said, adding mischievously, "Is your dad here?"

"Yes, I'm here." said Andrew joining the group and kissing his daughter, and then turning. "Michael, congratulations, a proud day for your family." again, turning to smile at Rachel.

"Hello Andrew." she said working hard to process all that was happening. "I see Laura got a first, you must be very pleased."

"Yes, thank you Rachel. Actually, Laura has persuaded me to look for another place. Still in Edinburgh but in a different area, more modern."

"So, everyone knows everything." thought Rachel. Before she could respond, he added. "Yes, it was high time, and Mrs Grey is retiring, she has found a small place in Kilmarnock, near to where her sister lives."

Peggy saw that Rachel was scrambling for words and came to the rescue.

"It all sounds very exciting, another chapter in these young people's lives." she said looking at Michael and Laura.

A bell rang and a voice shouted over the din.

"Ladies and gentlemen, the buffet is now open."

People started to move in the direction of the voice. Peggy corralled the two graduates, leaving Andrew and Rachel behind.

"Your friend is very intuitive." said Andrew.

Amongst other things." replied Rachel smiling.

"I've been planning what to say for weeks." said Andrew." I'm sorry about your visit, but it shook me into action. I had a long talk with Laura and she urged me to make some changes. I also told her about my feelings towards you Rachel."

"Let's not rush into things Andrew, I'm pleased you have decided to make some changes in your life but I want you to be sure."

"I am sure."

"O.k." she replied, "but before you say any more, why don't you come and stay with me at my house for a few days and we'll take it from there."

"I'd really like that, Rachel."

"That's settled then, let's get something to eat, I'm starving." Linking his arm, she led him towards the tables.

Peggy had held Michael and Laura in conversation about this exciting city but Laura had kept her eyes firmly fixed on her father and Rachel until she saw the pair approaching. Their countenance told the waiting group everything they needed to know.

CHAPTER 13

Michael returned to the cottage a week after his graduation, the same day as a handwritten letter with a perfumed envelope. Rachel thought she knew who it might be from as she placed it on the fireplace.

"What are your plans love?" she had asked before he went out that Sunday morning.

"I thought I might take a job on the farm to earn a bit of money whilst I apply for jobs."

"That sounds like a good idea," she had said. "I think Tom still works there."

"Haven't heard from him lately. I'll go for a little walk, see if we can catch up."

"O.K. love, dinners at 6."

Michael hadn't indicated who the letter was from, just a friend, he had said brushing his hair back with his hand. "He still does that when he's unsure about something. "she thought.

He was late." He's never late for dinner." thought Rachel. "Something must have happened."

Rachel put her coat on and was about to leave when Michael arrived back, slightly worse for drink and not looking happy. He was a man now but Rachel had never been good at scolding her son anyway.

"I'm afraid your dinners ruined, but you can try it if you wish." she offered in that quiet voice of hers, but then she noticed that he was upset.

"What is it love?" she asked.

This triggered an unexpected response, he started to weep.

"It's Tom," he sobbed. "He had an accident at work and he's now crippled, with a wife and two children."

"Oh Michael, what happened?"

"The tractor he was working on toppled over on the hill to the top field."

"O love, that's awful. How are they managing?"

"They're not. He's had to apply for Invalidity benefit but these things take an age, so they're existing on unemployment benefit."

"Did Mr Jones pay him anything?"

"Just a fortnight's pay and his cards. Reckoned he was messing about before the accident."

"and was he messing about?"

"I don't know mum; he just looks so ill."

Rachel embraced her son. I'm so sorry. "she said, hating to see her son so upset but at the same time sort of grateful that this was giving her the opportunity to hold him, something she had not been able to do this for years.

"Can he find any other kind of work, do you think?"

"He can't walk mum, he's in a wheelchair. He was never much good when it came to paperwork, so I don't know. I just hope he can get back on his feet. He hadn't been out since the accident so I took him down the pub and bought him a few drinks, there was no-one in at that time but when some of our school friends came in, he wanted to leave, he didn't want to be seen like he is."

Rachel retrieved Michael's dinner from the oven and made some fresh gravy. He picked at it for a while but then said, "I think I'll have an early night mum. See you in the morning."

Rachel sat half listening to the radio for the rest of the evening, thankful that it wasn't her son who had to face life coping with such a huge disability and also wondering what the future held for all of them. Life could be so unpredictable.

Always wishing to leave the place tidy before retiring, Rachel straightened the cushions on the settee and noticed something shoved down the side. Lifting it out she saw it was the letter addressed to Michael. As she moved to place it on the mantel piece, she was curious. The envelope was of quality, hand written and had a local postmark. Holding it to her nose, she recognised the fragrance. Sophia. Holding it, she sat and agonised. Should she risk reading it? She didn't want Michael hurt again, especially not now, on the brink of a career. In the end she stuffed it back into the end of the settee without reading it; she knew that its contents would be written on her face and she wouldn't want Michael to know that she had read his letter. Anyway, he would tell her when he was ready.

Next morning over breakfast, Michael was quiet, processing his thoughts.

"What will you do today love, it looks like it's going to be a nice day."

"I thought I would head into town to see if I can get some temporary work, maybe at the greengrocers where I had my Saturday job."

"Good idea, the shops will be busier now the schools are closed for the summer." said Rachel relieved that he wouldn't be working on the farm. "Try not to worry too much about Tom, I'm sure things will get better for him."

And then trying to cheer him she asked, "Have you heard anything from your university friends?"

Michael tried to refocus." The letter was from Sophia."

"Oh yes, how is she love?" thankful that she hadn't read it, it would have shown.

"Well, she only managed a third at Oxford." he said. "Her father wants her to go to a school in Switzerland for a year, like the debutants used to, but she is resisting. She wants to meet."

"How do you feel about that love?"

"I'm not sure, I don't know if I want to be dragged into family stuff. Not like last time."

Rachel didn't want her son to be hurt again but thought if he didn't meet up, it would eat away at him and he would always wonder. But she didn't want to influence his decision one way or another. But Sophia had kept her promise not to contact him until after he had graduated and she liked her for that.

"Maybe you should meet up love, but be careful. Did she say how to contact her?"

"She wants to meet in Faye's Café in town on Monday morning at 9 when it's not too busy. She said that if I didn't turn up that she would understand and not try to contact me again."

"I see." said his mother, not adding anything. She liked Sophia very much and a part of her wanted Michael to meet with her but she would worry about what would follow; if they did decide to continue where they left off three years ago. It would cause trouble; damn this class divide.

The telephone rang, it was Andrew. Rachel intended to ask him to ring back. But he wasn't ringing from home, he was ringing from the hospital.

"I've sold the house." he said excitedly.

But Rachel couldn't cope with two relationships at the moment; so, she asked him to ring back in the evening as she was late for work.

"Please don't worry about me mum." said Michael recognising his mother's anxiety. I know the situation with her family and I'll not do anything stupid. I've got my future to consider."

Rachel was late for work. Peggy recognised that look.

"O'K. ducs, what's the matter?"

"Oh nothing" replied Rachel but then, "I'll tell you later." getting on with her work. It was month end and there was plenty to do.

Peggy enjoyed Rachel's accounts even more now, since she had met the main characters in her life, Michael and Andrew. She sighed thinking of the man she had met in Liverpool, so distinguished looking and ruggedly handsome and most of all available. She buried herself in her work, that way lunchtime would come quicker and she could resume her inquisition. "I wish something romantic would happen in my life." she thought thinking of her husband and then sighing again.

"There, you're now up to date," said Rachel over their lunchtime sandwiches

Peggy stared open mouthed at her friend. "What do you mean, you can't cope with two relationships? Hears me wishing I had just one, I sometimes think mine needs the kiss of life."

Rachel loved her friend; she was so funny and always knew what to do.

"Leave Michael to make his own decisions, he knows what he's doing. Concentrate on dishy Andrew and help him find his new house, after all it sounds as though you could well end up living in it."

"You think?"

"No, I don't think, I know. He's sold his old house because he would do anything to get you. So, get on with it girl before he changes his mind."

"Do you really think that."

"A blind person could see that; he's infatuated with you."

"Alright, when he rings tonight, I'll set a date for him to visit."

"Good, and make sure Michaels out of the way."

That evening, Rachel discussed her plan with Michael. He had always been a thoughtful lad and immediately said that he would arrange to visit a university friend.

"There's no need love." Rachel had said trying to hide her embarrassment.

"It's fine mum. I've been meaning to do it for a while. And I've also decided to meet up with Sophia on Monday."

"Things were moving fast," though Rachel but Peggy was right, she had to get on.

The week end passed quickly. Rachel and Michael left the house at the same time, she on her way to work and Michael to his rendezvous with Sophia. Next week end was a big week end, Andrew would arrive Friday night and Michael would leave during the morning to visit his friend in London.

Opening the door of the café triggered the sound of a gentle bell. It had been over three years since he last saw Sophia. He was ten minutes early but she was there already, sat in the corner behind a small vase of summer flowers. A waitress he recognised from school was attending.

"Hello Michael." Both girls had greeted him in unison and with obvious delight.

Realising that he had come to meet another, the waitress retreated in disappointment. Sophia rose from her seat. She wore a summer dress similar to the one she had worn and that day five years ago when they first met. Her blonde hair shone like it had that day. But Michael was no longer that shy little lad who stuttered to get his words out. He was now this confident six-foot-tall university graduate.

"I'm so glad you came Michael." she said softly holding out her hand.

"So formal," Michael replied smiling and gesturing her to sit. "How are you?"

"You look great Michael."

"You look exactly the same Sophia, just like the lovely girl I met playing the piano."

"You still blush, I see."

"Yes, I can't help it."

"I still like it," she said, another beautiful smile breaking across her lips.

Michael had earlier decided that he wouldn't allow himself to be hypnotised by this lovely girl but he couldn't help it. Trying to put a brake on his emotions he gestured to the waitress.

"Tracey" he called. And then looking at Sophia he said "Tea?"

"That would be lovely." she replied.

"A pot for two?" asked Tracey, sadly realising that she could not compete with this girl.

Breaking the protocol, she had been taught to strictly observe, Tracey said to Michael. "Have you heard about Tom? I don't know how they will manage."

Just then, a lady, Michael judged to be the owner appeared and Tracey quickly hurried away.

"Is that Tom whom I met at the dance?" asked Sophia looking concerned.

Michael explained what had happened to his friend.

Eventually Michael asked Sophia if she would go to Switzerland.

"I don't know, what do you think?"

Michael was dreading this question. He would have loved to have said. "Of course not. Come and live with me and have my children, but he couldn't and gave the sensible answer.

"What do you want to do Sophia?"

Like Michael, she would have loved to have said. "Let's run away and get married. "but she couldn't.

"I'd like to go to the cinema with you." she said in the end.

Michael broke the serious atmosphere and laughed. Continuing the fantasy, he said. "How about tonight?"

"What's on?" she asked, not caring what it was, but now knowing that yes, he did want to see her again.

"West Side Story, I don't know what's it is about but I've heard its good."

"It's a modern Romeo and Juliet story set to music and dance." said Sophia looking straight at Michael with love clearly showing in her eyes."

CHAPTER 14

As they left the cinema the couple danced along the pavement, each laughing at their partner's missed steps.

"At least you have had ballet lessons." shouted Michael as he provoked another fit of giggles from Sophia. "I would never have thought dance could be such fun,"

Sophia looked at Michael thinking her heart would burst with happiness. Yes, this was the man she wanted and her father would have to accept it. She didn't want a spoilt hooray Henry, even if he did come from the right kind of family. As they continued to walk along the now quiet streets the pair fell silent, each with their own thoughts until Sophia started to hum the song from the film, There's a Place for us, somewhere a place for us.

"Do you think we'll find that place?" asked Michael quietly.

"I know we will." Sophia said firmly, as she stopped abruptly to kiss him tenderly.

"I hope so." replied Michael, "I hope so." he repeated, a frown forming on his young forehead.

As soon as Michael had left for his weekend in London, Rachel worked furiously cleaning the house from top to bottom. New summer curtains that she had made, went up in the living room and front bedroom. The carpets were hoovered, kitchen floor washed and furniture polished, cushions plumped and table cloths ironed. Last inspections carried out, she made herself a cup of tea while she checked things off in her mind.

"All done." she said at last, looking at the clock on the mantel. Andrews train should be arriving soon. "I'd better get ready." she thought looking at herself disapprovingly in the mirror.

As Rachel walked towards the railway station, she spotted Mrs Murray on the other side of the road, looking her up and down.

"I wonder where she's going all dolled up like that?" thought Rachel predicting the gossip's thoughts.

The train was on time, even though this was rush hour. Andrew emerged from the steam of the train, carrying a tartan travel bag and a bunch of summer flowers. He looked well, in spite of his long journey from Scotland. She was on her own ground this time and confident that this visit would be so much more successful than the last time. Linking him, the couple made their way back passing Mrs Murray once more. Rachel held her man closer and waved. "This is my friend Andrew; he's come to stay for the weekend." she shouted knowing this would give her plenty to chew on.

Rachel was beaming as she showed Andrew around her cottage, she had not felt this happy in a long time and the anticipation of what was to happen later made her skin tingle as she showed him her bedroom.

"It's lovely." Andrew had said looking at Rachel.

" Dinner won't be long" she announced turning to hide her blushes.

After unpacking, Andrew descended the stairs carrying a bottle of Drambuie.

"I thought you might like a wee dram later, "he said, with a cheeky glint in his eye.

Lovely, Rachel had said not knowing what the drink was, but suspecting it was a kind of Scotch whiskey.

Dinner comprised of roast beef, Yorkshire pudding, boiled and roast potatoes and buttered cabbage and broccoli. A bottle of red wine and a vase, containing the flowers Andrew had brought, sat between them on the white, embroidered tablecloth.

"I like it here in the country." Andrew said as he ate. "I don't hear the birds in the city."

"Perhaps you should choose your new house outside of the city." Rachel suggested. "Where the air is sweeter."

"That was superb. "Andrew exclaimed, as at last, he lay down his knife and fork.

"I thought we'd leave pudding until later; would you like to go for a little walk to help you digest dinner?"

"Aye, I would Rachel." he agreed.

Rachel took him the short distance out of town to the wall which marked the edge of Hazlehurst Manor.

"You remember his Lordship." said Rachel with distain.

"How could I forget." he replied laughing. "I bet he has given you a wide berth ever since."

After a pause Rachel said "I think they're back on."

"Michael and the daughter?"

"Sophia, yes. I mean she's a lovely girl but I worry that it's going to cause a lot of problems. Michael didn't say much after their meeting in town last Monday but I could tell they were back on. He was so happy."

"Well true love usually finds a way Rachel, take us two for instance."

Rachel was surprised at this overt declaration of Andrew's feelings and took a moment to consider.

"Did he just say that he was truly in love with me?" thought Rachel but choosing not to respond at that moment.

The sun was setting over the hills on the far end of town as the couple made their way back in silence. Andrew wondered if he had spoken too soon. He hoped he hadn't ruined another weekend, but then, to his relief, she linked him and they resumed their conversation. As the couple walked along the unfamiliar road, Andrew stumbled as he mounted a kerb but Rachel managed to save him from falling.

As the clock struck ten, Rachel poured them both another Drambuie and they sat in front of the open fire which was now settling into a crimson pile.

"A cup of tea Andrew?" asked Rachel standing.

"I'm fine thank you hen." he replied finishing his drink.

"Then shall we take the bottle upstairs?" she asked quietly "I like this stuff." she said smiling seductively.

Andrew felt an immediate hardening and stood, lifting the bottle.

Rachel had remembered Peggy's instructions of how to deal with this moment but decided she could manage quite well on her own, even though it had been twenty years.

As the couple reached the bedroom door, Rachel turned to face Andrew and said. "Did you mean what you said earlier, about true love and us two?"

"Aye, I did lassie."

Before he could continue Rachel kissed him full on the mouth and brought him into the room.

The bed had already been turned down as she turned and asked him to unzip her dress. He did so with trembling hands, the smell of her perfume now more intense.He then proceeded to undo his shirt buttons. Slipping out of her underskirt to just bra and frilly panties, she glided into bed and watched Andrew as he neatly laid his trousers on the back of a straight chair that had been conveniently placed at the foot of the bed. His manhood bulged as he removed his socks and underwear before slipping into bed next to her. With strong arms he lifted Rachel over him and undid her bra allowing her breasts to fall onto his chest. Her nipples hardened as he removed her panties before swinging her on to her back. The dim light from a streetlight briefly shone on her face as he told her that he loved her.

"I love you too." she replied as he entered her fingering her silky black hair.

"Did he have a hairy chest?" asked Peggy on Monday morning. "Did he snore?"

"No to both, "answered Rachel beaming.

"I'm so jealous." said Peggy, "When are you seeing him again?"

"I'm not sure. He's going to ring me tonight"

"You must bring him over next time he comes down. Maybe we can all go out together."

It was Tuesday evening when Michael returned home with news.

"I've been offered a job in London." he announced. "How do feel about me moving up there?" he asked.

"I thought it wouldn't be long." replied his mother lovingly straightening his pullover.

"What kind of job?"

"It's with a publishing house in Chelsea. I said I would let them know by Friday."

"And what would you be doing love?"

Michael had now judged that she wasn't entirely against the idea, her face would have given her away. "It's assistant to the editor in the travel section, they publish magazines that gives insights into foreign travel, a bit like National Geographic."

"It sounds really interesting, foreign travel is starting to become popular, my friend Peggy was only saying the other day that she and her husband are talking about going to Spain this summer."

"Yes, it's the future mum, air travel is set to take off."

The unintended pun broke the tension and they laughed.

"And where would you live Love?"

"Oh, they said they would take care of that, new flats are being built in the area." said Michael, allowing his enthusiasm to show.

"Then you must take it love." said Rachel closing to hug him.

"Will you be O.K. mum?" he asked. "I could try and get work around here."

"I'll be fine love." she said, trying to smile through her emotion. "Anyway, there's not much work around here for a graduate, especially one as brilliant as you.

Next morning Peggy said to her friend, "You'll miss him."

"I will." agreed Rachel." But I could never stand in his way and anyway he left home three years ago when he went off to University."

"And who knows what the future holds for you girl, you and Andrew."

"Yes, who knows, although I haven't heard from him since he went back on Monday morning."

"Oh." said Peggy, "Have you rang him?"

"I thought I would do that this evening, after dinner."

"I'm sure he'll be fine. Emergency at work or something." said Peggy doing her best to sound confident.

That evening, Michael had announced that he was going to visit his Friend Tom so Rachel decided to leave ringing Andrew until later. As the clock struck eight, she stood, intending to make the call but as she entered the hall the phone rang. She relaxed the teneseness that she had been feeling thinking it would be him.

"A female voice asked from seemingly far away. "Is that Mrs Flynn?"

Rachel tensed as she quietly answered, "Yes, this is she."

"Rachel, this is Laura, Andrew's daughter."

Rachel's stomach muscles tensed even more as she waited with bated breath for her response to leave her lips.

"Laura, lovely to speak to you." she replied automatically. And then" Is everything alright?"

"He had a fall on Tuesday, tripped over a curb on his way home from work."

"Is he hurt?" asked Rachel clearly anxious.

"Well, he suffered mild concussion after his fall and has been kept in hospital for a few days for tests and observation. It's not the first time he's had a fall. Has dad told you about his vision yet?"

"No, is he having trouble with it?"

"He promised me he would tell you. I expect he didn't want to spoil the weekend."

"Is it bad?"

"I should really let dad tell you about it, but yes, I'm afraid it is. I think he will be home by Friday at the latest and he will call you then."

"Are you alright love?"

"Yes, I'm o.k., just worried about dad."

"Alright Laura, thanks for letting me know, try not to worry too much love, I'm sure it will be alright."

Placing the receiver down, Rachel fell, deflated, onto the settee and recalled Andrew stumbling on their walk last Friday evening. At the time she had put it down to the poor street lighting but now she wondered if it were a symptom of a more serious condition.

CHAPTER 15

Sophia knew London well. Her father had many contacts there and had taken her there often to meet his friends in their social set. She found it exciting as a young child, but as a teen she found it a duty rather than a pleasure as she realised that she was being paraded in the hope of finding her an eligible future suiter.

But now London looked different, it was where her beloved Michael lived. Since starting his career here, she was a frequent visitor, delighting in showing him the sights and lesser-known places where they could be themselves and, most importantly, free from her father's scrutiny. Although Michael's flat was tiny, it was a perfect little love nest. Autumn leaves decorated the many trees outside and a small gas fire kept them warm as they spent the evenings sharing a bottle of wine and talking about their futures. On the last weekend in September, they had dinner out at a small Chinese restaurant near the river.

"We need to be sensible." Michael said. We both need to have decent careers that we enjoy."

Sophia nodded in agreement but then burst out laughing.

"You look ever so funny when you talk seriously."

"Sophia." retorted Michael firmly. "There's a lot to consider."

"Yes Michael, sorry." And then after a short pause. "What about children."

"Children?" said Michael incredulously.

"Yes, plural. I don't know about you but I have hated being an only child."

"O.K., but what about?"

"What about what?, "asked Sophia mischievously having guessed what Michael meant.

"You know, don't tease."

"Ah, you mean mmm."

"Yes."

"Not here Michael. We'll talk later," said Sophia, allowing her smile to morph into a more serious look.

Michael had been oblivious to the people around them in the crowded restaurant and continued with his verbal jousting but Sophia briefly wondered at a man on his own,satat a table near the door. He was making notes and referring to his watch.

As they walked home along the embankment, shuffling through the many gold and brown leaves, they confirmed a couple of decisions they had made over the past month.

"The thing is Michael." said Sophia as the couple made their way along the embankment. "I have always promised myself to go to the alter as a virgin, as difficult as that may be, as difficult as it is."

That was what Michael so loved about this girl, her bravery and honesty.

"It would be so easy to make love to you Michael right now, but I want it to be special and for ever. I don't want a grand affair, father would probably disown me anyway, and that would suit me. We would wait for a perfect dawn in mid-summer, I would gather wild flowers into a bouquet and I would walk over the fields to the church, where we would meet and marry."

Michael stopped under a dim Victorian light that shone just enough to cast its soft beamsonto Sophia's face. She looked almost angelic.

"She's serious." thought Michael, "She means it."

"Sounds lovely Sophia, but do you think we can manage all that, and how long would it be?"

Sophia advanced and held both of his hands and looked into his face.

"We can do it Michael, you and I. As you say, we must first pursue decent careers. You have started yours and I shall go to finishing school in Switzerland as father wants me to, but only for a year and then hopefully he will come around. In that time, you will have established yourself in the publishing business and I will teach piano and compose. We can then marry and start our life together."

"Wow, "said Michael, "You've got it all planned, but we'll need a house and there's my mother to consider and your fathers not going to just do nothing." he protested.

"We can do it Michael." Insisted Sophia. "I'm of age and he won't be able to stop me, so if he doesn't want to lose me, he'll have to agree to the marriage or lose me altogether."

Sophia's expression was firm and Michael knew from experience that she meant every word.

The couple walked on in silence, unaware that they were being watched.

"You're quiet Michael." said Sophia after a few minutes silence.

"Oh, you know me, just thinking."

"Worrying you mean."

"Yes, I suppose I am."

"O.K." said Sophia stopping. "Do you love me?"

"You know I do." he replied.

"Well then, leave the worrying to me." she said pulling him to her and kissing him. "It's going to be fine."

The moon was full and seemed to celebrate the occasion as its light sparked on the river.

"10th June then next year, "said Sophia.

"As long as the weather is nice." replied Michael smiling.

The couple made their way back to Michael's flat where they spent a loving, but celibate, week end together. As Sophia went to draw the curtains on the last evening, she saw a man across the road, stood by a dimly lit lamppost. When he realised that he had been spotted he moved on. She wondered if it might be the same man sat alone in the restaurant that night. She decided not to say anything to Michael, she didn't want him to worry.

CHAPTER 16

"To tell you the truth Peggy, I'm angry. He should have told me."

"Yes, he should have girl." agreed her friend, "but if you finish it now, it might seem that you've done it because of his health worries. You need to ask yourself if you love him and if the answer is yes, then you need to ask yourself another question."

"And what would that be?"

"Do you love him enough?"

"Yes, I see that. He'll probably not be able to continue to operate on patients. And maybe he won't even be able to look after himself. It depends on his prognosis."

"Everything O.K. ladies?" asked Mr Melcher.

"Yes, thank you Mr Melcher." replied Peggy smiling. "We were just saying how well you look today."

"Why thank you ladies." he said trying to smile. "And may I say how well you both look this fine morning." moving his gaze to stare at Rachel for just a moment too long."

As Mr Melcher returned to his desk, Peggy said under her breath "There's always Mr Melcher, Rachel, you know he fancies you, don't you?"

This remark made Rachel shiver and both tried to stifle their laughter.

That evening, Rachel made her regular call to Michael and after the usual enquiries to each other's health Michael said in his solemn voice.

"I have something to tell you."

Rachel braced herself for another shock. "What is it love?"

"Sophia wants us to marry."

Rachel relaxed a little, relieved it was not more bad news, "How do you feel about that son?"

"That's what I wanted to ask you mum?"

"I want what you want son."

"Well, I love her and she loves me. If only it were that simple. And there's you mum."

"Now listen Michael, I'm fine. It's her father that could be the problem."

"Sophia said to leave that with her. She's going to agree to her father's wishes to go to Switzerland for a year, on condition that he won't interfere with her seeing whoever she chooses. She's not going to tell him about us just yet; that would be just too much for him at this stage."

"I see. She's a sensible girl and I'm so happy for you. I like Sophia and she'll make you a good wife. Just be careful when it comes to her father, he could cause trouble."

"I will mum. How did your weekend with Laura's dad go?"

"It was nice love but Laura rang me to tell me about him having an accident, a bad fall."

"Was it due to his eyesight?"

"You know about that?"

"Laura told me about it before we graduated."

"It seems we both have complications with our relationships son."

"I want you to be happy mum, but I don't want you to be tied to someone who could be dependent upon you for the rest of your lives. I've seen how Tom's wife looks at him, more pity than love."

"Yes, well we don't know how bad it is yet. I don't think Andrew's is the type of man who would try to deceive, but we must wait and see."

"O.K. mum, but just remember, I'm always here for you, you know that."

"I do son, but listen." Rachel said firmly. I'm the parent here and it's for me to worry about you, not the other way round."

"O.K. Mum but I'm a man now and it's my turn to look after you."

"Do you think she's pregnant?" asked Peggy after Rachel had told her about the phone call.

"No, of course not." replied Rachel indignantly. "Sophia's got very clear ideas when it comes to that sort of thing; she wants to arrive at the alter intact."

"You mean Virgo intact; I take it." said Peggy trying to stifle a laugh. "I remember trying that. It didn't work. Well, it was during the war."

Rachel loved Peggy, she was so intuitive and made every situation potentially funny.

"And what about Andrew, have you heard from him yet?"

"No, not yet, he's probably still recovering from his fall."

"Have you worked out how you feel about."

Rachel cut her friend off short. "No not yet, it depends on what he has to say."

But Peggy always had to have the last word. "Look Rachel, just don't let the fact that you've, you know, done it together, influence you too much. You don't owe him."

That evening Andrew rang.

"I'm sorry I haven't been in touch. I've only just been discharged from hospital but I gather Laura rang you."

"Yes, how are you now Andrew?"

"Ach, I'm fine Lassie, such a fuss about a little fall."

"But it wasn't just a little fall, was it?"

Andrew hesitated before answering in a low voice. "No darlin, Laura said she had told you; about my eyes that is."

"How bad is it?"

"Ach, It's no too bad."

"That's not what Laura told Michael."

"Look, I'm in London in two weeks' time; why don't you come up and join me and we'll have a good talk then."

Rachel thought quickly and then said, "Alright Andrew, I'll do that."

"Cheer up darlin, it's going to be fine, I love you."

Rachel dreaded him saying that he loved her. But he had said it. She needed to think. Life had taught her to be cautious and she was not going to commit until she knew exactly what she was getting into, so she simply said. "O.K. Andrew, I'll see you then." and quickly placed the receiver on the cradle.

Feeling wretched, she needed to speak to someone, but not Michael, she wasn't going to worry him with this, but needing some words of comfort she rang Peggy."

"He said he loved me but I just couldn't say it back. I don't know if I can do this."

"You did right girl, he shouldn't have said that he loved you, he had no right, not until he knows more. He can only expect sympathy but not love, you did right"

Rachel felt relieved that her friend understood. She was not a heartless person only there for the good times, she had only known him for less than a year and the implications of him being disabled were huge.

Rachel thought of little else during the following two weeks. She had spoken to Michael several times and he had not mentioned having heard any more from Laura and she herself had not said anything. He had however, heard from Sophia; almost nightly and she reported having spoken to her father about her relationship with Michael. As predicted, he was against it but surprisingly not as fiercely as he had been previously. He was pleased that she had agreed to go to Switzerland and had said that if she felt the same about Michael in a year's time, he would not oppose them seeing each other. She had not however mentioned their unofficial engagement, this might have been a step too far at this stage.

"Some good news for a change." Rachel thought and it gave her a temporary solution to her own predicament. "She would give herself a similar length of time to mull over how she really felt about Andrew.

The two weeks passed quickly as Rachel found herself on the late afternoon train to London Victoria and her meeting with Andrew. She felt nervous and wasn't sure how she felt about only the second man in her life that she had slept with. This had been a big deal for her.

Andrew met her at the station as arranged and kissed her on the cheek. He looked exactly the same as he had a month ago, except for some slight bruising to his face.

"I've booked a table at a little place in Covent Garden, near the Royal Opera House." he said looking at Rachel for any sign of how she might be feeling about their relationship now. She smiled and said simply. "That's nice Andrew."

The restaurant was much less grand than Arabian Nights had been but it was a cut above anything she would have been able to afford. The conversation centred on Michael and his relationship with Sophia and on how Laura was getting on. Andrew had chosen a soft red wine and as the evening progressed Rachel felt more relaxed and remembered what an attractive man Andrew was and how tender he had been during their love making. The evening was progressing nicely and Rachel had allowed herself to wonder if that experience was to be repeated that night. Their conversation movedon to his search for a house outside the city of Edinburgh and what she thought about it. Rachel had never had the luxury of deciding what kind of house to live or where it would be, she just counted herself lucky to have a roof over their heads. Now she had a say in what he should buy and where. Her cheeks flushed as the waiter continued to fill her glass and she found herself wondering about furnishings and even curtains. A young man started to play romantic tunes on a violin, to the obvious delight of the guests in the packed venue. There was no mention of Andrew's eyes until he reached for his half full wine glass and accidentally knocked it over. The red wine spilled rapidly across the white embroidered table cloth. The reality of what this meant hit her like a slap across her face. After the inevitable fuss of the waiter clearing up and refilling their glasses, Rachel asked, her demeaner now having changed completely,

"So, Andrew, how is it with your eyes?"

"Ach, they're fine Lassie."

"Are you sure about that, what did the hospital say?"

Repositioning himself on his chair and sweeping back his hair as he always did when he was uncomfortable, he replied quietly "Well, they said I have a mild form of Macular Degeneration.

"Your eyes are degenerating? she asked.

"Mildly."

"Are you able to continue with your work, as a surgeon, I mean?" Rachel looked at Andrew intensely looking for any sign of hesitation.

The waiter attempted to top up her glass but she placed her hand over it.

"Oh, please don't let this matter spoil our evening, Rachel."

"Andrew, you have to be completely honest with me. Are you going blind?"

"Absolutely not. They told me that my sight would decline over time but that would be a long time off."

"Is there any treatment for it?" she asked, now feeling that she needed to re-address how she felt about her future with this man.

"Well," he replied with hesitation in his voice. "There is some research being conducted here and, in the States, and I am optimist about the outcome."

Rachel had heard optimistic talk many times before in her life and had learned the hard way not to rely on it. Her heart was now sinking fast. Yes, she liked Andrew a lot but was it enough to commit? She couldn't say at this moment, she needed to think.

"Oh, my goodness," she said looking at her watch, which hadn't worked for years, "Is that the time? I must go, I promised Peggy, I'd help her out this weekend."

"Rachel, please don't go, I'm sorry it's been a shock. I had hoped you would stay over at my hotel tonight."

Rachel felt wretched all over again, she was leaving this lovely man who had been so generous towards her, so charming. He stood as she stood. He looked so forlorn, so sad, so unhappy.

"I, I need time to think Andrew. I like you very much."

"Then please stay Rachel. I don't expect anything of you, just stay this one night. In the morning I'll take you back to Victoria and if you then want to call it a day, I'll totally understand."

Looking at this desperate, wonderful, gentle man, who had shown her nothing but kindness, Rachel sank slowly back into her chair. Was this love or pity, she needed to know.

Michael B McLarnon

CHAPTER 17

Nearly a year has passed. Michael was doing well at work and has been given his first foreign assignment. One of his company's established authors Greg Singer, has asked for an assistant to accompany him to the northern lakes in Italy.

Arriving early at Gatwick airport he had been told to meet his client at the check in desk. He was to hold up a card with the name of his publisher on it and they would make contact. This was to be the first time in an airport, let alone flying from one. Checking his passport for the third time Michael checked the time, 10.50. Check in closes in five minutes. "Where is he?" he asked himself again looking around anxiously. A middle-aged stout lady with a single suitcase approached him. "You must be Michael." she said, holding out a gloved hand.

"Yes, and you are?" he replied nervously.

"Gloria Savage." she replied rather stiffly, "but you'll know me as Greg Singer. Not a great idea, but after twenty or so rejection letters, I thought I'd try my luck as a man.

"Final call for flight BA 203 to Verona" came the announcement over the tannoid.

"Shakespeare never went to Verona you know." said Miss Savage as the plane taxied towards the runway.

"Really." said Michael remembering that Romeo and Juliet was set there.

"Strange when you consider." started Miss Savage but her words were drowned out by the scream of the engines as the plane hurtled down the runway for take-off."

As the aircraft levelled out Michael finished her sentence "When you consider he never went there."

"Quite." she said looking at her young travelling companion in a new light. He wasn't just a pretty face.

"Do you know Italy Michael?"

"No Miss Savage, I've never been."

"Call me Gloria." she said abruptly. "Wonderful country" she continued in a military sort of way. "I've wanted to set one of my novels here for many years, such a romantic place, the food and the flowers. You'll have noticed, I like food, particularly the sweet confectionaries."

Michael struggled with a diplomatic reply. Yes, she was a large lady and had struggled to get into her seat, but he couldn't possibly comment. After thinking of a few combinations of words he decided not to say anything.

Shortly after Gloria had downed two gin and tonics, she excused herself and struggled to get out; Michael had vacated his seat two minutes earlier.

"You may take the window seat, "she said as she started along the isle. "The view makes me feel nauseous.

Michael hadn't had time to examine his feelings about his first ever flight but looking down he wondered about the people who lived in the small villages tucked away far below at the base of the snow-capped mountains. Small white clouds hung prettily around and above the peaks of the Italian Alps that stretched in all directions below a beautiful blue sky.

"That's better." announced his travelling companion as she gave out a loud burp before sitting.

Michael smiled politely as he wondered how someone like her could write such wonderfully romantic novels. Michael's boss had described him, who turned out to be a her, as a very successful writer of romantic novels.

"Remember Michael, this writer is highly prized by us." his boss had briefed. "He makes us a great deal of money so treat him with the utmost consideration, nothing will be too much trouble. Got it?"

"I'm flattered to be asked to go sir but why me?" Michael had asked.

"Well, he asked for a fresh young energetic and intelligent young man, so as you fit the bill, I decided upon you."

"May I ask what he's like sir?"

"No idea" he replied "Never met him, I just look at his sales figures, that's all I need to know."

Leaving the mountains behind, the aircraft gradually reduced altitude as it approached Verona airport over olive groves and vineyards.

"I think I'm going to like it here." thought Michael as he made his way through the airport to collect their luggage. Gloria followed him complaining about the heat and that her ears were blocked, in spite of having sucked several boiled sweets on the plane. A taxi driver was waiting for them holding a large card displaying the name G. Savage.

"Ello Mr Savage." said the black suited man to Michael, this way please, gratzie."

"Don't bother." boomed Gloria, intercepting Michael's attempted correction.

The journey to Limoni skirted the lakeside town of Riva before speeding along the elevated and winding lakeside route. Gloria explained the road had many tunnels that had been cut through the mountain side on the orders of Mussolini and named after his many mistresses. Michael listened courteously as he admired the many flowers that bordered the route and also the waters of the lake that sparked in the sunshine. This was indeed a romantic place and he could well understand why Gloria had chosen it for inspiration. What he wasn't sure of was his role. Why had he been brought here?

The taxi drew up outside Hotel Splendid Palace. Gloria marched to the main entrance as Michael and the taxi driver followed with the luggage. Looking at the grand entrance Michael thought that, yes indeed this was a splendid palace. Michael turned to thank the driver but he had already returned to his shiny black limacine. "He must have been paid already." thought Michael as he approached the reception desk which was staffed by two pretty receptionists, dressed in white tops and black skirts Gloria was checking in.

"Yes dear, two bookings for two double rooms with balconies."

Michael sighed his relief. "Whew, he thought."

Placing the cases down he brushed back his hair with his hand and proceeded to sign the register under the smiling gaze of the black-haired receptionist.

"I hope you have an enjoyable stay with us sir, "she said in perfect English, her Italian accent making her words sound romantic in themselves.

"See you at dinner Michael." Gloria said as a bell boy whisked her case away leaving him to wait for the boy's return. Another guest was checking in speaking German. The receptionist effortless switched from English to fluent German. The other receptionist leaned on the desk and smiled at Michael as she enquired if he was on vacation.

"Working I'm afraid" he said in his very English accent.

"Perhaps I can show you around in your spare time." she replied in a slightly pleading way. "My name is Lucia."

Michael was struggling to reply when the bell boy returned saving him from making an excuse, had he wanted to, that is. "This place has got it's temptations." he thought as he followed the boy. "But there's only one girl for me."

His room was spectacular. Classic paintings of the area adorned the walls. The double bed looked inviting; its duvet decorated with lemons. The bathroom had a large bath, toilet and bidet. A separate ornamental wooden door led into a Romanesque marble floored wet room. Turning to the window, a slight breeze inflated the net curtains and revealed a balcony. Stepping out on to it, the full panorama of the lake and bordering mountains was revealed.

"This must be what heaven is like." he thought. "This is where Sophia and I will spend our honeymoon."

Dinner with Gloria was hugely embarrassing due to her obvious dislike of foreign male waiters, in fact of anyone who wasn't English.

"Hey, Luige, where's our dinner?" she shouted across the crowded dining room.

The staff were eager to please and diplomatically tried to inform Gloria of their names, such as Andre or Pedro, but to no avail: they were all Luige as far as she was concerned.

Michael would have loved to reprimand her but this was his first foreign assignment and he didn't want to receive a bad report. He did however try to apologise to one of the men when she made a trip to the cloakroom. He had graciously accepted in a very professional way.

The following morning Gloria didn't show for breakfast but a handwritten message was waiting for him in the dining room. It said simply

"M,

I'm working on my novel today in my room. See you at dinner.   G"

"This is going to be a good day." thought Michael as he sat for breakfast.

Leaving the hotel through the rear exit he walked the short distance along the flowered pathway which emerged by the Lake; the waters of which sparkled in the sun. A large ferry boat approached the short landing stage that jutted out from the land. A church bell sounded. Its chime was different to the church bells at home, they were lighter in their tone. He followed the sound and saw the lemon-coloured church perched on a large rock on the other side of the small town. It was 10 o'clock. Passing the small harbour, he observed a dozen small colourful boats dancing on the swell caused by the ferry. The sky had a few cotton-wool clouds and the whole place looked beautifully cheerful, so different to London. Climbing the steep steps to the church he turned and admired the view over the lake to the opposite shores which were guarded by high, snow-capped mountains. The beauty of it all almost took his breath away. He would tell Sophia all about it in his next letter; he would write this very evening. The church, he noticed was dedicated to the French saint San Bernadette. He entered; a Mass had just started. Sitting at the rear he was impressed at the obvious devoutness of the congregation, that he judged to be mostly local. The elderly ladies were almost all dressed in black wearing either headscarf or hat. The men were dressed in simple coats and trousers. In contrast, the young priest had a colourful vestment and the four angelic looking altar boys wore white Cassocks with red coloured shirts. Fabulous works of religious art adorned the walls and a mixed choir sang their hearts out. This seemed to be so different to the class ridden church in his town back home.

    Michael enjoyed the rest of the day sat on his balcony. He wrote two letters, one to his mother at home and the other to Sophia at her school in Switzerland. His tone, was of course, very different in each. To his mother he described Gloria as a most unlikely author of love stories and ventured the opinion that her love life was confined to the pages of her books. He didn't mention his companion at all in his letter to Sophia, devoting it largely to describing Limoni and imagining himself walking along the shores of the lake hand in hand with his beloved. He also said he had found the perfect church to be married in and that there would be no need to bring flowers as they were everywhere.

    Handing the letters over to the receptionist, who he had encountered the previous day at check-in, she asked in a flirty sort of way if they were for his girlfriends. Smiling back at her, he replied that they were, before making his way to the dining room. Gloria was already seated at their table. Michael was courteous as ever and asked how her writing was progressing.

    "Good." she replied, then asked if he would like to hear an outline as far as it went.

    "I'd love to." he replied, hoping this would occupy her and distract from her bullying the waiters.

    Looking straight at Michael with a stare that defied any deflection, Gloria launched into her story, transforming her appearance completely. Imitating the voices of her characters she related the story, all without referring to any notes. Her concentration was complete. Michael listened in a trance like state, fascinated at this woman's talent for creating and relating.

    "This woman has multiple personalities." thought Michael who was transfixed. She not only imitated her characters, she actually became them, from gentle ladies to fierce young men. Waiters approached and retreated, as they recognised that any interruption would be more than unwelcome. A brief return to the present and then a pause, as Gloria announced, "Chapter Two." And then "perhaps tomorrow."

Michael lay in bed that night thinking about this extraordinary woman who he had completely misjudged. He would have loved to have recorded Gloria's performance at dinner. Even her face seemed to change with the characters, it had been quite extraordinary. His thoughts were interrupted by a squall that blew up suddenly and fiercely blew the balcony curtains. Rising he looked at the angry waves on the lake, illuminated by a full moon tinged with an orange glow. He closed the balcony doors and as he headed towards his bed he heard and then saw the knob on his room door slowly rotate. The bedside clock said 1am.

"Who could this be at this hour?" he thought apprehensively. "What should I do?"

Deciding that the best thing was to do nothing, he returned to the comfort and relative safety of his bed. But he was now wide awake and wondering. He remained in that state until he eventually fell asleep. Waking at 7.30, he slowly recalled the night's events as he showered and dressed. Still wondering who his late-night visitor might have been, he made his way down to breakfast. "If it were Gloria, perhaps she would give him a clue. Desperately hoping that it wasn't, because it would mean the end of his association and possible job, he decided that he wouldn't mention it at all and just hope that it would all go away. As he passed reception the girl who had asked about his letters said,

"Good morning sir, did you sleep well?"

He replied quickly that he had, but then asked himself if it could have been her. Looking back towards the desk, she seemed to confirm that it was indeed her, as she gave him one of her special smiles. Feeling relieved and thinking he could handle this, he carried on to breakfast. Gloria didn't show. Not sure what to think, he ordered breakfast and looking through the window onto the lake decided that this had the makings of another glorious day. On leaving the dining room Michael approached the pretty receptionist who leant on the desk and greeted him once more with a beautiful smile.

Trying to maintain his professional manner he asked if she would kindly connect him to Miss Savage's room. She did so and then leaned on the desk with her face close to his.

"Hello Gloria, Michael here, are you O.K. I was expecting to see you at breakfast."

A few moments later, Michael handed the telephone back to the receptionist, a subtle smile appearing on his face.

"Miss Gloria not coming Michael?" she asked, her eyes sparkling.

"No, she's working on her book again."

"I finish at 10." she said, "Would you like to spend the day with me, I could show you around." she added invitingly.

Michael said nothing but thinking how tempting she sounded and not really wanting to spend another day alone he responded. "Why not, I'll see you by the ferry at 10.15"

"10.15." she replied with a huge smile. "I am Lucia, see you, ciao."

Wondering if he had done the right thing, Michael strolled along the passage way into town. The smell of the flowers hanging in baskets along the way was almost intoxicating. "At least I won't be alone." he thought. "I hate being alone, even in a place as beautiful as this."

Sitting on a bench by the lake he stared across he waters and let his mind wander. Wishing that it was Sophia he was to meet, he wondered what she was doing right now, maybe trying to walk in a straight line with a book on her head. I bet she was good at it, whatever she was doing. A large ferry boat approached the pier and a queue began to form outside the ticket office. The people were mainly elderly and almost exclusively made up of couples. "I want to be one of those couples in fifty years or so, Sophia and me." he thought.

"Ciao Michael." said a voice. It was Lucia. She kissed him on both cheeks as she reached for his hand. "Let's go to Mount Chesne." she said dragging him to the ticket office. "You will only need one ticket; my brother works on the ferry."

A couple of tall young men guided the passengers on board. One of them kissed Lucia, "This must be her brother." thought Michael as she jumped from the gangway into his arms.

"Come Michael, let us go upstairs." she said leading the way, the skirt of her lemon dress billowing in the breeze. "This was a beautiful girl." thought Michael, "So much like Sophia in her ways. Today she will be my Sophia."

Michael B McLarnon

CHAPTER 18

Sophia sat in her room in Lausannereading Michael's letter. Smiling, she loved his description of where he was staying on Lake Garda, it sounded similar to her, situated as she was on Lake Geneva. If only they could be together. Sighing, she opened the door leading onto her small balcony and looked over the lake. Lausanne was indeed a beautiful place but it would be so much more if Michael were here. She wondered what he was doing today, was he lonely like her, was he longing to see her again.

The tinkle of the bell being rung along her corridor gently called her to the next lesson, deportment. She enjoyed this part of her day, walking across the ballroom floor and up the steps on the other side. She still found it highly amusing when one of the ladies lost concentration, and allowed the books placed on her head to tumble onto the floor; It often had a domino effect, resulting in much laughter as it allowed a cathartic release for her fellow students. Joining her friend Odette afterwards, the girls strolled down the hill to the town, chatting about their day. They were both looking forward to Thursday evening when the young gentlemen from their sister college were coming to practice ball room dance. They were from similar backgrounds to the girls, from privileged families in Europe and North America. Giggling, Odette fanaticized as to the partner she would be allocated.

"He will be tall and so handsome and we shall fall in love at first sight."

Sophia smiled. She guessed it would be her first encounter with a young man. Not so with Sophia.

"I hope you have better luck than I have had in the past." she said. "They were mostly overprivileged Hooray Henries, used to always getting their own way. But perhaps it will be different here in Europe."

"I ope so." replied Odette with a look of disappointment.

"I hope so too. Just watch that they don't step on your feet and watch where they put their hands, especially the Italians, they tend to be oversexed."

Laughing, Odette replied. "Thank you, Sophia, I will watch them carefully, but I don't think I will be too strict."

Thursday evening was a hive of activity. Cries of delight could be heard along the corridors as the young ladies prepared for their encounter with the young men in the grand hall. As two mini buses pulled up outside, all faces were pressed to the windows to catch a first glimpse of their prospective partners.

"Calm yourselves ladies." came a command from Madame. You must conduct yourselves in the manner you have been shown.

A collection of twelve equally excited young men, all dressed in evening suits, emerged from the buses and gathered around their master for a final briefing. They were then greeted by the principal, Madame Grace who led them through to the ballroom where they were offered light refreshments. Meanwhile the ladies, in evening dresses were corralled in the corridor and after being reminded how they were expected to behave, they were led in a straight line by the deputy principal Madame Hope down the staircase, across the hall and into the ballroom whence a silence immediately descended.

After brief introduction the young ladies' names were called, one at a time by Madame Grace followed by the Master from the young gentleman's college who called the name of one of his young men. Each young man stepped forward and bowed to his partner who duly curtsied.They were then ledto the side of the ballroom.

A quartet of musicians provided the music. Madame Grace looked down from the gallery above the dance floor. Her deputy, Madame Hope had arranged each couple one metre in from thee edge and two metres apart, so that they formed an egg-shaped formation. Each couple was carefully inspected to ensure the young men had their right hand around their lady's waist and their left hand elevated holding the gloved hand of their partner. Any hesitation by the young men was firmly corrected by the firm hand of Madame. Only then was the quartet allowed to play the first piece, a slow waltz. As Instructed the young couples proceeded to dance in an anti-clockwise direction. Sophia was an experienced dancer and was pleasantly surprised at her partners proficiency, who was clearly experienced also. They managed a few steps before the music was stopped by Madame Hope loudly clapping her hands and exclaiming, "No, No, No., Ladies, Ladies."

And so, the evening stuttered on until half an hour later when the couples had managed to complete one circuit of the dance floor. At the end of the two-hoursession, they were approaching something like proficient and the gentlemen were no longer constantly looking at their feet and the ladies were managing to smile sweetly as instructed and the music quartet managed to play a whole piece without being abruptly stopped by Madame Hope. The ladies and their partners were then directed to follow Madame into the dining room were twelve tables for two had been arranged under a ceiling of six glittering chandeliers and art covered walls. They were then instructed on the art of entertaining on the part of the gentlemen and the ladies on how they should respond. A troop of young waitresses, dressed in black dresses and white frilly pinnies appeared, like a troupe of ballet dancers and approached the gentlemen to take their orders.

CHAPTER 19

Lucia linked Michael throughout the twenty-minute journey to the other side of the lake, excitedly pointing out points of interest from their vantage point on the upper deck of the ship. Feeling like the preverbal million dollars he snatched glances at the beautiful girl on his arm. She was so vibrant with a warm personality and gorgeous smile to match. The girls at uni weren't like this, they were mainly English with the odd Scot or Irish girl and although they could be very friendly, especially after a drink or two, they didn't come close to this Italian lass. Mind you, he thought, this weather helped a lot. As the ferry docked in the colourful little harbour, Lucia skipped down the stairs holding Michael's hand. Her cotton dress swirled in the breeze and she held him close as they reached the lower deck. Laughing she pulled him along the gangway to the shore. Turning she waved to her brother who was staring at Michael as if to warn him to be careful with his little sister. Feeling somewhat overdressed in his suit and tie Michael slipped off his jacket, revealing his white shirt. Slinging his jacket over his shoulder he allowed Lucia to pull him along the cobbled road that was bordered by little shops selling mostly leather goods and ice cream.

As the road steepened, Lucia said enthusiastically, "Come on Michael, I'll take you to the cable car that will take us up the mountain."

Michael was drinking in the beauty of this place and his companion who seemed to be a natural part of this flower filled landscape. As the couple approached the entrance to the cable car, Michael looked up at the summit of the mountain. It was covered in snow which dazzled in the sunshine. He reached into his pocket for his sunglasses. Lucia had hers perched on her head just in front of her red ribboned hairband. "You will need to put on your jacket when we reach the top, "laughed Lucia as they entered the cable car.

   The journey was in two parts, the first part took them half way to a landing stage where they had to change cable cars for the trip to the summit. So far, the journey had been over mainly grassland and wild flowers but the second part was over rock and then snow-coveredland. As the couple left the carriage, the temperature was much colder, in spite of the sun being strong against a powder blue sky. Looking at Lucia in her beautiful but flimsy dress, Michael draped his jacket over hershoulders.Lucia looked at him with surprise, she was not expecting the gallant gesture and hugged him. He could feel the heat of her body and suddenly felt protective toward her, a feeling he had not experienced before and wasn't expecting. Crunching their way across the compacted snow the couple viewed the lake below and the small settlements that clung to its shores. The entire lake was surrounded by mountains and only a small area had ledges onto which small towns, like Limoni had been built. Deciding to head back down, the couple left the cable car at the half way landing and headed for hotel they had seen on the accent. Sitting outside under a pergola covered with flowers they decided on café latte and apple strudel. Michael had sat opposite Lucia at a small table with four chairs, but she immediately changed seats so that she could be next to him. Deciding this wasn't close enough she pulled the armless chair right up to his and leaned in, putting her arm around him. The waiter smiled broadly; he would have been forgiven for thinking that this was a couple on their honeymoon. Lucia ordered and also said something in her native language that Michael could not understand. Whatever it was the waiter laughed vigorously, said something in Italian and then kissed her hand twice. He had recognised a couple of words, one being England and the other Lamour. Smiling, Michael asked Lucia what it was the waiter had said.

"He said it was very nice to see an English man so very much in love with an Italian beauty."

Michael blushed which set Lucia off on a rapid series of embarrassing comments.

"Oh Michael, is it true, are you in love with me?" she said leaping onto his lap and kissing him passionately on the lips.

Michael desperately tried to pull away but Lucia had him pinned firmly to his chair. In the end he just had to wait until she unlocked her lips from his.

"Lucia", he said trying to regain his composure and gasping for breath "Of course, I like you very much but I am engaged to be married.

At that point, the waiter returned with their coffee and strudel and was surprised at the dramatic change of mood. Lucia had turned on her chair and with folded arms sat with her back to Michael; she was weeping softly.

Deciding it was best not to say anything, the waiter quietly placed the order on the table and left. The other guests, who had had witnessed the scene turned away, but continued to steal the odd glimpse.

Michael was at a loss what to do. He felt that he was co-staring in a romantic drama and wished he could just run away. Placing his hand on Lucia's shoulder he just said.

"Would you like your strudel?"

The elderly man sat with his wife at the adjacent table tried unsuccessfully to muffle a laugh, with his wife saying "Shush Harold."

Lucia took the handkerchief offered by Michael and slowly turned back to face him.

"Don't you like me Michael, not even just a little bit?"

"Of course, I like you Lucia, I like you a lot but I love my fiancé, Sophia. Where I not engaged, things would be different, I find you very attractive."

"You are an honourable man Michael, I understand, but can I have you for just a short time while you are here?"

Going against his better judgement and unable to hurt this beautiful girl further he said.

"Well, I am here on a working assignment, but in your free time and mine I don't see why not, but just as friends."

Lucia dried her tears and just like a little girl who had just been scolded and forgiven, she picked up her fork and broke a small piece of strudel. The audience of fellow diners, deciding that the drama was over, continued with their lunch, pretending that they had not been glued to the scene.

Lying in bed that night, Michael could not stop thinking about Lucia. He had never met anyone like her, so vivacious and beautiful, he could easily have loved her. But he could not betray Sophia, she had been his first love, his only love, but this trip had shown him what a big world was out there, so many opportunities, so many beautiful and talented people. So many here were multi lingual. He had heard Lucia switch seamlessly between her native Italian, to English, German, French and even Spanish. When he returns to England, he will learn Italian, such a beautiful romantic language and maybe German as well. Looking at the balcony, he could see the full moon reflected on the lake. This place cannot be real, were his last thoughts before succumbing to a dream filled night. He slept so soundly that he did not hear the door knob turning or see the two figures enter his room.

Michael thought he was dreaming of being kissed but it was no dream. Lucia had slipped into his bed and kissed him passionately. Waking, the room was flooded with light from a full moon. Sitting up in his bed he recognised Lucia's voice saying she was sorry. She was naked. Then several flashes blinded him and the figure next to him rose, pulled on a top and quickly left the room.

CHAPTER 20

"Well, you've got a lot to think about girl," said Peggy, after Rachel had brought her up to date with the details of her trip to London.

"Did you sleep with him?"

"No," replied Rachel. "I wanted to but that would have been tantamount to saying that I wanted our relation to carry on and inevitably deepen."

"So, does that mean a no?"

"No, it just means that I haven't yet decided."

"Well, this is a big decision," said Peggy looking grim. "But whatever you decide make sure it's for the right reasons. What you need is a lover and a companion, not a patient; because, believe me girl, you will need to love him a lot and you are no Mrs Grey"

This last comment struck Rachel like a hammer blow and it showed.

Seeing the effect her words had, Peggy added. "I'm sorry love, but you are the dearest friend I have ever had and I just want you to be clear about what you are facing. You have both got a lot of living to do and I'd hate myself forever if I didn't say what I thought. Love is fierce when you experience it like you have, but it can wear off pretty quickly when it is tested, day after day with no hope of life getting any better during the long years to come. I love my Ralph in my own way, but there is no way I could be his full-time carer, I'd soon resent him for stealing my life."

Michael B McLarnon

Rachel loved her friend Peggy and thought deeply about all she had had to say. She would consult with Michael when he got back from Italy but would leave out what her friend had had to say.

CHAPTER 21

Michael turned up for breakfast next morning feeling sick with worry. For once, he was glad that Gloria was there.

"O.K. Michael, what is it?" she asked, showing uncharacteristic concern in her speech and demeanour.

Michael could cope with many things but not this. He told her the full story from the beginning, including how he had met Sophia.

"I can't lose her Gloria" he ended. "Sophia's father is behind this."

"This sounds like one of my novels," she said at last, finally acknowledging the waiter who had been waiting patiently for her order.

"Send Miss Lucia to see me please."

"I regret she hasn't reported in today," he replied, clearly having heard part of Michael's story.

"Very well, I shall see the manager after I have had my breakfast. Now come on Michael, you'll feel better with something inside you."

Michael felt a little better, telling himself that if anyone could sort this mess out it would be the formidable English woman sat opposite.

"How long have you been employing agent provocateurs at your hotel?" Gloria asked the Hotel Manager in a very loud voice outside his office.

Anxious to get her into his office away from the Reception Desk where several people were attempting to check in, the manager danced around her pulling back a chair for her to sit.

Before he managed to close his door on Michael, he heard her say, "My publisher, who incidentally publishes several travel magazines, is going to be very interested in your reply." Boomed Gloria.

Waiting outside, Michael looked over to the now quiet Reception Desk. The young woman who was on duty beckoned Michael.

"Lucia has left town with an older man. I think he is a private detective. He arrived the day after you checked in. Like you, he is English"

Michael thanked the girl; her name badge said Maria. "Although I am not supposed to I can show you his check in card."

Michael quickly copied the details and stuffed the note into his pocket, as Gloria emerged from the manager's office followed by the manager bent almost double with humble apologies.

Gloria motioned Michael to follow as she entered the revolving door out of the hotel.

"I managed to copy his check in card." said Michael.

"Almost certainly fake," she replied. "What's that?" she asked pointing at a long number.

"It's his passport number."

"Good, he can't of faked that," she said. "I've got my own contacts who'll be able to identify him. Now Michael, I suggest you have a quiet day. I've got some loose ends to tie up on my novel but I shall be ready to fly back on schedule the day after tomorrow. In the meantime, I suggest that you write an account of everything that happened including times and dates. And oh, get me a copy."

With that Gloria turned on her heal and headed back into the hotel, leaving Michael with his thoughts.

"No doubt, Lord Hazlehurst is behind all this, he will be delighted with the photographs and will waste no time in getting them to Sophia. I can't lose her," he thought. "I just can't."

The sound of the ferry hooter brought him back and he realised he was on the bank of the lake watching the people board. He saw Lucia's brother assisting the passengers and headed quickly towards the gangway to board.

"You remember me, Pedro? I was with your sister Lucia."

"Ticket, ticket?" he demanded.

"I don't want to travel, I wanted to ask you about your sister, Lucia."

"Ticket, ticket," he repeated.

Michael retreated down the gangway. "He either doesn't understand English or he chooses not to, "thought Michael.

As Pedro began to pull the gangway on board Michael shouted. "I'm going to the police, policia."

As the ferry pulled away the two men's eyes met and Michael realised that his words had been understood. Pulling his eyes away from the now distant ship, Michael walked for a while along the shoreline, once again deep in thought trying to formulate what his next moves should be.

Finding himself at the path leading up the hill to the church he made his way up. Hearing singing, he entered and sat on a bench at the rear. The choir were rehearsing at the front, near to the alter. They were comprised of six males and six girls, all seemingly teenagers. There were also about ten children, all junior school age, he guessed. An older woman, he placed at about the same age as himself was conducting. She had turned to see him as he opened the door of the church.

Sitting there, listening to the music and gazing around at the religious artwork and candle lit statues, Michael felt a calmness wash over him and a sense of peace descend. At the conclusion to a lovely piece, the conductor said something in Italian to the choir and they sat and opened their hymn books to look at the next piece. She then walked down the isle to where Michael was sitting and asked.

"Sie O.K.?"

"I'm sorry I don't understand," he said, I'm English.

"Are you Ok?" she asked, seamlessly having switched to English.

"Not really, but I feel a little better listening to your music."

She smiled sympathetically and then returned to her students.

Reluctantly, Michael dragged himself out of the church and returned to his room at the hotel. Sitting at a small table on his balcony he spent the afternoon writing his account of the day he spent with Lucia and his rude awakening in the night. He wondered if he should try and contact Sophia and tell her what was going on before her father had the chance to get the incriminating photographs to her.

"But what if she doesn't believe me?" he thought. "It would be difficult for her to believe that her father would go to such lengths to discredit him, even with his record of deceit."

Gloria was sat at their usual table for dinner. She looked smart and refreshed.In contrast Michael looked very tired and uncharacteristically scruffy.

"Have you got your account," she asked abruptly.

Michael handed it over and sat in silence as she read it.

"Do you think I should try and phone her?" he asked.

Gloria ignored the question and continued to reread the account.

"The photographer is a private detective, ex Met Police. My contacts tell me he is very professional and likely to have done a thorough job. It says here in your account that she was very friendly towards you, especially at the restaurant where you had lunch. He will have taken photos of you throughout the day that you would not have been aware of."

Michael gulped and reached for the water jug. Recalling images of him and Lucia at the restaurant he thought they spoke for themselves, there was no denying the mutual attraction.

"I'm done for," he said.

"Tell me."

Michael explained in detail how he had enjoyed Lucia's company and how he had been flattered by her attention and had temporarily forgotten himself but that at no time did he indicate to her that he wanted more.

"I see," said Gloria solemnly.

"Do you think I should try and give my side of the story to Sophia before her father gets to her?"

"I won't try and sugar coat this Michael."

"It's bad, isn't it."

"It depends how much she trusts you, Michael. You'd be asking her not to believe the evidence clearly shown in the photographs, and more than that. "you'd be asking her to believe that her father is a liar. Whichever way it goes, it will leave a legacy of mistrust."

"Sounds like I have little choice," said Michael, head bowed.

"That's about the size of it I'm afraid, "said Gloria beckoning the waiter. "Why don't you ring her now. Charge the call to my room."

Michael left the dining room and asked the receptionist to call a number in Switzerland and to put it through to his room. As he entered his room the phone rang.

CHAPTER 22

Rachel reached for the bottle of Drambuie to refill her glass. Finding it empty she laid it down. It was 9p.m. and she was tired, very tired. The battle between her head and her heart had been going on for days and she could still not decide. Trying to block it all out she climbed the stairs; she would have an early night. As she reached the landing, the telephone rang. Hesitating, she decided not to answer it.

"Why did this have to happen?" were her last thoughts before falling into a deep sleep. The telephone rang again.

At Hazelhurst Manor his Lordship was relaxing with a glass of wine when the butler knocked softly on the oak door and entered.

"Special delivery m'Lord," he said handing over a large envelope.

Opening it, his Lordship smiled as he flipped through the photographs.

"Will that be all?" asked the butler.

"No Benson, get my daughter on the phone, will you?"

"Yes sir, will you take it in here?"

"Oh yes," said his Lordship making no effort to hide his joy at the images before him. Benson left the room wondering, not for the first time, what he was doing working for a man like this.

In Limoni, Michael pressed the telephone close to his ear with such intensity that it began to hurt. Sophia was talking none stop and with obvious delight that Michael had rung her. Eventually she said, this call must be costing you a fortune, you must have something important to tell me. Michael hesitated thinking that the words he was about to say would impact massively on his future happiness, indeed his very existence. In his naivety he had allowed this girl, Lucia into his life, thinking that it would be without consequence and that Sophia would never find out about it anyway. Even if she did, there was nothing in it, just a day out with someone whom he had just met. But the fact remained that he had been out with another girl, a very attractive girl, and in his arrogance, he had thought that this was O.K.

"Hello Michael, are you there?"

"Yes, sorry. Sophia, I have something to tell you."

The line went silent.

"Yes Michael, what is it?"

"I'm in trouble. I've been tricked."

"In what way?" asked Sophia apprehensively.

"There was this girl." Immediately regretting his choice of words, Michael continued.

"I was lonely." Tightening his grip on the telephone Michael smashed his free hand, which was clenched, onto the bedside table in frustration at another more devasting choice of words.

"Michael, are you saying what I think you are saying?"

"No, no. I was tricked. I never touched her. She let herself into my room and there was this man taking photographs," he stammered, then added, "I'm sorry."

The phone line from Switzerland went dead.

The next morning, a distraught Sophia received an envelope containing photographs and a note simply saying, "from a friend." The postmark was clearly visible "Limoni, Italia."

When a distraught Michael finished relating his account of his phone call, Gloria simply said in her usual forthright manner.

"Well Michael, I'm afraid Lord Hazelhurst himself couldn't have done a better job."

CHAPTER 23

"Did you decide anything over the week end," asked Peggy sitting at her desk.

"I did have one thought," answered Rachel unsurprised that her friend was on her case from the off. I thought that I might suggest to Andrew that we live together, without committing to anything. That way, I wouldn't feel trapped.

"Good," said Peggy. "That way you could leave without any bitterness on either side."

"I wouldn't leave." added Rachel.

"What do you mean?" asked her friend.

"I wouldn't leave because I would ask him to live with me, not me with him."

"Wonderful, "said Peggy, "that way I wouldn't lose you.

Mr Melcher coughed loudly, so both ladies got on with their work, Peggy happy that she wasn't going to lose her friend, and Rachel content that she had, at last, made her decision.

As Rachel turned the key on her front door, she heard the telephone ringing. It was Michael, not sounding his usual happy self.

"Are you alright love?" she asked

"Is it alright if I come to you on Friday, I'm flying back late on Thursday."

"Of course, you can come. Is everything O.K. love."

"I'll tell you about it when I see you. I called you last night but you were out."

"No, I wasn't out love. I had a headache and went to bed early."

"I'll see you on Friday then."

"Alright love, I'll see you on Friday."

Rachel had planned to ring Andrew that night to put to him her suggestion of him living with her, but things had changed. She would wait until she spoke with Michael about his problems, he still came first.

In Edinburgh, Andrew sits on a straight chair in the otherwise empty front room, fingering the letter that had arrived that morning. Looking at the portrait of his late wife Margaret hanging above the fireplace he spoke.

"Well, darlin, looks like this is it, I've been suspended from carrying out further operations. We had great dreams didn't we Lassie, back in the day, you, me and wee Laura. And those dreams came true, didn't they, until that dreadful day when you were taken from us. How I managed to get back on an even keel, I'll never know. And just as I was getting there, my eyes start to go. You always said life was so precious and wonderful and I was just about starting to believe that again.

"Excuse me sir," asked the removal man, "we are ready to go, shall we take the chair and the portrait?"

"Just the chair." replied Andrew, "the portrait stays."

As the man took the chair, Andrew stood in front of the fireplace and looking up at the portrait, said with tears forming in his eyes, "Goodbye my sweet love, until we meet again."

The week passed slowly, too slowly for Rachel; she couldn't rest until she knew what was troubling Michael.

Peggy had done her best to cheer her with various theories of why he was coming, maybe Sophia is pregnant after all and the wedding has been brought forward, or maybe he has found a sexy Italian girl, or maybe. Rachel laughed at the absurdity of her friend's suggestions but secretly worried that Michael might be in some kind of trouble.

On Thursday morning as Rachel walked to work Lord Hazelhurst jaguar passed her. He waved to her from the back seat.

"He's never done that before," said Rachel to her friend. I don't trust him, somethings not right."

"Well, I'm sure you'll find out soon enough," replied Peggy looking worried for her.

When Rachel returned home, she found out the reason. On the mat was a letter from the Hazelhurst estate. She opened it feeling apprehensive. It was from the estate manager increasing her rent by nearly half and effective from next month. As she slumped into her armchair, the telephone rang. It was from the one person she didn't want to speak to at that moment.

"Hello darlin, its Andrew." He was bubbling with excitement. "Well, I've done it, I've moved out. I'm living with Laura until you help me choose a new place."

Not for the first time Rachel put him off but also lied.

"Andrew I'm so sorry but I have company at the moment, my friend Peggy and her husband. And Michael is due home on tomorrow, can I ring you back on Saturday?"

"A deflated voice on the other end said quietly, "Of course."

"O.K. Andrew, speak to you then, "said, Rachel hurriedly.

"You'll need the number, Rachel." he protested.

"Yes, Just, a moment. O'K. I've got a pen."

As she placed the receiver down, Rachel felt tired, very tired. Tired of fighting, tired of powerful people wanting something from her.

In Lucerne Sophia looked at the envelope on the bed and once more wept. The photographs were explicit and devasting., there was no need to look at them again, they were imprinted on her mind and on her heart.

A soft knock on her door was followed by, "Miss Sophia."

It was Susanne, her house mistress. "Can I come in?"

Sophia had no one in this whole world that she could talk to that she could trust, now that Michael, her one and only true love, had betrayed her.

Susanne opened the door without invitation and entered. She was shocked at the state of her charge.

"Oh, my poor, poor girl. Whatever is the matter?

Sophia tried to answer but once more, she was engulfed in her sorrow and her tears fell unabated. Susanne lay down the breakfast tray that she had brought and held Sophia.

"My dear girl, please eat something, it has been two days." Take a sip of coffee and then tell me what it is.

This was not the first time Susanne had comforted one of the students. Over the years she had become an excellent listener and counsellor. Sophia had talked to her about Michael many times and she was very surprised to hear the details and see the photographs. Several coffees later Susanne started to speak, in her soft French accent but in a very firm and deliberate way, almost like a detective summing up a case.

"First of all, this does not sound like the Michael you have spoken of these months I have known you. Also, the envelope the photos arrived in is postmarked Limoni, where Michael is staying and the note saying it's from a friend is not signed. Therefore, as you do not know anyone in Limoni, it is definitely not from a friend. It is from someone who wants to see you split from Michael. Do you know of anyone who would like to see this?"

Sophia grasped desperately at this piece theory. "Only my father, but it couldn't have been him, he is at home in England."

"Could he have arranged for someone to do this?"

"You mean pay someone?"

"Well, would he?"

Sophia remembered the stranger in the restaurant in London and later, outside Michael's flat.

"It's possible, but some of those photographs show Michael and the girl enjoying themselves on a mountain, during the day."

"Yes, my dear, but that also could have been contrived"

Sophia was now deep in thought. "Yes, I see,"

"Is there any way you could check, without asking your father directly?"

"He would deny it anyway. I could ask someone who works for my father, but that would put them in a very awkward position and at risk of losing their job."

"I'll let you think about that my dear," said Susanne rising. "Now please eat something, "she added looking at the breakfast tray.

Sophia, now full of hope, eagerly reached for a croissant.

CHAPTER 24

The journey home to Gatwick was uneventful. Gloria had gathered all the information she needed for now and was well on in planning her novel. Michael had only one thought, Sophia. The evidence against him was overwhelming. The photographs told their own story, how could he have been so stupid, Lucia and her photographer colleague had stitched him up, good and proper. Such a beautiful place, now tainted forever. He could never return; it would always be the place where he had lost his dearest love. Although this was only his second flight, it held no interest for him and before he knew it, the landing lights reminded him to fasten his seat belt, but he had never loosened it, so deep were his thoughts.

As Gloria said her goodbyes, she thanked Michael for his assistance on the trip and seeing the forlorn look on his face said.

"I'm sorry what has happened to you, I'll do what I can to try and find out who hired the detective who took the photos but I can't promise anything. And if the worst comes to the worst, you must get on with your life Michael, you have a lot going for you. You are young with a lot of living to do. I'm afraid life is not always a bed of roses; I can attest to that."

With that Gloria hailed a taxi and left.

It was late afternoon when Michael arrived at his mother's house. Rachel was waiting.

"Your room is ready for you love," she said. "Dinner won't be long, are you hungry? you must be tired."

"No mum, not really mum, but I am a bit tired." he replied tears welling up.

Rachel held her son close. "What is it love?"

Michael related the events of the last week. Rachel knew her son better than anyone and knew from the pain in his face that that he was telling the truth.

"It doesn't take Sherlock Holmes to work out who is behind all this," said Rachel eventually. "He must be desperate to have sunk so low."

"It was partly my fault mum. I was flattered by Lucia and being a bit lonely, I"

For a terrible moment Rachel thought that Michael might have succumbed, but then he continued.

"I agreed to her showing me around but there is no way that I would have, you know, gone with her."

"I know son, I know. I'm afraid his Lordship is a nasty piece of work, the type of person we are not used to dealing with. I just hope Sophia will realise that, but if she doesn't know you by now, it might be as well that you've split. Since we've been involved with that family it has brought us nothing but grief."

"No mum, I can't lose her, I just can't."

The telephone rang, Rachel looked at it but made no effort to answer. She couldn't deal with Andrew at the moment, she had enough on her mind.

"Are you expecting a call, Michael?"

"No, no one knows I'm here mum.

" It will only be Peggy; I'll ring her later." lied Rachel.

The weekend passed slowly, both mother and son nursing breaking hearts. Michael left on Sunday evening for his flat in London unaware of his mother's problems. She had kept them from him, he had enough to deal with.

Back at work on Monday morning, the boss called Michael into his office for a debriefing.

"Right then, how did it go with Mr. Singer then." he asked.

"Who?" asked a pale faced Michael, feeling nauseous with the constant build-up of his stress.

"Mr Singer, the author you went to Italy with." said his Mr Grainger angrily. "Are you alright, come on, wake up."

"Yes sorry, tummy problems, with the travelling. No, sorry, Miss Savage seemed happy," he offered meekly.

"Who the hell is Miss Savage?" yelled his boss, his voice now audible to the staff on the main floor. This pushed Michael's stress levels beyond his control; he vomited into his hands before rushing out to the toilets.

Monday morning, Rachel was alarmed when her friend Peggy, didn't turn in to work, she was the only person who could possibly have given her any solace. Mr Melcher told her that she had phoned in sick.

"Don't you worry Rachel," he said. "I'll sit with you at her desk, there is so much to do."

"It never rains but it pours, "thought Rachel, smiling through gritted teeth. And then "Thank you Mr Melcher."

"Please, call me Graham," he replied smiling. "I'm very happy to help you, Rachel, "he added in his creepy fashion dragging Peggy's chair right up to hers."

Rachel spent the rest of the day trying to fend her boss off whilst constantly pulling up her top and pulling down her skirt.

Home time couldn't come quickly enough and after making excuses as to why she couldn't accept Mr Melchers offer of a lift home, she made her way through the heavy rain and cold wind to Peggy's house.

"You look like I feel girl." said Peggy as she opened the door dressed in her winter dressing gown.

Rachel launched herself into a torrent of words and tears at the sight of her friend.

"Slow down girl, first let's get you out of those wet clothes and then you can tell me all about it."

Ten minutes later the two friends sat on either side of the roaring open fire with matching dressing gowns and hot mugs of tea.

Rachel related her tale of woe to her best friend, her only friend.

Peggy listened carefully, as she always did, but sneezing violently every few moments.

"I'm so sorry Rachel," she said, "This blasted cold."

"No, it's me that should apologise, coming around here, telling you all about my troubles, and you off work ill."

"Little steps girl, little steps," said Peggy ignoring the apology. "Nobody has died."

First of all, ignore Melcher, he's a pest but not really dangerous, just say something like, "My boyfriend wants to thank you personally for being so helpful, he said he might call in before going to his boxing club on Friday."

"Now, as for Michael, there is nothing you can do, just be there for him when he needs you. If Sophia really loves him, she will believe him given a bit of time and space.

And, if she doesn't love him enough, then it will be for the best anyway.

Rachel was already feeling better, "What would she do without her friend?" she thought.

Peggy was just about to ask about Andrew when she heard the key turn in the front door, it was her husband, Ralph.

"Hello dear, how are you feeling now?" he called from the hall.

"I'd better be going." said Rachel.

"Ralph darling," called Peggy, launching into another sneezing fit. "Rachel has called to see how I am, will you be a love and take her home."

"Ralph was no Humphry Bogart but he is a nice man," thought Rachel recalling her friend's description of her husband that time in Liverpool. "Peggy was fortunate to have him. There's a lot to be said about stable relationships even if they did get a bit boring."

It was dark as Ralphs car turned into her road and the car lights showed that the rain was getting heavier. During their short journey Ralph had thanked Rachel for being such a good friend to his wife. "She thinks the world of you, you know." he had said as he stopped outside her house. Still wearing Ralph's dressing gown and slippers, Rachel stepped out of the car. She waved and smiled as he pulled away, but her smile turned to a frown as she noticed that Mrs Murray had happened to be passing just at that moment with umbrella raised and torch pointing straight ahead.

"Could this day get any worse," thought Rachel as she turned the key in her front door. The phone was ringing. Thinking it would be Michael she rushed to answer it.

"Hello darlin, it's me," said the familiar voice cheerfully.

"Andrew," said Rachel in a slightly surprised tone, thankfully blocking the words "I thought it was Michael."

"How are you," she asked automatically, giving her time to gather her thoughts.

"I'm grand," he replied impatiently. "I've got my eye on a lovely place near the river just outside Edinburgh, you must come and see it."

"O.K., "thought Rachel, "the moment had arrived, make or break."

"Actually Andrew, I've been giving this matter a great deal of thought," she said, quietly wondering if she was doing the right thing.

Andrew held his breath "conscious that what she was about to say would dramatically affect the rest of his life," He heard Rachel take a deep breath.

"Well Andrew, as I said, I've given this matter a great deal of thought and I was wondering if you would like to come and live with me, see how we get on." Rachel gripped the telephone even harder. "There, I've said it." she thought.

Andrew let out the breath he had been holding. He wasn't sure what to think but she hadn't called the whole thing off. Feeling that he should say something he said in a subdued way. "If you think that is best Rachel."

"I do," she said firmly, in a voice that was both strong,yet caring, a skill she didn't think she possessed.

"Right, I'll call off the viewing then," he replied in a voice that had lost its initial enthusiasm.

"O.K. then Andrew, you'll have a lot to arrange; work, Laura and so on. Call me at the weekend."

As Rachel moved to replace the receiver, she thought Andrew had started to say "Love

CHAPTER 25

"At least you won't have to worry about the rent increase." Peggy had said.

"True enough," thought Rachel as she began to think about the future. "I won't mention Andrew's contribution to the household bills until he asks. I don't want him to think that this is the main reason for me asking him to move in."

The first day of December saw a change in the weather, it was beginning to get much colder. The wireless had said it could be a white Christmas. As Rachel brought a fresh bucket of coal into the house from the coal bunker she worried.

"Everything seemed to be going up in price. She had already broken into her savings to pay the increased rent and her pay at the council could not keep pace." As the fire began to take hold, she took her coat off and sat by the grate. The telephone rang and she reluctantly made her way to the hall, it was cold.

Rachel felt relief, it was Michael.

"Hello mum," he said, "How are you."

"I'm fine love, how are you?"

"Work's better, my boss heard from his top grossing author today, Gloria Savage. Apparently, she gave me a good report on our trip to Italy."

"That's good love, I'm pleased for you. Have you had any thoughts for Christmas?"

"Yes mum, I'm really looking forward to coming home, Is that alright?"

"Of course, it is love, why wouldn't it be?

"Well, Laura rang me last night and told me about her dad moving in with you."

"Oh, I wanted to tell you first. But listen, it won't affect you at all. Your room is ready for you and always will be."

"O.K. mum, but you must put yourself first, as I've told you before."

"I know love."

Rachel paused and then said quietly, "I don't suppose you've heard from Sophia at all?"

"No mum, nothing."

Aware that this last question had upset her son, Rachel quickly changed the subject, going on to say that Andrew and her were going to give it a go and see how it went. Nothing would be written in stone.

Friday, 15th December 1972 was to be a special day. It was the day Andrew was to move in. He was coming by train and arrive at 5.30 p.m. Rachel had gone to work as usual but today was going to be special, so she had a spring in her step. Peggy was almost as excited and the two best friends chatted and laughed the day through, with the occasional attempted but unsuccessful interruption by their boss, Mr. Melcher.

The train arrived on time. Andrew emerged from the first-class compartment carrying two suitcases. Rachel tried unsuccessfully to take one from him but their lips met in a tender kiss.

"I've organised a taxi," said Rachel leading the way.

"That's grand Lassie, "he said, "The rest of my stuff is coming tomorrow. Don't worry it's not much, just a small desk and some papers."

"That's fine Andrew, I just need to call at the shops for something for dinner, I've come straight from work."

It was dark as the taxi eventually pulled into the road where Rachel lived. As she emerged from the taxi, she groaned loudly.

Andrew was by her side instantly. "What is it darlin?"

"Look." she said, pointing to a large notice attached to a wooden pole in the front garden."

"For Sale," by order of Hazelwood Estate.

He's really out for revenge," her friend Peggy said on Monday morning. "I don't suppose you can afford to buy.

"I would never get a mortgage." replied Rachel."

"But you know a man who can and before you say anything, I don't mean Michael."

"You mean Andrew. He has already offered to buy it outright but you know it would be like buying me with it, and I don't want that."

"O.K., I understand why you wouldn't want that, but you don't want to end up homeless either."

"Well, it's Christmas in a couple of weeks and I'm determined his lordship is not going to spoil it. If you've not made any other arrangements, I'd like you and Ralph to come to Christmas dinner at my place." As soon as the words left Rachel's mouth, she wondered how much longer she would be able to call her home, my place.

In London, Michael tried desperately not to think of Sophia but it was hopeless. She dominated his thoughts from the moment he woke in the mornings to last thing at night. The bus journey to work each day was short but Sophia was always on his mind, so much so that he missed his stop at least twice a week whichextended his walk to the office. Since arriving back from Italy, he had been put on the proof-reading team. It was monotonous work requiring maximum concentration. With his thoughts often elsewhere, he made mistakes, too many and he was moved into the public relations department. There, it was his job to draft out replies to management mail. These were letters from the press, letters from solicitors, politicians and the like. Replies had to be carefully drafted and then passed to the senior manager they had been addressed to, like the Chairman, Managing Director etc. This suited Michael better and after a while he became good at it with fewer and fewer being rejected. Just as his pain over Sophia began to ease a little, he received his daily batch of mail to deal with. The mail was always heaviest on a Monday morning as it contained Saturdays as well as Mondays. As the boy dropped it on his desk, he noticed a bright yellow envelope among its midst. It was handwritten, international, addressed to him and bore the postmark, Limoni.

He opened it with trembling hands.Several hundred-euro notes fell onto his desk.

Picking up the letter, which seemed to be covered in stains, he read,

Dearest Michael,

Michael B McLarnon

I am writing to say sorry, very sorry.

My confessor has said that I must do this and ask for your forgiveness. What I did was unforgiveable, but I hope in time that you will be able to forgive.

You must be really angry with me. I did this terrible act because I was offered a lot of money, 500 euro, by an Englishman who said his name was Mr Smith. At first, I refused, but when you let me show you around, you did nothing but talk about your betrothed, Sophia, but I also loved you,but you rejected me, and I wanted revenge.

To show you that I am sincere, I have enclosed the money I received. Please use it as you wish or give it away.

I do not expect you to reply Michael but for the sake of my soul and family honour, I hope you will forgive.

See how my tears have fallen on the paper.

Lucia

Michael's mind raced with the possibilities this raised. "I'll send this to Sophia, she'll believe me when she sees it, she must."

CHAPTER 26

Rachel called from the kitchen, "Andrew, come and help."

Excusing himself from the happy company, he hurried off. Michael felt a strange feeling, one he had never felt before, a faint touch of jealously perhaps. His mother had always called his name at Christmas dinner as it was normally just the two of them. Now there was a new man in her life. Peggy noticed, but understood; it was natural.

"Michael, how is your work going?" she asked, diverting his thoughts.

"Good," he replied automatically. Smiling. "I get to meet many of our authors."

"A mixed bag, I bet," added Ralph, trying to expand the conversation. Peggy had kept her husband abreast of developments in her best friend's affairs. He knew all about Rachel's love life and also about Michaels and had been warned not to take the conversation in that direction.

It seemed to do the trick.

"Yes, they certainly are. Many of them have pseudonyms, some men have women's names and vice versa, I have to be careful as to how I address them. Some are very sensitive."

Ralph continued the conversation. "I hear you've been to Italy. How was."

He aborted the sentence quickly after receiving a hard kick to his ankle delivered by his wife.

"Sorry darling," she said loudly, "I seem to have my leg stuck."

Michael saw through the ploy and said, "I'll just check if mum needs any more help."

Entering the kitchen unannounced he was embarrassed to see Andrew and his mum in a tight embrace. Withdrawing he made his way upstairs to his room, his head flooded with mixed thoughts and emotions. He was happy for his mother, of course he was, but seeing her so close to another, he couldn't help feeling so alone. He had sent Lucia's letter to Sophia at the manor house over a week ago but he had not received a response. This only added to his sadness, but this was Christmas and he must put on a brave face for his mother's sake, he didn't want to cast a gloomy shadow over proceedings. Hearing the telephone, he raced down the stairs to answer it.

"Hello Michael, it's Laura, can I speak to dad please?"

"Yes of course, I'll get him."

Michael, feeling thoroughly sorry for himself and thinking no one wanted him, tried hard to crack a smile as he re-joined Peggy and Ralph.

"Cheer up," said Ralph seeing through the false smile and lifting a colourful Christmas cracker from the table added, "Here, have a pull."

It was so ridiculously unfunny Michael burst out laughing, quickly followed by Peggy and then Ralph, relieved that he wasn't going to receive another physical reprimand from his wife.

Rachel entered the room to announce that dinner wouldn't be too long now and was delighted to hear her son laughing.

Andrew then announced that Laura had just rung to say that her friend has got flu so she's driving down join us.

"Is that alright Rachel," he asked.

"Of course, it is Andrew, we will be one big happy family, just as it should be, at Christmas."

Over at Hazelhurst Manor, his lordship was busy planning his daughter's future, now that his tenant's son was out of the picture. He had received several acceptances to his invitations from several aristocratic prospects, chief amongst them the athletic Lord Milburn.

Sophia could not refuse this man, a charming,30-year-old bachelor, extremely rich, blonde hair, 6 foot tall and the only son of Lord and Lady Milburn of Bedfordshire. He had always had an eye for a pretty girl, evident by the number of paternity claims reputed to be filed against him. Lady Milburn would jump at the chance to marry her son off to the virginal Sophia and produce an heir.

The butler opened the great door; it was Sophia looking pale and tired.

"Miss Sophia, how wonderful to see you home for Christmas, are you well?

Ignoring his question and handing him the keys to her red sports car she said simply, "Thank you Benson."

Lord Hazelhurst had heard the doorbell and was stood by the Christmas Tree that reached almost to the high ceiling of the hallway. Embracing his daughter, he led her into the sitting room where a fire was burning in the grate. Sitting, he got straight down to business.

"Jonny Milburn is coming down for Christmas, you remember him from London?"

"Yes, I remember him father, I don't like him so if you have any thoughts of matching us up, forget it. He must be at least eight years older than me and we have nothing in common."

"Give the poor man a chance dear, he's very keen to meet up with you again. I thought he might come with us to Midnight Masstomorrow;it could be interesting, we have a new vicar, Charles de Courtney."

Christmas eve was a happy affair in the Flynn household. Laura fitted into the group as though she had lived with them for years. Michael knew her well from university and she had the happy effect of cheering him. Dinner was a success and after the Queen's speech the company played board games, much to the amusement of Rachel's friend Peggy and her husband Ralph who managed to inject a lot of fun and laughter into what was normally a bit of a bore. It was well into the evening when Laura asked Michael if he would take her to Midnight Mass. He was taken back a little at this request, as she had never been known to attend services whilst at university. Rachel overheard Laura and guessed why she wanted to go. She also remembered that Michael had vowed never to go to the local church again after his bad experience there a number of years ago. Attempting to rescue the situation she said, "Michael, I hear the church has a new vicar and that he's very nice."

Still, he hesitated but then, seeing his mum gesture a yes, he agreed. It was a little while before he came up with the answer to his unspoken question. Of course, she was thinking of her dad and his eye problems. Michael's demeaner then changed, from being a reluctant escort to happy to do anything that might make his mum happy, that's why she said what she did about having a new vicar. Rachel opened the door to see the couple off. It was cold with a few white flakes dancing in the air. Laura linked Michael and instantly became the happy carefree girl he had previously known her to be. As they walked along Church Street, dimly lit by the ancient street lights, they saw families and couples approaching the church. The early snowflakes falling from a black sky together with the tall Christmas Tree decorated with coloured lights made the scene like that from a seasonal greetings card. As the couple came in sight of the church entrance a large car drew up. Michael recognised it. The chauffeur quickly alighted and opened the door for the passengers to alight. Michael froze as he recognised the shape of his Lordship. Following close behind a tall blonde man helped a lady from the car, it was Sophia. Gasping for breath he alarmed Laura who held him close asking if he was alright. Sophia turned and saw Michael seemingly being hugged by a young woman adorned with beautiful long flowing hair. The sight of her beloved Michael in the arms of another made Sophia almost wretch. Her blonde companion gripped her arm and led her towards the church. Like his Lordship, Jonny Milburn knew that appearances were everything. Lord Hazelhurst saw and hurried back to assist as did the vicar who had been standing at the entrance welcoming.

"Do you want to go home Michael?" asked Laura looking concerned.

Michael's shock at seeing Sophia with another quickly turned to anger as he saw his Lordship. He wasn't going to give him the satisfaction of seeing him scuttling away and anyway, he was here for Laura and her father.

Mrs Murray cut a lonely figure as she followed the group into church. She was the only person who had come alone. She had witnessed the scene and although she didn't know what provoked it, she was happy to make it up for the sake of a juicy bit of seasonal gossip.

His Lordship and his party took their privileged seats in gated pews at the front of the church. The service was heavenly pleasant for some, listening to the Christmas Carols sung by an angelic choir. For others, like Michael and Sophia it was unbearably long. The vicar's sermon focused on the humility of the Holy Family with the King of Kings being born in a stable, in stark contrast to the aristocracy of the time. which he noted could be compared with our current society. Michael heard the words but his thoughts were otherwise directed as he contemplated losing his beloved Sophia to the aristocrat sat beside her, chosen, no doubt by her father. The service ended with the traditional hymn, Thine be the Glory. In line with tradition, his Lordship was allowed to leave first, processing down the aisle in front of his daughter who was linked by the blonde chosen one. As Sophia passed Michael, she looked at his stricken face, a tear escaping his eye. Sophia looked incredibly beautiful but pale and extremely sad, as though she was marking the end of a fateful chapter in her young life.

CHAPTER 27

By the end of March 1973 both Michael and Sophia had accepted that their mutual love could not be, each believing that the other had found new love partners. Michael had wondered if Sophia had received his letter containing Lucia's confession, but perhaps she had decided to move on anyway. The pressure from her father together with Jonny's constant attention had now got to her and as she hadn't heard from Michael, she finally accepted Jonny' s proposal of marriage. Andrew had seen the formal announcement of her engagement in the Times and told Rachel, who received the news with a heavy heart. She had liked Sophia very much and at one time wondered if she would re-unite with Michael against all the odds. But it was not to be. "Perhaps it was just as well." she thought. "Her son had been hurt enough by that family."

In late April, Andrew returned to the cottage with news.

"I've got a surprise for you darlin," he said to Rachel, a huge grin on his face.

"It must be good," replied Rachel, "from the look on your face, come on, don't keep me in suspense."

It was a Saturday and the couple had no plans for the day. Andrew handed Rachel a large thick envelope.

"What is it?, "she asked.

"You'll need to open it to find out darlin."

Rachel sat and slowly withdrew the contents from the envelope.

It was a parchment of some kind. As she unfolded it the words, Deeds of Property appeared. The colour left her cheeks as she realised, they were the deeds to her house.

"What have you done Andrew. What in God's name have you done?"

Feeling his legs turn to jelly, Andrew sat, the shock of her words hitting him like a bolt of lightning.

"I thought you'd be delighted. It means that bully Hazelhurst can't evict you. I know how much this place means to you."

"But how?" There is no way Hazelhurst would sell this house to me or anyone connected to me."

"I knew that, that's why I got my family solicitor to handle it for me. I knew you wouldn't accept the house as a gift, so it is in the name of my solicitor, but to all intents and purposes, the house is mine."

"Andrew, I know you did this with the best of intentions but I don't feel comfortable about it. You know our agreement, if things don't work out for us then, then."

"I do Rachel, I do. But look, as far as I am concerned the house is yours. If it doesn't work, I'll transfer the deeds to you and I will go back to Scotland, I still have enough money to buy another place."

Rachel knew Andrew to be a man of his word and reluctantly accepted the situation.

"Alright Andrew, I'm still not sure how I feel about this but it is done now. It feels strange that this place is no longer mine.

"As I said darlin, just say the word and I'll transfer it over to you."

On Monday morning at work and mouth agape Peggy asked "So what did you do then?"

"What could I do? This crazy, wonderful man had just bought me a house. I hugged him but made him promise, No more surprizes."

"So, are you now going to let him make an honest woman of you?"

"How can I, it would look as though he had bought me."

"Well, he can buy me anytime girl." laughed Peggy.

When Rachel arrived home that evening there was another sign in her garden, it said Sold in large red letters.

Michael was out visiting his friend Tom. He had left home at 10 a.m. As he knocked on the door, he was worried at what he would find. The paint on the front door was peeling, the windows were filthy as were the curtains, one of which was hanging at one end only and the gutters were overflowing with moss and weeds. A young woman answered the door. Her hair was long and unkempt, a cigarette hanging from her lips.

"Yeh, wadda you want?"

"Gillian?" guessed Michael.

"Yeh."

"It's Michael, Tom's friend."

Michael could hear children in the house, one was crying.

"I was wondering how Tom was."

Gillian stared at Michael who was dressed casually but smartly.

"I remember you; you had a posh girlfriend didn't you."

"Yes, that's right; unfortunately, we are no longer together."

A rough voice came from the interior. "Is that you Mike?"

"I suppose you better come in." said Gillian reluctantly.

Michael entered which led him straight into the living room. It was in semi darkness and felt damp. Walking across the bare floor towards a shape sat in a wheelchair, he found his friend.

"You're looking good Mike," said Tom, "proper smart like."

"Yeh, I'm good thanks."

"I'd make you a cup of tea," said Gillian, "but we have no milk."

"That's O.K." retorted Michael.

"You couldn't lend me a fiver, could you?"

Tom tried to object but Gillian simply said, "Well you're not bringing in any money, are you?"

Michael reached into his back pocket and pulled out a few notes and handed them to her.

Gillian grabbed the money eagerly, then saying, "I'll give it back when Tom's giro comes. I'll go and get some milk." With that she left the house.

"I'm sorry about that Mike, but she's not well. Doctor says she's got depression."

Michael peered at his friend to get a better look at him. He was a shadow of his former self. He was pale and thin. Reaching for his cup he asked Michael to get him some water from the kitchen. As he ran the tap into the sink, which was full of unwashed dishes the smell of dirty nappies on the filthy floor made him wretch. He could hear two children playing in the yard and another crying upstairs. Bringing the cup of water back into the living room, Tom urgently swallowed several pills. Michael wanted to get out of this house and run, but he couldn't leave his friend. He stayed for two hours talking about old times when they were growing up. Still Gillian hadn't returned. Eventually Michael asked,

"Are the medics able to do anything for you Tom?"

"Haven't seen anyone for a year, last time I was at the hospital they said there was not a lot they could do for me."

"I'm sorry mate." was all Michael could say.

Another hour went by and at last Gillian came back, somewhat the worse for drink and no sign of any milk.

Walking home with tears rolling down his cheeks, Michael had a thought. Andrew was now working at the local hospital as a surgical consultant. As his eyes had been judged falling short of the standard required to perform operations, he was working in an advisory capacity only. He would ask him to have a look at Toms Xray's, to see if, in his opinion, anything could be done.

Arriving home, he was as surprized as his mother had been, on discovering who the new owner of his childhood home was.

In the following months Laura became a regular visitor, ostensibly to see her father, but Rachel noticed that her visits nearly always coincided with her son, Michaels visiting. She thought it would be a little if strange if they were to form a relationship at the same time as her and Laura's father, but if it made her son happy, she wouldn't do anything to discourage it. Rachel was thankful that the weeks and then months that followed were without further drama. Michael and Laura seemed to be getting closer and her father had mentioned that they had met in London on a couple of occasions. Rachel had been wise enough not to comment apart from saying "Oh that's nice." She had always been a great believer in not taking second best in anything, if you couldn't have what you really wanted, then better have nothing. She believed this was particularly true when it came to choosing a life partner.

CHAPTER 28

Sophia was increasingly unhappy. Her father had been acting suspiciously since the incident in Italy and it made her think of her friend, Susanne at her school in Switzerland. She had suggested that a third party may have been involved. At times like this she knew that she needed wise counsel, so just as the May flowers were starting to appear she arranged to visit her maternal grandmother in Sussex, Dowager Lady Grace Summers. Since the death of her mother, she was the only one she really trusted. She was so much like her late mother, wise and loving. It would also get her away from the estate and the constant observation she was sure she was under. Also, Jonny had been a constant visitor since their engagement. He seemed to need constant assurances that she would go through with the wedding, she was also tired of his never-ending pressure to have sex with her, something she was loathe to do. Nan would know what to do.

On a wet Wednesday morning towards the end of the month Sophia drove herself to her grandmother's home. She loved coming here, the place where her beloved mother had grown up. She always felt close to her here, as though part of her had lived on. As she passed the lake, a pair of swans were gliding down to land on the surface. On visits to nan's her mother would bring her down to the water's edge to sit for a while; just to look and listen. She remembered the time her mother related the story of King Arthur and the possibility that Excalibur might lie in the depths, waiting for a new king to arrive. She loved these stories but most of all she loved being with her mother. Climbing the steps to the grand entrance, Sophia turned to admire the view. The lake with its fountain was framed by green lawns and massive oak trees completed the magnificent scene. In her mind's eye she could see herself stood with her mother at the shore of the lake.

Reluctantly turning to face the present she waited for the great doors to be opened. The ancient maid showed her through to the garden room. Hugging her grand-daughter the pair looked at each other with the great love they shared. Although her nanna was now 82, she still had all her faculties and her complexion made her look much younger than her years.

"You are the image of your dear mother darling," were her first words as she held both of Sophia's hands. Leading her into the conservatory she asked the maid, who was only slightly younger than her ladyship to bring some tea. The sun broke through the clouds, instantly warming the room. A piano sat near the French windows, it reminded her of her favourite room at home and inevitably of her first meeting with Michael. The scene made her burst into tears; she had intended to tell her grandmother of the reason for her visit but in a more controlled way.

"I'm so sorry nan, so sorry," was all she could manage to say between sobs."

"My dear, dear girl. What is it?" said nan holding her and guiding her to the couch where she could be by her side.

Sophia relayed the whole story from her first meeting with Michael, interrupted briefly by the arrival of tea and biscuits delivered on a silver tray. Breeding allowed Sophia to recover her composure while the maid poured the tea into the bone-china cups.

As soon as Sophia had finished relating her story, grandmother said instantly, "It's your father."

The speed of her verdict took Sophia by surprise.

Lady Grace then went on to say that she had never really trusted her father and that it was a sad day when her daughter announced that she was pregnant with his child, no doubt due to the pressure he put her under.

"Thank goodness you take after your mother and not him. He was always ambitious to climb the social ladder and it sounds like he is engineering a similar fate for you, my dear."

Sophia sat and listened open mouthed to her nan as she related that he would stop at nothing to get his own way. "Now that you are of age darling, I suggest you get as far away from him as possible and for that matter this Jonny fellow too. You can live with me dear; this place will be yours soon anyway."

Sophia rose from her seat and hugged her grandmother tenderly. "Please don't leave me on my own nan, I couldn't bare it."

"Then get back in touch with your Michael, you clearly love him very much"

"But Michael has another, I saw them together at Midnight Mass."

"A rebound affair, I'm sure."

Sophia thought for a split second and realised that her grandmother was so right, she did love Michael dearly and she couldn't bear to let him go."

"Get him to come here dear, I'd like to look him over.

"Really nan, "questioned Sophia eagerly, "You'll love him."

"I know I will. He must be special if you love him darling."

"He is nan, and his mother too. They are different from all the others I have known."

Wednesday found Michael alone in his flat. He had just finished an unappetising supper and now his plate sat in the sink together with aweek's worth of washing up. The telephone rang. Picking up the receiver he hoped that it wasn't Laura again.

"Michael," said a familiar voice.

He had almost stopped hoping that she would ring.

"Is it really you Sophia?" he asked timidly.

"Yes Michael, it is me," she replied eagerly, "I believe you."

"You got my letter then," he answered.

"No," she said questioningly. "What letter was that?"

"The one in which I enclosed a letter from Lucia, confessing that she had set me up for money."

"No, I haven't received any letters from you, but you can tell me more later," she continued eagerly, "My nan would like to meet you. Can you come"

"Yes, yes I can," stammered Michael. "When?"

"Would Friday evening be O.K?"

"Yes, yes of course. "

Sophia rapidly gave Michael the address with instructions to ring from the railway station when he got in.

Sophia could hear Michael falling over a chair and saying "Ow."

She pictured Michael falling, in his rush to grab a pen and paper and she was still giggling when he breathlessly picked up the receiver.

When Michael confirmed that he had copied down all the information, Sophia said "See you Friday then."

"O'K.," he said, "see you Friday."

"And oh, Michael, "said Sophia.

"Yes," he replied eagerly.

"I love you."

It was only after Michael had replaced the receiver that he realised that he hadn't asked about her engagement. "She must have broken it off," he thought, "otherwise she wouldn't have said she loved me. If it's all true this is the happiest day of my life," he thought, before crashing over another chair. He now had two bruised shins.

It was late to ring his mother but he just couldn't contain his good news. She was happy of course but she cautioned him not to get too carried away, and there was

Laura to consider. Rachel had noticed how fond she was getting of Michael and she urged him not to say anything to her just yet. Andrew was in and she wouldn't mention this development to him until the situation became clearer.

    Michael considered what his mother had said but struggled to think of anything but Sophia. He found himself counting the hours and the minutes until he would leave the office on Friday afternoon. Friday dragged; he found most of his time was spent correcting the mistakes he had made the previous day and morning; such was his inability to concentrate on his work. He arrived at the railway station in his best suit which he had worn for work that day. It was only as he boarded the train that he realised that perhaps he should have brought a change of clothes as there was no way he could get back that night. Such was his enthusiasm to see Sophia that everything else was pushed to the back of his mind. Arriving at his destination he read the address he had hastily written on a scrap piece of paper. It simply said Nanna's house, 1 Grosvenor Avenue. It was now dark and he had been the only passenger to alight from the train. Following instructions, he made the call from the ancient red phone box to the number he had been given. Pressing Button, A, he heard the coins fall into an empty chamber. He shivered, remembering the time he had rang Hazelhurst Manor those many years ago when he had been so humiliated. The urgent beeping of the pips brought him rudely back to the present. An elderly female answered the phone just as a black Rolls Royce pulled up at the station entrance. Michael spoke into the receiver but it soon became clear that she couldn't hear him. He was still trying to be heard when the pips sounded loudly and he was cut off. It was now very dark and the only light came from the station entrance and the headlights of the car. It started to rain as Michael approached the driver to ask him how to get to Grosvenor Avenue.

He was surprised when the uniformed chauffer said. "You must be Mr Michael."

"Yes," he answered meekly.

"This way sir," he said opening the rear door.

Michael sat on the leather seats, the smell of which confirmed the world he had just entered. Trying to think of something to say he eventually asked, "Is it far."

"No sir, we will be there in ten minutes."

The car glided along the empty rural road and then slowed to enter the gates of the estate. Driving along an avenue of birch trees they emerged to pass a lake. The clouds had cleared and the moon shone on the water giving its surface a silvery sheen.

"It was as though he were being carried along as a spectator in a fairy tale," thought Michael. It was as though the dream continued as the car drew up to the bottom of the steps leading up to the great front doors of the Grand Georgian House. A lady stood at the top illuminated by the lights of the wide porch. He recognised the figure as Sophia. She was dressed in a long evening dress and her hair flowed behind her. It was clear she was waiting for him, a bride waiting for her husband.

There were no questions, no demands, no tears, the couple just embraced and Sophia led Michael through the doors to the chandeliered hall, past the grand staircase and into the garden-room where an elegant, elderly lady stood waiting for them.

"What do I say?" whispered Michael as they approached.

"Just be yourself," counselled Sophia.

"Nan, I'd like you to meet Michael."

Michael stroked his hair back and stretched out his hand.

"Pleased to meet you," he said feeling nervous and self-conscious.

"I'm very pleased to meet you Michael, Sophia has told me all about you. It must have taken a great deal of courage for you to ask my grand-daughter out all those years ago?"

Michael glanced at Sophia thinking that she really had told her grandmother all about him.

Michael was getting better at conversing with people he had once regarded as too far above his station.

"I have to confess it was my friend Tom's idea, he bet me I wouldn't dare."

"And was there money bet on it?" asked a stern looking Lady Grace.

"No, your Ladyship, it was just a childish game."

"And were you glad you did it?"

"I've never been happier with anything I've ever done," replied Michael firmly.

Lady Grace responded by smiling and linking him. "You must be hungry; shall we have dinner?"

Sophia beamed as she followed the pair into the dining room. She had received confirmation that nan did indeed like the man she loved.

CHAPTER 29

There was barely a day Rachel didn't think of her son.

"Would he be alright? Would he get hurt again. But Sophia was a rare prize, and had Michael asked her what to do, she would have said, go for it."

Rachel liked Sophia and knew she wasn't the type of girl to hurt anyone, let alone the one she knew instinctively was the person she was meant to be with. The thought of Michael and her getting back together filled her with unbridled joy. She remembered the day her beloved Jack had asked her to marry, the world was theirs for the taking. It wasn't the same second time around; Andrew was a lovely man but times were different, she was different. He probably felt the same about her, Mrs Grey had made that very clear. Still, they were content rather than madly in love and that, she thought, was probably was how most middle-aged couples felt. Yes, Andrew's eyes were a potential problem, a major problem, but she could cope with that if she had to. She no longer had any major financial problems and life was good. The telephone rang waking her from her thoughts, it was Laura. She was wondering if Michael was there as she couldn't reach him on his home telephone. Rachel thought quickly, there was no easy way of saying this.

"Oh Laura, Michael is away for the weekend. Apparently, Sophia had rung and invited him over to her nans."

The phone line went quiet.

"I'm sorry love. I'm sure Michael will be in touch soon. If he rings me, I'll get him to ring you."

"Thank you for telling me, Rachel, I sort of knew he wasn't over her, bye"

Rachel placed the receiver down with a heavy heart. Laura was a lovely girl and she hated giving her the news, but better now than further down the line. She would also have to tell her father; that would be awkward. She thought it best to get it out the way so as soon as Andrew arrived home, she told him.

"I was sort of expecting it", he said with an air of resignation. "Best now rather than further down the line. I'll ring her."

"Might be best leaving it for a while," counselled Rachel.

"Eye, you're probably right lassie," he had replied sitting.

"Tomorrow is Sunday and it's your birthday Andrew, let's go out for the day and celebrate. As for this evening, I've planned to make you a special dinner," said Rachel trying to take the conversation away from his daughter and her son."

"And maybe something special afterwards," said Andrew smiling and raising his eyebrows.

"We'll see," replied Rachel, blushing a little.

Monday morning at the office saw Rachel telling her friend Peggy of the latest developments in her son's love life and of the lovely day she had had with Andrew yesterday.

"I'll ring Michael tonight before Andrew gets home. I hope the weekend worked out for him."

"Well, it seemed to work out for you," said Peggy smiling.

Mr Melcher approached. Peggy and Rachel quickly resumed their work but it was not the expected reminder to get on.

"Rachel, the hospital has just rung. Andrew has had an accident; they have asked that you get down there as soon as possible."

The colour drained from the faces of the two ladies. Amid a flurry of activity Rachel grabbed her bag and coat, Peggy called that she would call her friend this evening.

The streets that, this morning had looked bright and welcoming, now looked grey and threatening. People were going quietly about their normal business. Rachel's mind was racing, what if it wasn't the usual trip or fall, what if he had really hurt himself. She had gotten used to him being around, looking after her, caring for her. She didn't want to be responsible any more, she'd had enough of that, worrying about how she would manage. At last, she had someone who wanted to look after her just because he wanted to, because he loved her. And all he wanted in return was to be with her.

The receptionist at the hospital asked her to take a seat whilst she contacted the Matron. Rachel searched her face for any clue as to how bad it was, there was none, she must have been used to these situations and she had learned from bitter experience that it wasn't her place to give out any information as what she thought might be the situation.

"Mrs Flynn," she called, "Doctor will be down to see you shortly."

Rachel was startled by the announcement, it woke her from her thoughts of how happy they had been lately, she had almost forgotten Andrew's prognosis, the one she had concluded, not the official one.

The hospital corridor, quiet and empty for so long, was now occupied by two white coated figures approaching. She recognised the younger of the two, she had met him at one of their social gatherings. He was the first to speak,

"Rachel, this is Mr Goldstein, consultant ophthalmic surgeon. Please," he said gesturing her into a side room.

Feeling her stomach hitting the floor she entered the small room.

"I'm afraid Andrew has suffered sudden and serious sight loss," began Mr Goldsmith, "the degeneration in his vision has accelerated to such an extent that he is now technically blind."

Shocked at this news, Rachel took a deep breath and then asked "What caused this sudden acceleration.""

"We are not altogether sure, "explained the younger doctor. "Has he
had any sudden shocks lately, something that could have affected him emotionally?"

"No, not that I'm aware of," she replied quietly. "I know that he was worried about his ability to carryon working due to his eyes, but that has been going on for more than a year now and we were both hoping that it wasn't going to get dramatically worse any time soon."

Grim faced, Mr Goldsmith beckoned Rachel to sit and then continued. "Well, apart from his eyes Andrew is physically O.K. and after a few more tests he can be discharged. I know this must have come as a shock to you but you must now turn your thoughts to Andrew's care. We can ask social services to assess the situation but I know they will need to ask you if you are prepared to be his carer."

Rachel knew that this question would be asked of her one day but not yet, please not yet.

"I don't know, I don't know, "she whimpered. This was too soon. She had asked herself this question so many times, so many times. And she had said yes most of the time, but this was real and it was now."

"There's no need to give an answer now, but perhaps you should give it some thought."

Rachel snapped back "Don't you think I've asked myself this question a hundred times. I just don't know the answer, we've been together for only a short time and I just don't know, I don't know if I could cope with it."

"Well, there's no need to make a decision straight away. Would you like to see Andrew now, he's in Turner Ward. Dr Simpson here can take you up."

Rachel had faced hardship before and was not one to run away from hard decisions. Regaining her composure, she nodded and stood.

CHAPTER 30

Lord Hazelhurst was furious, where the hell was she? Banging down the receiver he yelled for his butler, Benson.

"I'm afraid I don't know sir. Have you tried Lady Grace?"

"Four times, he yelled. Her old fool of a maid is as deaf as a post and I'm not getting anywhere."

"Perhaps Sir John Milburn will know," ventured Benson.

"Oh, get out man, it's him who's looking for her."

Benson turned to leave, a broad smile of satisfaction spreading across his face and thinking "This Jonny person is a thoroughly disreputable fellow, much like Lord Hazelhurst. Here's hoping Miss Sophia manages to escape both their clutches."

Rachel could see Andrew through the glass of the side ward. Her hand rested on the door handle as she stared inside. He was sat in a chair at the side of his bed. He wore a white nightgown and dark glasses. He looked vulnerable and scared. Bracing herself she entered.

"Who's there?" he asked meekly.

"It's me Andrew."

"Thank God," he blurted, holding out his hands. "I wasn't sure if you'd come."

This was exactly what Rachel was frightened of.

Andrew grasped her hands tightly and drew her to him. "Oh Rachel, I'm so scared."

Reluctantly she stroked his head and sat on the bed.

"I know we said that I wouldn't want you to put your life on hold to look after me, but at the moment I don't know which way to turn. Can I come home with you, I'm sure I'll be able to do certain things on my own. It's just that I'll need some help for a while. And I'll have my hospital pension. I'm sure we'll manage."

"Andrew please let go, you're hurting me," Rachel cried. "Yes of course you can come home, just as soon as they've finished all the tests." She then slumped on the chair. "What else could I do," she thought, "I just can't leave him like this. There'll be time enough to think things over."

By the time Rachel left the hospital it was dark and raining. She was about to start walking home when a familiar voice called her name, it was Peggy beckoning her to her car. The two hugged each other, Rachel with sheer relief and Peggy with genuine affection.

"Ralph let me take the car," said Peggy cheerfully.

"But you don't drive," retorted Rachel.

"Oh, I do drive girl," she replied," I just don't have a licence."

Rachel laughed, "Oh you're just what I need Peggy," she said before bursting into a flood of tears. Peggy held her friend close.

"Let's go back to my place," assured Peggy, "We'll have a drink and you can tell me all."

"Won't Ralph mind?" asked Rachel.

"He's in London overnight. What he doesn't know won't worry him."

The two women talked and drank gin and tonics late into the night and shared their troubles over and over until Peggy realised how very tired her dearest friend was.

"Why don't you stay the night," she suggested at last. Peggy gave her bed and slipped in beside her, kissing her forehead gently.

Next morning Rachel was awoken by her friend pouring tea by the side of the bed.

Seeing Peggy fully dressed Rachel asked, "What time is it?"

"It's half past eight."

"I must get up, I'll be late for work," said Rachel, pulling back the bed clothes quickly and then pausing to hold her head.

"You're not going anywhere," replied her friend. "I'll explain to Mr Melcher and I'm sure he won't mind in view of the circumstances. I'm going now, have your breakfast and when you get home, you'll need to phone Laura and tell her what has happened and also Michael if you can reach him."

Michael arrived at work at 9 a.m. tired but elated. It had been a rush getting back to his flat after his weekend with Sophia and her grandmother Lady Grace. He had no sooner arrived at his desk when he was summoned to his boss's office.

"It seems you have friends in high places Michael," beamed Mr Craig, his usual fierce demeaner not evident on this occasion.

Michael attempted to speak but was silenced by an outstretched hand, palm out.

"Sir Archibald, our chairman wants you to join us at our annual dinner at the Ritz next Saturday evening. He wants to meet you and your fiancé Lady erm," he hesitates to look at his notes and coughs, "Lady Sophia."

"I'd be honoured," Michael started to say before he was curtly dismissed with a "Yes, Yes, that's all."

Michael had to force himself to concentrate for the rest of the day, his life had turned around so quickly from despair to ecstasy. He couldn't wait to ring his mother tonight and give her all the amazing news, not least that he needed a ring.

It was dark and raining as he left the office. He took his normal route to the bus stop and stood in the queue which seemed longer than usual. At the rear stood four men who he hadn't noticed queueing at this time before. Over the months he had got to know many of the people who caught this bus at this time. They were new and it made him feel uneasy. This feeling increased as they followed him off at his stop. It would normally take him ten minutes to reach home but he decided not to walk down the unlit alleyway he normally took and stayed on the main road which was well lit and busy with pedestrians making their way home. It would take him double the length of time he had to walk but it was, he decided safer. As he placed his key in the door, he glanced back but found one of the men on top of him. Forcing him through his door the other three men ran and also entered the hall way of the entrance where they set about Michael punching him to the ground and then started to kick him mercilessly, leaving him bleeding and unconscious. He was found half an hour later by a young woman who lived in a neighbouring flat. She called an ambulance.

The telephone in Michael's flat rang several times that evening but no one answered.

CHAPTER 31

Rachel was in bed at 1 a.m. when the telephone rang downstairs. It didn't awake her because she was already awake wondering about how her future was going to look. Was this how it was going to be, caring for a man whom she wasn't sure she even loved, her worst fears had materialised. She didn't rush to answer the phone as she knew it would be the hospital about Andrew, or maybe Andrew himself seeking reassurance. Picking up the receiver a female voice said they were ringing from the hospital. Rachel tensed, but not greatly. The voice continued, "Saint Thomas Hospital London". Rachel stiffened. "Am I speaking to Mrs Rachel Flynn?"

Rachel opened her mouth to reply but nothing emerged. The voice repeated "Mrs Flynn is that you?"

This time Rachel managed to say weakly, "Yes."

"Please don't worry Mrs Flynn, we have your son Michael, he's O.K. but he has been severely beaten. He has regained consciousness but he has sustained cuts and bruises and he's currently undergoing tests for internal injuries but we think he will be alright."

Rachel took in a large breath and then said, "Can I see him?"

"Yes of course, we hope to transfer him to the general ward as soon as his test results are in."

The early train to Victoria Station was packed but she managed to find a seat in a compartment which contained a variety of people she guessed were daily commuters. Thankfully, she thought, no one wanted to engage in conversation. She managed to tick off her thoughts, Peggy would explain her absence to Mr Melcher and the local hospital would just have to hang onto Andrew for a while longer, Michael was her main concern. As her thoughts calmed, she was able to analyse her feeling more deeply. Her actions spoke for themselves, Andrew coming home was not something she was looking forward to but she would move heaven and earth to look after her son.

The ward sister directed Rachel to her son's bed after she had warned her what to expect. Even so, Rachel could not contain her cry of anguish when she saw him. His face was literally black and blue and his cut lips were swollen. Rachel's cry, although muted woke her son. He tried to speak.

"Don't try to talk son," she whispered, trying desperately to contain her tears. Holding his hand, she sat by his bed unable to drag her eyes from her beloved son's face. He tried to open one of his eyelids but it was too swollen.

"It's O.K. son, I'm here."

Michael tried to gesture for a pen and paper. Rachel rummaged through her handbag and retrieved a pen. Quickly emptying the grapes onto her lap from a brown paper bag she had brought, she handed it to her son. Without looking Michael wrote the name Sophia and the words, ring her.

"Where will I find her number?" asked Rachel gently. Michael gestured to his bedside. His mother searched the bedside cupboard and found his diary.

"I'll do it now son." she said rising from her seat. "The ward sister wants you to rest now. I'll stay at your flat tonight ad come back to see you in the morning."

On her way out, Rachel asked the ward sister what she knew about the attack on her son. "I don't know a lot", she said, "but the police said that the motive wasn't robbery, his wallet was found on him, that's how we identified him. It had your contact details in it. I expect the police will want to talk to him when he's up to it."

When Rachel arrived at her son's flat the first thing, she did was to ring the number Michael had given her. It was answered by the elderly maid at the residence of Lady Grace who upon hearing that it was Michael's mother who was calling suddenly regained her hearing ability and informed Sophia straight away.

Recognising the anguish in Rachel's voice she responded.

"Is everything alright?"

Rachel quickly explained the situation. Sophia's response was calm but immediate.

"I'll come over at once."

On placing the receiver down, Rachel felt suddenly very tired and fell asleep in the chair.

It didn't take Sophia very long to drive her little red mini to the hospital. Parking in a restricted area she ran up the steps to the reception. After explaining that she was Michael's fiancé, a reluctant receptionist gave her the name of the ward. Before the receptionist could add that it was now outside visiting hours, Sophia had flown down the corridor to the lifts. She never ever pulled rank but deciding that this was beyond urgent she addressed herself as Lady Sophia Hazelhurst to a startled ward sister.

Rising from her desk, in deference to her ladyship, the ward sister pointed to a bed with the curtains drawn around it. Before she could explain that the police were with him, she was off. Pulling back the curtains and ignoring the two plain clothed police officers, she crouched by the bed.

"What have those brutes done to you my darling, my poor darling."

The two male officers sat observing this lovely young lady dressed in a pale blue top and darker blue skirt loving caress the young bruised young man in the bed. A moment later a flustered ward sister arrived.

"Your Ladyship," she started "Mr Flynn needs to rest, he has two broken ribs and multiple bruises and the police need to finish interviewing him."

"That's alright sister, we've just finished," said one of them turning to address Michael. "You've been very helpful sir; we'll be talking to this jonnie chap very soon."

As the curtains were closed Sophia tried to kiss Michael but pulled back as he groaned.

"I'm so sorry my love," she said sitting on one of the chairs vacated by the policemen.

"Did I hear them they were going to talk to a Jonnie. It wouldn't be Jonnie Milburn by any chance."

"Yes, I told the police one of the men said as they walked away. "That'll teach him Jonnie."

"I think it probably was his Lordship, I don't know any else called Jonnie."

Michael B McLarnon

"Did he have a slight limp? Last time I saw him he told me he had been kicked by one of his horses."

"Now you mention I think he did." confirmed Michael.

CHAPTER 32

Rachel was joined by Sophia later that evening at Michael's flat. From there the pair visited Michael daily and fussed over him mercilessly, much to the annoyance of the ward sister who had to almost forcibly evict them at the end of visiting each session. On the Friday evening Michael brought up the subject of his employers' annual dinner.

"I'm afraid I won't be able to attend," said Michael "but I would love you to attend in my place along with Sophia."

"Oh, I couldn't possibly." Rachel started to say.

"Oh, please Rachel, please say yes. My father is due to attend and I want him to see that we won't be intimidated."

"Your father is due to attend?" questioned Rachel". Sophia nodded.

"Then I will go," confirmed Rachel with a fierce look.

"Now mum don't go causing trouble," said Michael trying to sit up but then wincing from the pain, he fell back onto the pillow.

Sophia and Rachel went shopping the next day principally at Sophia's favourite fashion house and came away with expensive evening dresses and a couple of accessories. Sophia had managed to overcome Rachel's reluctance to accept them as a gift by explaining that she had charged them to daddy's account. The two laughed and giggled like a couple of teenagers as they made their way along Regent Street.

Michael B McLarnon

On the evening of the publisher's dinner, the two women, dressed in their expensive evening dresses set off by taxi but first they went to the hospital to visit Michael.

They walked along the ward as though it were a cat walk. Heads of patients and visitors turned to follow the glamourous pair as they made their way slowly to Michael's bed. Rachel's long black hair contrasted beautifully with her red dress and matching heels. Sophia had chosen a light blue piece, her long golden hair flowing freely. Like Rachel she wore matching heels but unlike Rachel the necklace strung around her neck were genuine diamonds. Michael's eyes opened wide in astonishment at his beautiful Sophia and his amazing mother. He had dreamed that one day his mother would be able to enjoy her life without worrying about money. He knew it was going to hurt but he drew himself up to take in the view and what a view it was capturing the two women he loved most in this world.

On arriving at the Ritz Hotel, the two ladies joined the queue of elegantly dressed guests to access the dining room. They were greeted at the door by Sir Archibald Harrington, chairman of the publishing house. Lady Sophia explained to him that as her fiancé, Michael could not attend, his mother had graciously agreed to attend in his place. Sir Archibald escorted the two ladies to their places, Sophia was to be seated next to him and Rachel one seat along was placed with Lord Hazelhurst. Rachel recognised him immediately and steeled herself to sit but he was already on his feet racing to see his daughter.

Sophia greeted him with a smile as cold as the icy blue of her dress. As he regained his seat Rachel spoke.

"Good evening, Lord Hazelhurst."

His lordship paled as he recognised her and realised that his daughter had arrived with his ex-tenant, Mrs Flynn.

"You'll be pleased to know that my son Michael is recovering well in St Thomas Hospital. Tell me, "She continued coldly, "Has Lord Milburn received a visit from Scotland Yard yet. I hear they are anxious to talk to him."

Reaching for his glass of water he managed to splutter. "I have no idea what you are talking about."

Raising her voice just loud enough for nearby guests to hear she continued. "O come now your Lordship, I'm sure you know about the attack on my son by Jonnie Milburn and his fellow thugs."

The convivial chatter in the room ceased and all heads, including that of Sir Archibald and his wife turned to stare at Lord Hazelhurst. Rising from his seat he left the room, leaving behind his lady escort in a state of shock.

Michael was discharged from hospital a few days later, still in a fragile state but in the care of Sophia. Rachel seeing that he would be well cared for at his flat headed home. As she opened the front door, she picked up the post. Recognising the probable contents from the envelopes, she placed them on the telephone table. But there was a hand written envelope that she opened as she entered her living room. It was from Laura

"Dear Rachel,

I hope Michael is recovering well from his injuries and that you are also O.K.

As we have not heard from you, I decided to take my father home with me as he needs care. He has recovered from his injuries sustained in the fall but his sight is now very poor and although his vision has not gone completely it is limited and he needs looking after. He told me he does not want to be a burden to anyone, least of all to me or indeed you, so he has booked himself into a residential rehabilitation centre for the recently blind. He is due to go next Monday and I shall be taking him. Please ring us when you can but hopefully before he leaves.

Love,

Laura"

As feelings of intense sorrow and guilt swept over her, Rachel let the letter fall from her grasp onto the carpeted floor. Tears welled up in her eyes as she reached for the telephone, but she couldn't find the strength to dial the number and eventually she replaced it.

The next day was Friday and pushing Andrew to the back of her many thoughts she went to work. Peggy was her usual supportive self but even she said that she must ring Andrew as soon as she got home.

"What do I say" asked Rachel, "I have a great affection for him but I don't think I can cope with being his carer."

"Then you must tell him, "stated Peggy firmly. "I know its difficult girl, but you you owe him this. He must know in his heart how you feel, so it won't come as a complete shock."

After eating a meagre dinner that evening, Rachel poured herself a large Drambuie and sat by the telephone table. After swallowing half of it in one go, she lifted the receiver and dialled Laura's number.

"Hello." It was Laura.

"Hello Laura, can I speak with your father please." She asked meekly.

"Rachel, how's Michael?"

"He's coming along, he should be back at work soon, thank you for asking."

"I'll get dad. "Rachel was relieved not to detect any bitterness or resentment in her voice.

Rachel could hear what sounded like furniture being moved and then Andrew's lovely Scot's brogue.

"Hello darlin, it's so good to hear your voice. How's Michael?"

"He's good. I hear you are off for some rehabilitation on Monday."

"Yes, I'm looking forward to it, can't wait until I can get some of my independence back."

"I hope you can, "said Rachel softly," I really do."

There was a pause as they both tried to interpret what had just been said.

In an attempt to push the conversation on, Andrew changed the subject. "Have the police discovered who carried out the attack on Michael?"

Rachel was grateful for the change in tone and the relief it brought. She then relayed the story of the goings on at the publisher's annual dinner.

"That's my girl," said Andrew laughing, "I wish I had been there to see…" he didn't finish the sentence and the laughing ceased.

Rachel still had feelings for this man but couldn't yet commit so she simply said "I really hope you get on well Andrew. When you've settled in, give me a ring and we'll talk some more."

Realising the conversation was over for now, Andrew simply said, trying desperately to take the emotion out of his voice.

"O.k. darling, I'll do that. Bye for now."

CHAPTER 33

Easter Sunday 1974 was a time for quiet celebration although the guest list was anything to be quiet about. Rachel put on a fine dinner for Michael, Sophia, Sophia's grandmother, Dowager Lady Grace, Andrew, Laura, and Laura's boyfriend Nigel.

Getting to this point had not been easy for Rachel. She had not been pleased with Michael when he had announced that he had invited Lady Grace for Easter Sunday dinner.

"What," his mother had screeched. "A lady dowager coming here for dinner?"

"She's really is very nice mum, there's no reason to worry, and she's eager to meet you."

"But how am I supposed to put on a dinner for a dowager? I mean where am I going to get a silver dinner service. And then, I wouldn't know what wine to get and I can't pour it into our odd glasses."

"Mum, mum, it doesn't matter. Sophia has told her all about you and she's not a bit bothered about the cutlery or the wine. She just wants to meet us as a family."

"And there's Andrew, this is the first time he's been back here since, since…"

"It will be fine mum, really. Andrew will be good with it. Lady Grace knows all about him and his circumstances."

Michael had at least given his mother a bit of notice, two weeks.

In the council offices on Monday morning, Peggy's reaction when she heard the news was even more dramatic.

"Aah, you're joking."

Mr Melcher sprinted over to see what the emergency was.

"I'm terribly sorry Mr Melcher, I just bit my tongue, "said Peggy screwing up her face whilst curling her mouth. "But, thank you for your concern." And then, "you are such a kind man."

"Peggy was so good at turning things around, "thought Rachel as she tried desperately to subdue a laugh.

"Well, I like to look after my staff you know," he said in his creepy voice. And then turning to look at Rachel. "Do let me know if there is anything else I can for you ladies."

It was then Peggy's turn to stifle a laugh as their boss headed back to his desk.

Easter Sunday fell on the 14th April. Normally, Rachel loved Easter but today was a big day, one of the biggest days in her life. Unable to sleep she left her bed at 6a.m. and headed straight for her kitchen where she put the largest chicken she had ever bought into the oven. She then started on peeling and scraping the veg. The radio announced it was 6.30 just as she heard a knock on her front door. Opening it she was greeted with the sight of Peggy unloading another enormous chicken from the back of her car.

"Hello ducks," she said followed by "or should that be chickens." She laughed.

"Thank God you're here." gasped Rachel nervously.

"Calm down girl, calm down, it's all going to be fine." replied her friend.

"I hope so Peggy."

"Well, you've only got a dowager and a lady of the realm coming plus your blind lover and his daughter, your son Michael and me. What could possibly go wrong?"

Rachel held her stomach, "Oh Peggy, don't make me laugh please, I've got too much to do."

"Well then, we'd best get on with it then girl, hadn't we?"

With that, the two very capable women took the kitchen by storm chatting as they worked.

"How's the old man," asked Rachel working at pace.

"Ralph. Oh he's still not too well, or reckons he isn't. Just a bit of a cold if you ask me but I reckon it's just an excuse not to come to dinner. He's not one for royalty."

And so, the two friends laughed and worked producing a mountain of peeled potatoes and vegetables.

Over a cup of tea Peggy asked what time everyone was expected.

"Well," started Rachel, "Michael will be accompanying Sophia and her grandmother to church here in town, so assuming the service will be ending a little bit later than usual, they should be here about 12.30. Laura should arrive with her father and her boyfriend just before then. We should get changed about 11.30, just to be on the safe side

The nervous laughter continued as the two friends changed into their finest upstairs in the bedroom that used to be Michael's room. Peggy had bought an expensive dress for the occasion. The maroon velvet was perfect to show off her beautiful, long blond hair. A string of white pearls against her white skin completed the vision. Rachel's black hair shone, in contrast to the pale lemon dress with modest neckline that she chose to wear. Around her neck she wore a pendant with a sapphire stone that husband Jack had bought her for their wedding day. A hint of a tear approached her eye as Peggy fastened the clasp for her.

The front door knocker rasped at 12 noon.

Laura held her father's hand as she carefully guided him over the threshold. He was smartly dressed in white shirt and tartan tie under a navy-blue lounge suit Rachel recognised from the time she met him in London. Dark glasses hid his eyes. Rachel stepped forward and kissed him tenderly on the cheek before pointing out to Laura where they should sit. Laura's boyfriend Graham followed.

Over at the church, Michael sat with Lady Grace and Sophia near thefront. They were two rows behind Lord Hazelhurst who was in attendance on his own. He had greeted his daughter and mother-in-law with a courteous kiss. He offered a reluctant hand to Michael who took it saying, "Happy Easter your Lordship."

An ill looking Mrs Murray, sitting several pews behind was in raptures.

The vicar's easter sermon focused on forgiveness and as Sophia was leaving the church, she approached her father and looking him straight in the eye said softly,

"In my happiness father, I forgive you but this is Goodbye."

At Rachel's house Peggy stood by the curtains in the front room as the vintage Rolls Royce pulled up outside. She let out a muffled scream, "They're here, they're here."

Rachel opened the door. Michael helped Lady Grace from the car and said softly,

"Mum, I'd like you to meet dowager, Lady Grace."

"Welcome to my home your ladyship."

"I'm so pleased to meet you at last, please call me Grace, after all we shall soon be related."

Rachel led her ladyship into her living room and introduced everyone.

Sophia grasped Michael's hand and smiled as Rachel addressed her guests,

"Well now everyone, I'm so pleased to welcome you all here today, you are my dearest family and friends. My good friend Peggy here will be helping me with dinner, but first what would everyone like to drink?" asked Rachel eyeing the newly purchased matching set of wine and water glasses decorating the two tables that had been placed together and covered with Italian cotton tablecloths.

Peggy held up a bottle of red and a bottle of white wine indicating the extent of the available options. She smiled broadly as she added "We also have a large selection of soft drinks. "

Lady Grace smiled at Sophia with a twinkle in her eye, she liked fun people. Sophia, who was sat opposite recognised the smile for what it was, a sign of affectionate approval. Although Rachel and Peggy had resisted the temptation to place name tags on the table they had rehearsed where each guest should sit and had drawn out a rough table plan. Happily, the guests did not resist and obediently sat on the chair presented to them by Peggy.

Laura opposite Graham, a safe distance from Michael who was seated opposite Peggy on the other end of the table;

Andrew opposite Rachel; it would give Rachel the opportunity to observe him at close quarters;

Lady Grace opposite Sophia.

Rachel was pleased to see conversation strike up immediately. Andrew explained his recent history to Lady Grace without a hint of self-pity. After Laura had taken her father's hand and placed it gently on the various pieces of cutlery, he explained that he still had some vision and was appreciative of the strong electric light bulbs Rachel had put in. His recent stay in the rehabilitation centre had been a great help and with a little guidance he could manage most simple tasks. Lady Grace was hugely impressed by this gentle clever man and touched his hand as a sign of her respect and regard. Michael was entertained by Peggy who wanted to know all about his work and his trip to Italy with the famous author Greg Singer.

"I'm a great fan of Greg's," she said enthusiastically, "do you think you could get me a signed copy of his latest book, The Italian Affair?" Michael lost his smile and looked pale. Peggy realised immediately the gaffe she had made, "I'm so sorry Michael but I see that chapter is now closed, so to speak." Rachel had overheard the latter part of the conversation and came to the rescue. "Peggy, could you help me in the kitchen please?" Sophia had also heard Peggy and engaged Michael by saying what a great friend Peggy had been to his mother. Lady Grace joined in by saying how much she was enjoying the dinner with such genuine people, something she wasn't always used to. Sophia then chatted to Andrew and Laura about their lives in Scotland and saying how much she enjoyed her visits there with her late mother and grandmother, Lady Grace. When Peggy and Rachel returned with freshly opened bottles of wine, they chatted to Sophia about their dresses and her upcoming wedding planned for the following spring, much of which still had to be arranged. Bringing Laura into the conversation Lady Grace asked how she and Graham had met and about their careers. It turned out Graham was in his final year of a medical degree and would soon be working as a junior doctor in Saint Thomas hospital in London. Laura had started her career with a Public Relations and Advertising company in London, near to where she and her father were living. Peggy and Rachel kept an eye on the drinks and topped up the glasses as needed, together with making many trips to the kitchen to check on the chicken and vegetables. As the dinner progressed smoothly Rachel watched Andrew carefully and was pleased to see how well he managed. Conversation was never a problem for Andrew, he had been used to conversing with important people and his soft Scots accent drew people to like him instantly, not least Lady Grace. By the end of the evening Rachel began to wonder if it could work, he and her. "It's not as though he's in a wheelchair or bedridden, maybe it wouldn't be too difficult. Lady Grace was the first to leave along with Sophia who kissed Michael asking him to ring her when he returned to his flat in London. Laura averted her gaze; it was still painful for her to witness the man she had loved kissing another. As Rachel saw the pair into their chauffeur driven rolls Royce, Lady Grace turned and kissed her on the cheek and invited her to Berkham Hall, her family home, to discuss preparations for the wedding. Andrew left shortly after, assisted by his daughter Laura and Graham. Rachel kissed Andrew on the cheek and promised that she would ring him soon. As Graham passed, he gave Rachel a large envelope, saying that Andrew had asked him to give to her.

    For the next hour, Peggy and Rachel sat at the dining table drinking wine and going over what they remembered about the evening and laughing at the little things that had gone wrong, like the burned carrots and one or two burps from drinking the fizzy wine too quickly. Michael excused himself and said he was going to see how his friend Tom was getting on. Last time he saw him he was in a pretty sorry state. After he left the house the conversation between the two women took a serious turn as they remarked how well Andrew had coped and how he had lost none of his charm. Rachel didn't challenge Peggy when she remarked, "I think you might still love him girl."

Rachel was thinking what to say when Ralph called to pick up Peggy who was now just a little worse for drink. Looking at the pile of washing up Rachel decided it would keep until the morning, Easter Monday, thankfully a bank holiday. Before climbing the stairs, she spotted the large thick envelope left on the settee. On opening it, she pulled out the heavy sheets of parchment, it was the deeds to the house, they were in her name, it seemed that they had always been in her name.

Sleep came unexpectedly easily to Rachel considering everything she had on her mind but even so she was awoken in the early hours by a series of clattering noises from downstairs. Looking at her bedside clock it said 3a.m. As she descended the stairs, she recognised the sound of dishes being collected. It was Michael in the kitchen doing the clearing and washing up. He was facing the sink, his jacket placed on the back of a chair.

"I'll do them in the morning love, you get some sleep." Without turning Michael replied, "It's alright mum, it's given me time to think."

"I understand son."

"It's funny how things work out in life, I mean ten years ago Tom and me were just a couple of happy go lucky kids still at school, now look at us. Tom has a couple of kids, divorced and on invalidity benefit where as I have a degree, good job and engaged to a Lady of the realm. Life's not fair, is it?"

"I know son, it isn't. Look at Andrew, a brilliant surgeon one minute and the next, well."

"Tom told me that Andrew had got him in at the hospital to see a colleague of his who specialises in spinal injuries and he reckons he can help him."

"That's wonderful news Michael, is he going to have an operation?"

"Yes, next month; he's living with his children at his mother's. His sister is still at home and she's helping with the kids."

"I'm so pleased son; Andrew didn't mention that he'd helped Tom."

"I don't suppose he would, he's that kind of man, a very decent man, a good man."

"Yes, he is," replied Rachel thoughtfully, now off you go to bed, I'll finish up here."

CHAPTER 34

Over the next few weeks, Rachel agonised over what to do about Andrew. They spoke weekly on the telephone and she had visited him at his daughter's place in London just a month after Easter but was no nearer reaching a decision on whether to ask him to move back in with her, although she came very close to it on more than one occasion. And so, the year moved on inexorably until Autumn when Lady Grace rang and asked if she were available the following week end as she felt it was time to discuss the wedding. Rachel agreed, not knowing if she was free or not, you don't hesitate when you receive an invitation from a lady dowager.

"Excellent, my dear, I'll send my car to collect you."

Before Rachel could say any more, the call was ended, leaving Rachel reeling with a hundred thoughts, what to pack, what to wear, what to say. Her first rational thought was to ring Peggy.

"Help," she muttered down the phone.

"What on earth is it girl?"

"I've been summoned."

"What did you do? Was it shoplifting?"

"No, not that kind of summons, It's Lady Grace, she's sending a car to take me to her place next week end. Can you come around; I need help."

"I'll be right over, your grace," laughed Peggy.

Rachel then busied herself tidying and hoovering whilst she waited for her friend to arrive. It should take her 20 minutes to walk, five if Ralph brought her in the car. After an hour had passed Rachel wondered if her friend was O.k. or if she had misheard her. "No, "she thought, "she definitely said she'd be over straight away."

Rachel poured herself a cup of tea and thought what a good friend Peggy had been over the years she had known her. Nothing had ever been too much trouble; she had always been there for her and never asked for anything in return. She was faithful, funny and always there ready to help in any situation. The telephone rang and suddenly Rachel felt fear. Had something dreadful happened? She couldn't bear it if anything happened to her dearest best friend.

Tentatively she lifted the receiver and said timidly, "Hello"

It was Ralph. "Hello Rachel, I'm ringing from home, Peggy's in hospital, it sounds like she' broken her leg, apparently some kid on a bike ran into her on the pavement. I'm just leaving to go and see her."

"Thanks for letting me know Ralph, tell her I'll visit her in the hospital tomorrow, we should know a bit more by then."

Rachel's stomach was turning over with anguish not knowing whether to feel horrified or thankful that it wasn't any worse. But this incident had made her realise the extent of her feelings for her friend, she was irreplaceable. It was then that she realised; she loved her, she loved Peggy, the woman who yet again was coming to her aid.

The following day was a Tuesday and work was busy, having to do Peggy's work as well as her own. Mr

Melcher was in a panic; it was month end and several staff were off with flu in addition to Peggy. But at least it kept him busy and away from her, the last thing she needed was him leaching after her. She worked through her lunch break and was then able to leave early and go straight to the hospital. She didn't like hospitals, it brought back unpleasant memories of Michael and then Andrew being in there. But even though she was very worried about them at the time, this was different. She couldn't explain this feeling she had for her friend, it was unfamiliar and new, she had never experienced it before. Ralph was already there, sitting at the side of her bed, she wished he hadn't. Peggy's face lit up when she saw Rachel walking along the ward with an armful of flowers and a brown paper bag, she guessed contained grapes. Ralph stood to greet her and after explaining that he had been there for an hour left for home. Before taking his seat, Rachel kissed her friend tenderly on the cheek. She noticed that apart from looking a little pale, Peggy looked as glamorous as ever, she had obviously been busy with her vanity case.

"It's not broken," she said looking at the lower part of the bed, just badly bruised. I'll have to wear my dark stockings for a while."

Rachel smiled as she said how worried she had been.

"Oh, I'm fine ducks. Now, about this weekend you'll need a dress to travel, a dress for the daytime and then of course for the evening, I've got just the thing."

Rachel laughed. "Now lady, listen to me for a change, you

need to rest and get better, I can't hold Melcher off forever"

"Are you sure you want to?" teased Peggy.

"I'm going before I do something I'll regret," quipped Rachel standing and laughing at her friend.

"Give Lady Grace my felicitations," shouted Peggy after her friend.

The rest of the busy working week flew by. Friday evening found Rachel looking through the window of her front room at the dimly lit road. It was almost dark and a drizzle was falling. Her mother called it wet rain, because although it didn't look much it would wet you through in no time. Shivering at the thought, she looked over her shoulder at the doorway leading to the kitchen now in darkness. Yes, she had checked all around, gas taps and water taps were all off. As headlights lit up the road, she transferred the house keys from her right hand to her left and picked up the large suitcase. Waiting to confirm it was indeed the Rolls Royce she opened the front door and turned to lock her front door. She reached for her case but the chauffeur beat her to it and then held open the rear passenger door for her to enter and placed her case into the boot of the car. He then tipped his cap to Rachel and gestured for her to enter but was surprised when she asked if he would mind if she sat with him in the front. This was the first time in his long service to Lady Grace that he had been asked this.

"As madam chooses," came his somewhat stiff response.

Rachel placed him at about 60. She could see under his formal exterior that this was a kind person, he would have to be, to work for such a lovely woman as Lady Grace.

"How long do you think will it take to get there?" asked Rachel as they started their journey.

"About an hour and a half madam, but it depends on the London traffic."

Rachel was tempted to ask him to call her by her name but thought better of it. She didn't want to shock the poor man further; it was difficult enough for him to have a guest sit by him in the front. She noticed how careful a driver he was, he had to be, driving such a beautiful car around. After a while staring ahead into the rain filled darkness, Rachel felt uncomfortable with the awkward silence and judged how best to talk to him so she shared with him a number of things including her friend, Peggy's recent accident and how lovely she found Lady Grace. He gradually relaxed and Rachel was able to ascertain that it was largely him and his wife who looked after her Ladyship. She also had an elderly maid who had been with her for many, many years. His wife, Jane would see to all the household duties including cleaning and catering. Whenever she had a social function, his wife would arrange for outside caterers to come in, but as for the day-to-day duties like shopping and cooking, they took care of all that.

Towards the end of the smoothest car journey she had ever had, Rachel heard the tick tick of the indicators as the car entered the gates of the Berkham estate. The rain had stopped and as Thomas turned off the windscreen wipers, she saw ahead the lights of the grand entrance reflected on the surface of the lake.

Thomas guided Rachel out of the car and then pulled the chain on the outside of the great doors. As they opened, assisted by a noisy electric motor, the light from the entrance hall chandelier flooded the scene. Lady Grace stood there in a kind of grand isolation.

"Welcome, welcome my dear," she said, her elderly maid standing by her side. "Come, we have a lot to get through. "Gesturing, she guided her guest into the library where a large fire was roaring in the grand fireplace. "But not tonight, you must be tired after your journey." And then gently addressing her maid "Dorothy, we'll take tea in here please before we come through for dinner."

Sitting in large armchairs at either side of the fire. Both ladies started to speak at the same time asking the same question. "How are you?" This broke the mild tension and made them laugh. Lady Grace then explained that she and her maid, the chauffer and his wife now occupied only a small part of the house.

"Is Sophia here yet," asked Rachel.

"No, my dear, Sophia isn't coming, I planned it to be just us two this weekend. I wanted you to understand a few things about my family. It's wonderful to see these two young people so much in love, but you and I know that life is not always the fairy tale we want it to be."

Rachel wasn't expecting this and tensed.

"Oh, don't be alarmed my dear, my granddaughter has no deep, dark secret, not like her father anyway."

Rachel breathed a sigh of relief, "I wondered what you about to reveal, their passage so far has not been straightforward as you know."

"I know my dear, you and Michael have come through it all with great credit, I admire your determination and good grace. I was particularly impressed with your Easter Sunday display of loyalty and love for your family and friends. No, I just wanted you to know a little of our history. But that can wait until tomorrow."

As if by arrangement the maid entered and announced that dinner was ready to be served.

"Thank you, Dorothy, "said Lady Grace rising and then to Rachel, "shall we go through?"

The dining room was huge and cold and smelled somewhat musty. In the centre was a long, polished dining table, Rachel guessed it could seat at least thirty people but she was pleased that places had been set for just two opposite each other in the middle. Large paintings of ancestors hung on the walls. They were mostly of seriously looking people ranging in age from early twenties to elderly. Their dress suggested that that they had been hung in historical order starting at the entrance. Rachel sat opposite a portrait of a very beautiful young woman dressed in a pale blue ball gown. Lady Grace said, "My daughter, Sophia's mother. It was painted only months before she was presented to the queen. You'll have noticed the striking resemblance to Sophia."

The maid entered with two shawls and offered one to Rachel who gratefully accepted. She placed it around her shoulders before doing the same for Lady Grace.

"I know it's cold in here my dear but I do like to keep up standards."

Rachel gave a little shiver as she nodded.

"I don't expect Sophia to keep this place on after she has married but it's too late for me to move out now." Raising her hand to the wall behind her, she continued. "After all, all my family are all here on the walls and in the cemetery at the back of the house, just by the chapel gardens."

Dorothy entered with a tray on which two bowls of soup balanced.

When she had served and left, Lady Grace explained that she had been with her over fifty years now. She lived in a little flat in the house. It was warm and cosy, "much more comfortable than the rest of the house."

Rachel sipped the soup, it was cold.

Seeing her quest's expression, Lady Grace apologised,

"I'm sorry my dear. It would have been hot when it left the kitchen but it takes Dorothy a little while to get here."

Rachel couldn't contain herself any longer and started to laugh. Lady Grace laughed also, until the pair almost cried. To Rachel's relief, the main course was served piping hot by Thomas and his wife Jane. After dinner the two ladies returned to the warmer and much more comfortable library. Dorothy appeared and left a bottle of Drambuie and two whiskey glasses on the small table which was in reaching distance for the two. Remarking that this was her favourite tipple Rachel warmed even more to the elegant lady opposite. Several logs had been added to the fire which was now roaring in approval.

"So," started Rachel "how long have your family lived here?"

"Since the English Civil War. My ancestor was a royalist, loyal to King Charles. After the war, he lost his estate to the Parliamentarians but when Charles 11 came to the throne, it was reinstated."

Rachel looked along the long line of portraits on the far wall.

"Cromwell is the most miserable looking one," said Lady Grace. "I'm all for good moral behaviour but the Puritans took it all too far. I couldn't live without music and dancing."

Rachel tried to remember her history from her school days.

Lady Grace guessed what Rachel was trying to do and said "Oh don't worry my dear, it was all a very long time ago. So, back to the present, do you know what your son's thoughts are about what kind of wedding he would like?"

"Actually, I have no idea, he hasn't discussed it. I think he is happy to go along with whatever Sophia would like to do."

"Very gallant. Is that what you want Rachel?"

"Well, yes, I suppose. Michael is my only child and apart from him I have no other family. I would just like my friend Peggy and her husband to be invited to the wedding."

"What about Andrew and his daughter?" asked Lady Grace earnestly.

"Well, yes, I suppose."

"You don't sound too sure my dear, are you still friends."

"Oh yes," replied Rachel a little too quickly. "It's just."

"He wants more, is that it?"

Rachel bowed her head slightly and then revealed all. "Yes, he's a wonderful, generous man but I don't know if I can give him all he wants."

"I think I know how you are feeling. After my George died, I had no shortage of offers, but none that came anywhere near replicating the feelings I had for my husband. Once I realised this, I was resigned to living the rest of my life as his widow. Who knows, we may meet again on the other side."

Rachel felt a tear well up in her eyes as she looked at this wonderful woman, this lovely lady and realised that she did know, she did understand.

The following day dawned bright and soon after a leisurely breakfast, the two ladies strolled in the grounds and continued to talk not just about the wedding but about everything, ranging from their childhood sweethearts to their favourite clothes and music. Rachel told her ladyship about the time in London when Andrew had booked a special evening at the Arabian Nights Restaurant but that her dress had been ruined in the rain but that the girl working in the hotel had found her an amazing dress in lost property. And later about encountering Sophia with her father in the restaurant and how she took him to task over him humiliating her son.

Lady Grace applauded and continued, "Do you know he wanted to turn my home into a high-class casino? The thought of it made me feel quite ill. I soon put paid to that idea and told him I thought those places to be evil, leading to untold misery and despair. But he didn't care about that, he just wanted to enrich himself and his disreputable friends."

All too soon, the weekend came to an end and it was time to say goodbye. She had very much enjoyed her host's company. Thomas took her home in the Rolls, in the back seat this time. She didn't talk much on the journey, she had had a lot to think about. She reflected on the warmth and character of Lady Grace, they were similar in many respects, not least on their ability to judge a person's character. Yes, she now had two firm friends, Lady Grace and Peggy, two people she could trust completely.

CHAPTER 35

Laura's flat in London was small, but small meant that her father could find his way around more easily and she was happy with that. His rehabilitation Centre had equipped him with certain skills such as making a cup of tea and preparing simple meals but the loneliness was beginning to get to him. Being alone all day, every day whilst Laura was at work was crushing for a man of his intellect. Calls from past colleagues had dried up and when he rang them, they were always busy or "not available". Rachel was always kind and gave him time but lately his calls were not answered even when he knew that she would have finished work for the day. Laura was wonderful but her work as a secondary school teacher in Peckham kept her busy and she often had to do marking and prepare lessons in the evenings, and when she wasn't working, she naturally liked to spend time with her boyfriend Graham, although he had sensed that things weren't all that good between them lately. The doctor had prescribed anti-depressants but he wasn't ready to go down that road, not yet anyway. He was beginning to think that everyone would be better off if he wasn't around anymore. No one could say that he hadn't tried to cope with his sight loss. In his frustration he had tripped many times in the flat and fallen to the floor. On one occasion his head had collided with the table and he lost consciousness. The cut on his forehead had bled profusely and he had been unable to wipe all of it away. When Laura had returned home that evening, she cried at his appearance. She wanted to ring Rachel but Andrew had begged her not to. After that incident Laura only left the flat for work and never to socialise. Graham had called on her several times and sat with her for the evening. Sometimes Andrew had retreated to his bedroom to give the couple some privacy but Graham eventually found the situation unacceptable when Laura repeatedly refused to go anywhere with him outside the flat and ended their relationship. When Andrew discussed this with his daughter, she said that she had wanted to end it for some time. She went on to explain that she had only started the relationship after Michael had become engaged to Sophia, she now recognised it for what it was, a rebound reaction. After that incident Andrew sought to give his daughter her life back. He recognised that Rachel had realised that the same thing would have happened if she had agreed to have him back living with her. So, he had two choices, one was to end it all but this would have caused unbearable pain to the two people he loved most, his daughter Laura and the only other woman he had ever loved apart from his wife, the wise and beautiful Rachel.

    The other choice was to find somewhere else to live and if possible, to be useful. The following week he rang his most trusted friend, Dr Stephen Ward in Edinburgh and told him how he felt. The very next day his friend travelled to London to see him. He had been his best man at his wedding and knew Andrew better than anyone outside of his family. His first impression was one of shock and distress at seeing his friend, clearly blind and with a large wound on his forehead. Laura stayed with a school colleague for the next couple of nights so that Stephen could have her bed and talk freely with her dad. By lunchtime on the third day, Stephen, now fully aware of the situation began to formulate a strategy. Andrew needed to find a place to live and have a purpose in his life. A few calls later and the plan was in place. Andrew would move into a country retreat in Wilshire which had been converted into a home for the Rehabilitation for the Blind, not as a patient but as a medical consultant.

CHAPTER 36

Lord Hazlehurst sat in the library brooding about his life. Benson was wary as he entered, not sure what to expect. Since his Lordships carefully laid plans had been so spectacularly dismantled by his late wife's mother, he was like a bear with a sore head. Benson despised his master and would have left his service long ago but for the hold he had over him. Blackmail was a tool frequently used by his Lordship and it was this that kept Benson in his service. He had tried to leave after the death of Lady Hazlehurst a lovely woman in all respects, but his Lordship had threatened to report him to the police over a hit and run offence in which the victim had died.

"Benson, I want you to do a little task for me."

Benson stiffened. He had been asked to do little tasks before and they were never pleasant.

"I'd like you to befriend Mrs Flynn and find out the state of play between her urchin son and my daughter."

"Can't you just ask her sir?"

"I think we both know that she wouldn't give me the time-of-day Benson."

"I don't know if I'd feel comfortable doing this sir."

"I don't give a damn what you feel Benson. Just do it," said Lord Hazlehurst staring fiercely.

The butler retreated to his quarters a, a look of grim determination on his face. This was the last time he would take orders from this man. He recalled the last spiteful order he had been given, to destroy the painting of his late wife with her daughter Sophia. He had protested at the time but to no avail. Benson knew how important the painting was to Sophia, she would be devastated if it were destroyed, so he had hidden it in a place his Lordship would never find it, in the servants 'quarters. When his Lordship was next away, he had taken it to the local art dealer for them to pack and send to Lady Grace Summers. He had enclosed a letter of explanation asking her Ladyship not to disclose how she had come into her possession. It had cost him the best part of a week's wages but it was worth it. He wasn't sure which gave him more satisfaction, the fact that it would really please Sophia and her Nan, or really infuriate his Lordship if he ever found out.

Benson didn't sleep well that might, he was torn between his conscience and the thought of being exposed as the hit and run driver who killed the elderly man on that country road. He once again dreamed of the stormy night he returned to the estate with his Lordship in the back having picked him up from the casino in London. He had waited for hours for his Lordship to emerge and had taken a drink from his hip flask to warm himself, something he had never forgiven himself for. But the thought of the shame of being exposed was too much to contemplate and once again he pushed his conscience to the back of his mind knowing full well it would never cease to torment him. But his conscience would have to wait until he had enough savings to get himself a small flat in the village. Then he would go to the police and confess and hope for a non-custodial sentence. In the meantime, his Lordship would want a progress report on the job he had given him. Benson had never been one for the ladies and he wondered how on earth he would befriend the attractive Rachel Flynn. He guessed he was about the same age as her and reasonably good looking in a rough sort of way but he often got tongue tied and embarrassed in the company of women, especially the attractive ones. His ex-wife had said he was boring before leaving him for the insurance man. He wondered if she had thought the same after he had given her lover a good hiding when he came home early one day and found them in bed together. He cracked a smile as he remembered the sight of lover boy running to his car half naked.

Nights off were spent in the village local, The Red Bull. Over the years he had made a couple of acquaintances, not really friends but at least he had someone to talk to. He remembered Rachel coming in a number of times with a female friend, so he wasn't completely unknown to her. The problem was how to approach her, as she never came in alone. So, the next time she came in with her friend he made a point of saying hello to the two of them and made small talk until it became obvious that they didn't want him to join them. Rachel had given no sign that made him believe that she recognised him, probably because he was out of his chauffeur's uniform. This allowed him, when asked by his Lordship, to report that he had, at least made contact. But that wouldn't satisfy him for long, he would have to make his next move soon. So, the following Saturday morning he knocked on her door.

"Yes," she said," Can I help you?"

"I don't know if you recognise me," he said nervously, "We met briefly in the pub last Tuesday. I wonder if I can have a word.

Rachel replied, a faint smile of recognition on her face, "Yes, I remember you, "she added but standing her ground, she was not about to invite him in, "What is it?"

"Well," It's about your son, Michael."

Rachel stiffened "What about him, is he alright?"

"Yes, yes, I'm sorry if I alarmed you. It's just, just,"

Rachel looked increasing agitated and said again. "What is it?"

Looking up at Rachel who was stood on the high step, he blurted out.

" Look, I'm on your side Mrs Flynn. I work for Lord Hazlehurst and."

Before he could finish his sentence Rachel slammed the door shut.

"Please Mrs Flynn, hear me out," he shouted, "I promise you, I'm on your side."

Leaning on the inside of the door, Rachel trembled as she listened to the man who she now remembered as Lord Hazlehurst's chauffer.

Shouting back, she said "Why should I believe a word you have to say?"

"Because, I know the kind of man Hazlehurst is. I know how he has tried to sabotage your son's relationship with his daughter. I can help you."

After a long pause, Rachel unlocked her door and said cautiously "You'd better come in but keep your distance."

Benson saw the rolling pin in Rachel's hand and slowly entered, keeping his distance, he had seen this formidable lady in action.

"Thank you," he said before following her into the living room.

"Leave the front door open," she commanded.

Benson started to relate his story about how he started to work for his Lordship 20 years ago after leaving the army. He left out the bit about him being in special forces.

Rachel interrupted, firmly tightening her grip on the rolling pin., "Just tell me what it is you wanted to say."

"Yes, I'm sorry. Well, I have become disillusioned with his Lordship since the death of his wife, a truly lovely woman. He is not a nice man and I've seen the way he has treated you."

"Then why haven't you left his service if you are so disillusioned with him?"

"Well, "said Benson shuffling uncomfortably, "Can I just say that he has a hold on me at the moment."

Rachel knew a victim when she saw one and softened her stance, just a little.

"You'd better sit down. Now, what is it?" she asked, the firmness in her voice still evident

"Well, you probably know that his Lordship is estranged from his daughter.

Rachel stopped herself from confirming this, she was not sure of this man yet.

"Well," he continued, "He has instructed me to find out the state of play between her and your son Michael."

Rachel studied his rugged face; wrinkles had furrowed his forehead even though he probably wasn't that old. In other circumstances she could have liked this man.

"Do you really expect me to answer that question?" she asked.

"No, I don't, but if you were to say that Miss Sophia and Michael were back on, I know it would really annoy his Lordship," he said, a smile breaking across his face.

Rachel relaxed her grip on the rolling pin.

"Tea?" she asked, turning towards the kitchen, a hidden smile breaking across her lips.

Benson relaxed as he waited for the tea to arrive. It had been five years since his divorce and he had given up hope of finding happiness again with another woman, but Rachel was special; in addition to being beautiful, she was brave and more than a match for his pathetic boss. But she was probably taken and anyway she wouldn't look at him twice. Over tea and biscuits, Benson told Rachel everything about his life and time working for his Lordship. He told of how he had seen Sophia grow up into a beautiful young woman with all the qualities her mother had had before she was worn down by this womanising, gambling excuse for a man.

"Was it you who answered the telephone when Michael tried to speak to Sophia all those years ago and made him feel small?"

"I regret to say that it was. In my defence, I was being monitored by his Lordship the whole time to ensure that I followed his instructions

"Thank you for confirming that. I suspected as much. By the way what do I call you? And please don't say Benson, I dislike the pompous ways of the aristocracy."

"It's Nigel ma'am," he replied, a feeling of relief spreading through his body.

Rachel had begun to like this man.

The couple chatted a while longer but when Rachel started to clear away the cups, Nigel took this as a sign his audience was over and stood.

"Well thank you Mrs Flynn for listening to me and also for the tea. What should I tell his Lordship?"

"Call me Rachel. You can tell him that Michael and Sophia are back on and I shall expect to hear from you how he takes it, badly, I hope. Here's my phone number, "she said handing him a scrap of paper.

Nigel smiled. "Did she just say call me Rachel?"

Rachel smiled confirming that indeed she had.

As he reached the door, Nigel thought of asking Rachel if she was seeing anyone at the moment but decided it might just be too much at the moment. So, he just said, "I'll let you know how his Lordship takes the news."

As he walked away, he felt a spring in his step and started to whistle his favourite tune whilst trying to remember the last time he had felt quite this happy.

On Monday morning at work, Peggy hung onto every word. whilst closely studying her friends face.

"Has he rung yet, what's he like close up."

"He's alright I suppose," replied Rachel.

"You fancied him, didn't you girl?"

"Of course not." shouted Rachel loudly.

"You protest too much girl; I can tell you liked him."

"Don't be ridiculous Peggy, I didn't." protested Rachel unable to suppress a smile and then a giggle.

"O my, girl, what is it about you? You have men chasing you all the time."

"I do nothing to encourage them Peggy, I don't know why they seem to be attracted to me." replied Rachel, secretly enjoying her friend's observations.

The ladies' laughter had not gone unnoticed by Mr Melcher. He tried coughing loudly but they were far too engrossed in their conversation so he tried again. In the end he felt he had to intervene and approached their desks.

"Ladies, Ladies, I'm sure your chat is very interesting but I must insist you leave it until your lunch break or after hours."

"Sorry Mr Melcher." both ladies said in unison before resuming their work.

That evening, Rachel didn't have to wait long to hear from Nigel, he rang soon after dinner

"He took the news badly, swearing and cursing and threatening to cut Sophia out of his will. He blames her Nan, Lady Grace, "No ambition, no regard for my hopes and plans for my daughter, my daughter, not hers."

"What does he plan to do, did he say?" asked Rachel

"No but he can be dangerous when he's like this. I'll keep an eye on him and keep you informed."

"Thank you, Nigel, I'd appreciate that."

"Rachel, I wanted to ask you something while you're on."

"Yes Nigel."

"Well, I was just wondering."

Rachel had been half expecting something like this and was prepared having given it some thought the previous day.

Nigel summoned up his courage and asked gently.

"I was just wondering if you were seeing anyone at the moment."

"Well Nigel," she replied slowly "It's somewhat complicated. I would be quite willing to have you as a friend but as for a relationship, no, not at the moment."

"I understand." he said eventually.

"You can't possibly understand Nigel, you don't really know me. Why don't you come around next Saturday evening and I'll explain?"

"Yes, that sounds like a good idea." he said perking up. At least she didn't just say "No", or "on yer bike", he thought.

Rachel had dinner alone that Friday evening. She had spent the latter half of the week trying to analyse her feelings and put them in some kind of order. First, was Michael.? Yes, that meant she was O.K. tick. Next, was her best friend Peggy.? Yes, tick. Now, she could consider her own feelings towards Andrew, was he O.K.? Well, he was physically alright apart from his eyes that is, at least he was when he had spoken to her on the telephone last evening. His work was satisfying, he had got his self-respect and confidence back and he could find his way around the hospital and his accommodation well enough. But there was one thing. He had stopped asking how she felt about having him back in the house. Rachel had tried to separate her feelings for him from her feelings of gratitude to him for buying the house for her. But for him, she would be homeless and she would be eternally grateful for that, but was it enough? Some days she thought it was, he was a charming, good-looking man and she did love him, but some days she thought that she was still relatively young and she wanted to do the things she missed out on after the death of her husband. She wanted to dance and take long walks in the countryside, she wanted to run and sing and breath, she wanted to be desired and experience the thrill of the chase, and yes, she wanted to be caught and loved passionately. And maybe Andrew would be better off where he was, if he came back to live with her it would be too far for him to travel for his work and someone would have to take him. Also, what would he do, rattling around the house all day whilst she was at work? No, it wouldn't work and she was not about to give up her job.

"So, that's the state of play as far as I am concerned. I told you it was complicated," Rachel said after giving Nigel a brief, heavily edited explanation of her relationship with Andrew.

"Do you dance?" she asked before Nigel could react.

"Well, I'm no Fred Astaire but I do like to jive."

"Good, where would you like to take me?"

"Well," he replied stalling to think, after such a forthright question, "well,", he said again, there's always the La -Scala in Broughton."

"Good, you can pick me up next Saturday at 7."

"Right," replied Nigel a look of astonishment on his face. He couldn't believe his luck; he was actually going on a date with this beautiful woman. Even in his wildest dreams, which he had plenty of this week, he didn't think this could happen.

"Good, that's settled, Wine? asked Rachel.

The evening then trundled on at a slower pace much to the satisfaction of Nigel, who had to pinch himself several times to ensure that he was awake. The pair found that they were comfortable in each other's company and as the evening wore on, they revealed more about themselves, helped by the wine.

As the last of the bottle was consumed, Rachel stood as an indication that the evening was drawing to a close.

"Right," said Nigel "I'll see you next Saturday at 7. In the meantime, if his Lordship gets up to no good, I'll let you know."

"Thank you, Nigel," said Rachel showing him out. As he turned to say goodnight the streetlight caught his face and gave him a handsome glow; she found herself stepping forward and giving him a brief kiss on the lips. After she had slowly closed the door Nigel stood motionless for a moment on the street.

"What just happened?" he asked himself as he made his way to his car parked on the main road. How could his miserable life have changed so much in such a short time?

Michael B McLarnon

CHAPTER 37

Michael passed his driver's test first time and to celebrate he invested in his first car, a brand-new Allegro, a new model just on the market. Even though interest rates were climbing, he thought he had got a good deal from the bank. Work was going well and he felt good about the future. His wedding was only a few months away and he wanted to be able to drive his beloved Sophia around on their honeymoon. This is something he needed to do, stand on his own merits. Yes, his future wife stood to inherit a fortune, but he wouldn't rely on any of that, he had seen how too much money and privilege could corrupt. When his mother mentioned that she wanted to visit Andrew in the rehabilitation home he immediately volunteered to take her.

It was a crisp spring morning when Michael pulled up outside his mother's house.

"What you think mum?" he asked.

"Oh, it's lovely love, I love the colour."

Michael had chosen a light blue model precisely because it was his mum's favourite colour.

"I love it as well said a voice from behind." It was Sophia.

"Oh, hello love," said Rachel surprised to see her."

"I thought I'd come along to keep Michael company so you can spend some time with Andrew.

"That's very thoughtful of you Sophia, thank you."

Sophia hugged Rachel only then realising that she may have been disappointed to see her, wanting Michael to herself. To make up, she took the back seat allowing Rachel to sit in the front with her son.

"Thank you dear," said Rachel suddenly feeling old but shaking off the thought saying,

" Oh, I love the smell of a new car. This is so nice Michael. " and then after enquiring after Sophia's Nan's health, Rachel settled for the journey and allowed herself to think about the future. After the wedding, Sophia would occupy the front seat in Michael's life, she would no longer be her son's next of kin. Still, Sophia was a lovely girl and she was sure she would understand how she felt. As if to confirm this, Sophia said.

"Rachel, I know it's going to be a wrench in all of our lives so we want you to know that there will always be a place for you in our home should you ever feel the need."

"She had used the word we," thought Rachel. She had tried to make it sound kind and sympathetic but it still felt brutal. She was now on the outside; she was no longer the most important person in her son's life. "

What would her friend Peggy say? She'd say you're lucky girl. Some girls would cut you off altogether, taking the attitude that he was yours, but now he's mine, and you would be reminded of that fact every time you meet."

"Mum" said Michael, "we're here." "Mum, mum."

Rachel woke from her thoughts saying, "Oh, sorry love, I was dreaming."

Andrew had heard the car approaching along the gravel road. There was no point though in looking through the window because his vision was very limited and not capable of distinguishing between objects. So, he waited for the bell to be rung at reception. His hearing seemed to be improving at the same rate as his vision was declining.

"We are here to see Andrew Daglish, he's expecting us. I'm Rachel Flynn"

The sound of her voice had always excited him but curiously not so much this time.

"I'll just inform his assistant, Marie," he heard the receptionist say. "She will be right down."

The trio of visitors sat while they waited. Andrew was tempted to make his way to reception but didn't want his visitors to see him with his white stick tapping on the walls, so he waited.

After a few minutes a smart lady dressed in a tartan skirt and neat dark green top made her way down the carpeted stairs and along the polished oak floor towards the group. Rachel was impressed with this middle-aged lady's appearance and unhurried manner.

"You must be Mrs Flynn," she said in a soft cultured Scots accent whilst holding out her hand. Rachel noticed her brown hair was the same shade as the kilt she wore. "I'm pleased to meet you; Andrew has told me so much about you. And you must be Michael and Sophia, is that right?"

"Yes, that's right," replied Rachel temporarily stunned, thinking that a lot had happened since her last visit.

Marie stepped across the corridor and gently knocked on a door. "Andrew, your visitors are here."

"Thank you, Marie, will you show them in?"

Turning the wooden knob, she opened the door. Andrew was sat on a plain upright chair by the side of an enormous wooden desk that had a telephone on it and several books and what appeared to be a radio and rather large tape recorder. A large window looked out over the gardens and entrance road. The room was carpeted and there were several scenic paintings on the wall. When all three had entered Marie flicked on the light switch and closed the door as she left.

    After the expected kisses and handshake and enquiries as to each other's health, Andrew explained that the rehabilitation centre was a country house gifted to the organisation by the late owner and patiently converted for their present use. This was his office and the adjoining door led to his living quarters. The three listened as Andrew continued to explain about his role here but Rachel's thoughts were elsewhere, specifically on Marie. She didn't have a wedding ring on, was she widowed or divorced? she was too attractive not to have had a history, what was she doing in a place like this in the middle of nowhere? And what were these feelings that she was suddenly experiencing, was she jealous, of course she was.

    After about half an hour there came a gentle knock on the door. It was Marie carrying a large tray upon which lay a large pot of tea and a plate of shortbread biscuits. Rachel watched her every move, from placing the tray on the desk to pouring the tea, to adding one spoonful of sugar to Andrew's tea to carefully guiding his hand to his cup. "She has done this many times before," thought Rachel.

When they had finished their tea, Sophia, as perceptive as ever said to Michael," I'd love a walk around the grounds, leave your mum and Andrew to talk for a bit."

When the young couple had left Rachel asked in as casual a manner as she could manage, "So, what do you do here Andrew, you and Marie?"

"Well, I, we, encourage our residents to realise that they can still make a contribution, in spite of their condition. We encourage them to learn Braille," he said fingering the books on his desk. "We have a Braille printing press here and as we develop our courses; we print companion books to help. I record on the recorder here," he said touching the tape-recorder "and Marie does the typesetting."

"I can see that you get on," said Rachel fishing for information about his relationship with her.

"Yes, we do, "he replied quietly. "She is very good with the residents.

"And you, Lassie, are you O.K.?"

"Yes, I'm O.K. Andrew, content anyway."

"I imagine the wedding is taking up a great deal of your time, any more trouble from his Lordship?"

Rachel didn't want to mention the recent contact with his butler, it would complicate matters even more than they were already. "No, and I really hope we don't have any more. But we are always on the alert. At Least Sophia now knows what he is capable of." Reaching for the tea pot she poured what was left into her cup. It was cold but it gave her hands something to do.

On her way here today, she had been thinking that one day, not too far off, that she would want to end it with Andrew and how would she do this. But that was before she had met Marie. And if things didn't go well with Nigel she could well be on her own. So, she wasn't going to ask Andrew if Marie and he were close, she wasn't sure if she wanted to know the answer or if she really wanted Nigel, anyway, Andrew was so much more. But now he was fulfilled, he had a purpose once more and an assistant who would be so much better for him that she. And she was in situ. If she were to take Andrew home with her, he would be little more than a pet, shut in all day whilst she was at work. No, she realised that she could be selfish but she couldn't do that to a man who had been so good to her.

"Are you alright Lassie." Andrew asked after a pause.

"I'm O.K. Andrew," she replied quietly, realising that he hadn't asked about coming home with her, something he always did. Perhaps there was something between him and Marie. She had a lot to think about on the way home.

CHAPTER 38

Peggy arrived carrying two bottles of red wine.

"Here you are girl, get them open while I take my coat off."

Rachel smiled at her friend as she took the bottles and made her way to the kitchen shouting back. "Thanks for coming out on a Sunday evening, I'm sure you had better things to do."

Peggy joined her in the kitchen and said "Well, there's nothing on the telly to compare with the continuing saga that is your love life. Also, Ralph wanted to watch the football, so we're both happy."

"You have a good marriage Peggy, I envy you."

"I suppose we have, in a boring sort of way but you can't have everything and let's face it, we have been together so long that we both look forward to bedtime for the sleep these days rather than anything else."

"You mean, you don't, you know."

"Have raging sex anymore?"

Rachel laughed at her friend who was showing the mischief in her face.

"Well, it starts off as a rage but it doesn't last long, he goes a bit limp in the second round and can't get back up before the count."

Rachel's giggles then turned into a full scale burst of laughter.

"I don't suppose you have that trouble girl, do you?"

"Chance would be a fine thing," quipped Rachel, which triggered another bout of laughing.

Eventually, Rachel ushered her friend into the living room and they sat by the open fire with the wine placed within easy reach on a small oak table that had seen better days. The nights were drawing in so Rachel drew the curtains and turned on the two wall lights that complemented the glow from the fire. Both had great affection for each other and the light from the fire gave both their faces a soft quality, rather like an oil painting might give.

"I think we can both still give the younger girls a run for their money," said Rachel. "I mean you can still turn the odd head; I've seen it."

"Mr Melcher you mean."

"Not just him, I've seen men in the Red Bull give you the once over on a few occasions."

"O.K." said Peggy perking up and smiling. "But enough about me, it's you I've come to talk about. How did the visit go with Andrew?"

Rachel's face dropped as she refilled the wine glasses.

"I might have missed the boat there Peggy. He has this lovely new assistant. Marie's her name and she's Scottish."

"How do you mean, missed the boat?"

"Well, I've been too selfish, just thinking about myself and how I would manage with him here, instead of thinking about him and his wishes. Here is a man who loved me to bits. A man who would do anything for me, he even bought me this house, no strings attached."

"You said loved as though it were past tense."

"I'm not sure, but I think I've kept him waiting too long and now he has this new life, a life with purpose and also a very attractive assistant who I could see is quickly falling in love with him. And why not, he is a man who you could fall in love with very easily, even in his present state."

"I see," said Peggy after a pause. "Do you want to let him go. I'm sure if you really wanted him, you could have him back."

"Oh, I really do want him back", replied Rachel lifting her head, "but I think I love him too much to do that to him." she said tears appearing in her eyes, "But what would he do here, shut away in this little house all day whilst I was at work; no, he would go mad with frustration and boredom, he still has so much to offer. I mean to society. No, I couldn't."

Peggy reached over to her friend and held her. "You are a very special lady Rachel, but I think you are right.

Rachel held onto to Peggy for a few moments and then sank back in the chair.

"And then there's Michael, soon he'll be married and go off to live in Sussex or London and I'll be here on my own."

"You'll never be on your own Rachel, "said Peggy quickly. "You'll always have me girl and this fellow, what's his name? the butler man, if you want him."

"Nigel," said Rachel starting to laugh at her friends stumble over her words.

"And I bet it won't be long before Michael provides you with grandchildren" added Peggy, desperately trying to cheer her friend up. "You. should start thinking of names now girl. John for a boy, after his dad and Rachel for a girl."

This did the trick and cheered her friend. "I think Sophia might want a say in naming her children."

"Well O.K., Two Rachel's might be a bit much if you are anything to go by" conceded Peggy.

CHAPTER 39

Fr Larry turned up in his battered old ford. It was evening and the spring light was fading. His arrival appeared almost secret as though Catholic Priests still had a bounty on their heads. Dorothy met him at the front door and guided him into the library where Lady Grace was awaiting him. A cold supper had been prepared and lay on the coffee table by the fire. The couple embraced and sat straddling the fire in the grate.

"You look tired Larry" said Lady Grace after she had had a good look at him."

"I'm fine, I'm fine" he said impatiently in his lovely soft Irish accent. Lady Grace knew he didn't like to be fussed over so she left it at that, observing the end of his dog collar that he had clearly stuffed into his navy-blue jacket. He had a shock of white hair that belied his age.

Dorothy appeared with a large tea pot and sat it on the tablemat.

"It's lovely to see you father, "she said, "Should I pour you a cup?"

"No, no, I'll see to it Dorothy, I see you are still hurrying around like a spring chicken."

"Oh, thank you father, "she laughed, "Not as fast as I used to be though "she added.

"Well, that will make you easier to catch maybe."

Both Lady and maid laughed, showing their enormous affection for each other.

Dorothy left the room glowing with happiness.

"Well now Grace, your lovely Sophia is to marry. That's grand, you must be happy that's she's found a young man who will look after her. I often think of her mother, such an angel of a woman."

"Yes, she was Larry. Happily, Michael, that's her fiancés name, is so different from her father. He is as honest as the day is long and she loves him very much."

"Well Grace, you have always been a good judge of character, I look forward to meeting him. Will his Lordship be giving her away?"

"That's up to Sophia, you know how he tried to break them up, that business in Italy."

"I do, "replied Larry, "A nasty affair. You told me it almost worked but thank God it didn't."

"I'm sure that you had something to do with that."

"Well let's say my prayers were answered."

"Yes, and her mother's too" added Grace.

"Now Larry, I want to know that you're looking after yourself."

"Well, there aren't as many of us as there used to be and we have to stretch ourselves more thinly but Mrs Doyle looks after me well enough, but like the rest of us, she is getting older."

Lady Grace looked at his blue shirt collar, it didn't look as though it had been ironed and his pullover was worn and almost threadbare in places.

"Well, I've put you in the front room, it was Helen's room. The décor is the same as she had it and the floor is carpeted, so you should be comfortable. It has a good view of the lawns and the lake."

Fr Larry helped himself to another biscuit and sank back into his chair." I'm always comfortable when I come here Grace, it has an air about it, a peaceful air and when I sleep my dreams are gentle."

Lady Grace smiled as she touched the bell on the side of the fireplace.

"We'll talk more in the morning."

Fr Larry sighed as he entered Helen's room. "What an angel that girl was" he thought thinking of Grace's daughter. "You certainly work in strange ways Lord."

Leaving the curtains open he looked across the lawns towards the lake and the little island that seemed to float on the surface. The moonlight gave it a magical appearance.

"Sleep well princess and fear not, God and I will keep an eye on Sophia."

The room had a natural fragrance about it and a peace that he had not experienced before. He tried to savour this rare feeling but sleep came over him ever so easily and indeed his dreams were gentle.

A knock on his door woke him as the sun's rays entered the room. It was Dorothy.

"Good morning father, I've brought you a fresh shirt. Lady Grace will expect you for breakfast at 9."

Reaching for his watch, it showed 8.10. He couldn't remember the last time he had been so late to rise.

"Thank you, Dorothy, I'll be there."

As he heard Dorothy's footsteps travel along the corridor he rose to the sound of birdsong and the fragrant smell of the spring flowers left in a crystal vase. "To be sure I've woken up in Heaven" he thought.

The ensuite shower was an added luxury, so much better than the clanking antique at his presbytery which alternately shocked him with freezing and then scalding water. The constant flow of soft warm water felt like a blessing from the lovely soul who once enjoyed the comfort of this room.

Refreshed and free from the arthritic pain in his knee Larry made his way down to the breakfast room where Lady Grace was waiting for him.

"Did you sleep well?" she asked a smile on her face.

"I did," he replied, "ever better than I do when the bishop sends me on a Retreat. Here, prayer is optional," he added with a smile.

"I'm glad Larry, but your whole life is a prayer."

A rattle of cutlery alerted the couple to the arrival of Dorothy carrying tea cups, saucers, spoons, jug of milk, a bowl of sugar and a tea pot.

Fr Larry stood and took the tray just as it started to tilt.

"Oh, thank you father," said Dorothy breathlessly.

"You should have asked Thomas to bring it." said Lady Grace.

"Oh, he's taken father's car into the garage in the village for some repairs and to have the tyres checked."

"That's very kind of him Dorothy, please thank him for me please."

"Yes father, I will, he said it wasn't very safe and he didn't want you to be locked up before the wedding."

Lady Grace smiled at the maid as Father Larry muttered something about not having the time to do it himself.

After breakfast Lady Grace linked the priest and they strolled around the back of the house to the small chapel set in the grounds of the family cemetery. She pointed out her husband's grave under the branches of a great oak.

"This is where I shall join him," she said" when the time comes."

The couple entered the ancient chapel. It was a very simple stone building with oak supports under a slate roof. The alter was a smooth granite block cut many years ago on Dartmoor. The windows were mainly plain glass but at the back there were three stained glass windows depicting scenes from the bible.

"I particularly like this," said Lady Grace pointing to the one showing Jesus with the children gathered around him. "As a small child, I imagined myself as one of them."

"What will happen to this place Grace when you are gone?" asked Larry.

"Good question. As much as I love this place it is a burden what with the upkeep and so on. I wouldn't want Sophia to carry this burden so I suggested to her that she might want to hand it over to the National Trust with the proviso that they allow part of it to be occupied by her and Michael and any children they might have."

The rest of the morning was taken up with discussing the wedding arrangements and after lunch Fr Larry's car arrived back from the garage gleaming, having had a full service and new tyres. After another cup of tea Fr Larry said his farewells with a kiss for Lady Grace and a kiss for Dorothy.

"I'll see you in July then ladies. God Bless."

CHAPTER 40

Tom gingerly collected the post from the doormat as he arrived back at his mother's house after dropping his children off at school. He still had a little stiffness in his back. Amongst the brown envelopes and circulars, he picked out an envelope which was addressed to him. It was greeting card sized but unusually thick and of good quality. As he walked slowly into the lounge his mother asked, "Something interesting dear?"

Tom had opened it and was reading. He looked somewhat quizzical.

"It's a wedding invitation for me, you and the girls from Michael," he said slowly. "I'm not sure," he hesitated.

"Not sure about what Tom?" she asked, an enquiring look on her face.

"Well, it looks like a posh do mum, here, take a look."

Tom's mother put her glasses on and sat in the armchair by the open fire and studied the card. It was beautifully designed and bore a crest she was later to learn was the crest of Sophia's maternal grandmother. It read,

The Lady Grace, Marchioness of Sommerwood requests the pleasure of Tom, Charlotte and Daisy Blunt at the wedding of her beloved granddaughter Sophia, to Michael

Flynne at 11a.m. on the 7th July 1973 at Sommerwood Hall. On the opposite side of the card was a handwritten message written in fountain pen.

"Tom, I'd be honoured if you would agree be my best man on this the happiest day of my life. Michael. Hoping you are well and improving."

"My goodness Tom, you seem to know some important people. It hardly seems possible that this is the same Michael who called for you every day on your way to school."

"It's the same person, mum. He's done so much for me and the girls, I can't refuse him. I've got a bit saved and I'm sure it will be enough to buy a new suit."

"And I'll see to the girls. It will be July and fairly warm. I've had my eye on a couple of new dresses for them anyway, down at the Co-Op."

Tom's mother was beaming. Her face showed her age and the wounds of much suffering over the years, not least when her son had been so badly injured on the farm. But life was now on the up, her son was able to walk again and the girls were now thriving and happy. Yes, there had been hard times but the sun was shining through her face once more.

"I'd better be going mum," said Tom smiling, "My shift starts soon."

"Alright son, take care on that bike, I don't want you getting injured again."

"I'll be careful mum, "he replied on his way through the back door. "See you tonight."

Tom's mum lifted the invitation to take another look at it. Never in her entire life had she seen or felt anything finer. Tom had been so good to her son. She would never be able to thank him enough, not least his friend, the surgeon who had been able to give her son his life back. No doubt it was it was his influence that had gotten Tom his job as a porter at the same hospital. Placing the card on the mantel piece in pride of place she looked back to admire it and what it meant. She would pick the girls up from school later and give them the good news about being invited to uncle Michael's wedding.

Tom enjoyed his job at the hospital, he liked talking to the patients and staff and knew many of the nurses by name. There was one in particular, Nancy. He would bump into her often and exchange a few words in the corridor whenever their paths crossed. She was on the paediatric ward. Tom loved children and when his work took him into the ward, he would pull funny faces as he passed their beds. It was this side of his character that attracted Nancy to him and it was she, not Tom who made the first move.

"Do you fancy going to the dance on Saturday?" she had asked one day, trying to hide a blush.

Taking her aside he replied, "I'd love to but you should know that I am divorced with two young children."

This had taken Nancy by surprise and it showed on her young face: she simply said "Oh, I see." And walked away, fussing over one of her patients by way of hiding her shock.

Equally embarrassed, Tom pushed the now empty wheelchair towards the ward exit. He had been attracted to Nancy for a while but had no expectations of forming a new relationship with anyone, let alone this lovely girl. Her enquiry about the dance had taken him completely by surprise and he had just blurted out his reply, something he instantly regretted. He thought that everyone must have known his history of disability and divorce and that he was distinctly undesirable. But he couldn't disguise the fact that when he thought about it, most people seemed to like him. That evening when he told his mother she confirmed this.

"You are likeable Tom, very likeable", she had said "It's time that you forgave yourself for past mistakes and get on with your life. You are young and healthy again, so rethink what you are going to say to Nancy and go for it, she'd be a very lucky girl to have you."

CHAPTER 41

Nigel was beginning to notice that his lordship's behaviour was becoming more and more erratic. He was becoming worse tempered and impatient. That morning he demanded to know what progress Nigel had made with that woman.

When he had asked if he was referring to Mrs Flynne, his lordship had screamed, "Of course Mrs Flynne, how many whores do you think I know?"

"Nigel struggled to hold back, even though he would have loved to have punched the man. Well, there were quite a few whores in his lordship's life," thought Nigel, but Mrs Flynne was not one of them, she was a remarkable woman, the finest he had ever met.

"Well, shouted his lordship."

"Well," replied Nigel struggling to hold his composure" We are seeing each other and I've a feeling that things are not going well with Michael and Sophia," lied Nigel.

His lordship's countenance changed immediately as he waited expectantly for more details.

Nigel had to think quickly. "Well, they haven't seen each other for a few weeks and Rachel, I mean Mrs Flynne seems to think that their feelings for each other are cooling somewhat."

"Very well then, keep me informed," said his lordship dismissing Nigel with a wave of his hand.

"Very good m'lord" said Nigel leaving the room with a contemptuous smile on his face.

That evening Nigel reported the conversation to Rachel word for word.

"Good, she had said, "he's not so dangerous when he thinks things are going his way. I'd like to be a fly on the wall when he finds out the truth but I think it's best to keep him guessing until after the wedding."

Rachel had asked Nigel to stay for dinner but still she wasn't sure about what she wanted. She was torn between the two men. Andrew and Marie seemed to be getting closer and if she was going to choose Andrew she would have to act quickly before he committed to her. But then she would disappoint Nigel andshe still needed to keep him onside for Michael's sake. Losing concentration, she allowed the potatoes to boil over. Nigel was by her side instantly when he heard her cry out.

"What a mess," he said loudly, here, let me see to dinner, you go and sit down."

Rachel allowed him to take over but strangely this interventionallowed her to make her decision. She didn't want to be rescued. This was her domain and she had always had to make her own decisions about everything and she wasn't about to let a male outsider, someone she hardly knew take over, least of all in her kitchen. Andrew had never tried to control her in any way and it was him who needed her, not the other way around. What was she thinking letting him go, she had never met a kinder man, of course she loved him. There would be a lot to consider, about where they would live for a start, he needed to do the job he had at the Home. She had been too selfish in the past. And no, she would not consult her friend Peggy about this decision, this was something she had to do herself and do it quickly.

Dinner was delicious but Rachel told herself she was not looking for a chef, she wanted a partner, a husband. Nigel sat on the settee after dinner but was disappointed when Rachel didn't join him. She busied herself with the dishes and when she eventually came back into the lounge, he could see that she had something on her mind.

"Nigel," she started "I'm afraid I have something to say to you."

As he leaving, Nigel turned and said, "I'm sorry you feel that you don't want to continue seeing me. I had thought that we had a connection, that it was going somewhere. If you change your mind, you can always contact me via the Red Bull. And don't worry, I won't tell his lordship anything, I may well leave his employ shortly and take my chances on whatever he decides to do."

Shrugging off her feelings of guilt, Rachel lost no time in taking her next step, she picked up the telephone and dialled Andrew's number. A female voice with a Scots accent answered.

"Can I speak with Andrew please."

"He's on his rounds at the moment, can I tell him who called?"

"You know perfectly well who's calling," thought Rachel "It's Mrs Flynne," she replied curtly, "I'll call later" she added before placing the receiver down quickly.

In bed that night Rachel's mind raced, "Marie isn't going to make this easy, she's not about to give Andrew up, I think I might have a fight on my hands." Her last thought before falling asleep was, "I'll ask Peggy tomorrow what she thinks, she'll know what to do."

CHAPTER 42

The following week end, Sophia wanted to spend a quiet few days with her grandmother so Michael went home to see his mum. Rachel was delighted to have her son home and made the usual fuss over him. On the Saturday night Michael arranged to see Tom and the two old friends went into town for a drink. Tom told Michael about the nurse at the hospital, Nancy and about how he thought he had put her off with his blunt reply to her invitation to go dancing.

"I see," said Michael trying to think of some encouraging words to say. In the end he just said, "Maybe when things settle, she might ask you out again."

Tom looked at his friend's face hoping that he could fix it but judging by his expression this looked like wishful thinking."

"I'm sorry Tom, my record in this field isn't good as you know from the things, I've told you about my love life."

Just then Nancy came into the pub in the company of a young man, a very good looking, smartly dressed young man. Tom looked across at the couple as they stood at the bar. Nancy was dressed in a floral dress and a powder blue coat, open at the waist. She looked across at the two friends and after a moment's hesitation she smiled and gave a short wave. Tom returned the wave and then said.

"Looks like I have missed the boat there Michael."

"I'm sorry Tom, she looks really nice. Tell you what if you get to know her, you would be welcome to bring her to the wedding."

Tom spent the next half hour glancing over to see what Nancy and her male companion were doing. She seemed to be enjoying herself, laughing and generally enjoying her male friends company. They left as Tom looked at his watch, it said 8.30.

"Looks like they're going to the dance," said Tom, "The one she asked me go to."

"Fancy going Tom?" asked Michael.

"Yes, let's go," replied Tom already heading for the door.

The dance hall was just across the road and its neon lights spelt out the letters THE SCALA. Both lads felt excited, it had been a long time since they had been to a dance. A group of young men dressed in Burtons suits with bright linings headed in before them followed by half a dozen girls all dressed in bright tops and rock'n'roll skirts. Michael brushed his hair back with his hand just like he used to. Tom was dressed casually in jeans and tea shirt and shivered with anticipation in the cold wind.

"Just like the old days," said Tom as they stood at the top of the stairs leading down to the dance floor. Clouds of cigarette smoke rose to the ceiling as the band played a Kinks song that started with "All of the day and all of the night."

Michael spotted Nancy on the dance floor with her date, she was clearly enjoying herself. A young woman approached; Michael recognised her from his class at school.

"Hello Katy", he said "It's been a few years since we've met."

"I'm impressed, "she replied, "You've remembered me. Are you married yet?" she asked hoping the answer would be no."

Michael didn't answer instead saying,

"I see you are," looking at her wedding ring.

"Yes but no children yet thank goodness, I don't want to be tied down just yet. Come on, let's dance."

Michael followed her onto the dance floor and stole a closer look at Nancy. She was pretty, he thought, and seemed very nice, so different from Tom's ex-wife. Katy danced well and took Michael's hand and rocked from side to side.

"Come on" she said, "Put some life into it, I don't get out very often and I want to make the most of it."

Michael apologised and speeded up his moves twirling Katy around and around remembering how much he enjoyed the rock music. At the end of the dance, Katy held onto to Michael and said "Another?"

Meanwhile Tom noticed Nancy was standing alone. Taking advantage of this opportunity he asked her if she'd like to dance. She seemed to hesitate but then agreed and took to the floor. It was a slow ballad so Tom held her close and the couple proceeded to move slowly.

"I can only have this one dance, I'm with someone." Nancy said looking across to the side door for her partner to return.

"I understand Nancy, "replied Tom "I just wanted to say sorry for the abrupt way I spoke to you at work."

"That's O.K. Tom. Sorry for taking you by surprise that day. Perhaps we can start again."

"I'd like that, he said as the dance ended and Nancy's date returned."

The two lads then had a few drinks and left before the end. Katy had been interested in Michael but he didn't want that. Tom had reset his relationship with Nancy and he was happy with that, hopefully it could go somewhere.
checked thus far

CHAPTER 43

Rachel had asked her friend Peggy if she could visit her after work this evening to discuss a matter of importance. Despite Peggy pressing for details at what seemed half hour intervals, she refused to tell her friend any more whilst they were still at work.

It was 7.30 when she knocked on Rachel's door.

"O.K., spill" she said leaning on the door smoking a cigarette and imitating Lauren Bacall's voice.

Rachel laughed and dragged her friend into the living room. A bottle of red wine and two glasses sat on a coffee table. Peggy sat opposite her friend on an easy chair, she wanted to search her face for clues as to what was coming.

"I've dumped Nigel and I want Andrew back." Rachel announced firmly.

Peggy re-engaged Lauren Bacall. "You don't beat about the bush baby, I like that. So where do I come in?"

"Well, it's quite simple honey," said Rachel taking the part of Humphrey Bogart. "You're going to tell me how to do it."

"That's a tall order, it'll cost you, "replied Peggy, clearly relishing the challenge." O.K., let's see what we've got," she continued "What do we know about Marie?"

"Not very much," said Rachel "apart from the fact that she's lovely, gentle and altogether very attractive and Andrew likes her, likes her a lot."

"Right," her friend replied coughing, "It's not going to be easy, let me think."

Rachel refilled Peggy's glass and waited.

At last Peggy spoke. "O.K., what does a very attractive woman, who could have her pick of any number men want with a blind ex surgeon who is living in a home for the blind in the back of beyond?"

"Good Question," replied Rachel.

She has to be running away from something," said her friend.

Rachel took a drink as she marvelled at her friend's thought processes. "What do you think it is?", she asked.

"My Ralph has a friend in the police, an inspector, I think. I'll get him to ask him to maybe do a discreet background check."

"I don't want him to get into any trouble Peggy."

"Oh, don't worry, my Ralph can be very discreet."

After Peggy had left, Rachel felt a pang of conscience at what she had set in motion. Marie appeared to be a lovely woman and Andrew could be very happy with her, but she couldn't bear the thought of losing him for ever. It was late when Rachel climbed her stairs. It was quiet in the house but the sounds in her head nagged and wouldn't let her rest, but she didn't want to end up an elderly old woman, alone with her thoughts for the rest of her days. No, she had done the right thing and tomorrow she would ring Andrew and set up a visit. It was only then that she felt settled enough to sleep.

CHAPTER 44

Whilst Nigel continued to earnestly search his brain trying to think why Rachel had dumped him so suddenly, he missed the bell summoning him to the study. It was only when his lordship appeared at the entrance to the kitchen that he came to. A red-faced Lord Hazlehurst screamed at him,

"Where the hell have you been Benson, I've been ringing for the last five minutes."

"I'm sorry sir, I didn't hear."

His lordship seemed to stagger and hold onto the wall for support.

"I need you to take me to see my doctor, now."

"Very good sir, I'll bring the car around."

As Nigel scurried to get the car, he turned his thoughts to his employer and how he didn't seem to be himself lately and had been taking rather a lot of painkillers, and there were the trips to the hospital. Yes, he was still a nasty piece of work, even nastier than usual but maybe there is something seriously wrong.

The trip to Harley Street took just over an hour. His lordship said nothing but Nigel noticed in the rear-view mirror that he was holding his head as though in pain. After letting his passenger out, Nigel thoughts multiplied. Yes, he was devastated when Rachel had ended their brief relationship but he still admired her and would continue to care for her even though he accepted that there was not much hope of getting her back. It was about an hour later when a traffic warden was about to move him on, that an attractive young woman in nurses uniform knocked on the glass and asked.

"Are you Lord Hazlehurst's chauffer?"

Nigel nodded and wound down the window.

"I'm afraid his Lordship won't be returning; we are awaiting an ambulance to take him to St Mary's Hospital."

"Can you tell me what's wrong?"

"I'm afraid I can't at the moment, we should know more in a day or two."

"Thank you." said Nigel, "I'll inform his daughter."

It was about 10.30 in the evening as Rachel answered the telephone. Recognising the voice, she started to say, "I'm sorry Nigel I have nothing more to say."

"No Rachel, It's about his Lordship. I need you to contact Sophia, it could be serious."

When Sophia received the message, she considered the possibility that her father was faking his illness just to find a way of reconnecting with her, but her instinct told her that she couldn't take the risk of ignoring it. Her grandmother agreed, but be careful she had said, "We both know that he cannot be fully trusted."

The traffic was reasonably light that cold November morning as Sophia made her way through London to Saint Mary's Hospital near Westminster. The receptionist confirmed that her father was an inpatient and gave her directions to the ward and added that there were no restrictions on visiting hours. An anxious feeling in her stomach told Sophia that no restrictions on visiting times meant that her father was in a serious state. As she negotiated the long corridors, she feared for him in spite of the way he had treated her and her late mother. Perhaps he genuinely thought he had been doing his best for her. Perhaps, he...Her thoughts came to an abrupt pause as she reached the entrance to the ward. A middled aged nurse sat at the desk. She noticed her name badge, Sister Adams.

"I've come to see my father, Lord Hazlehurst." uttered Sophia.

Sister Adams looked up and observed Sophia's impeccable appearance dressed as she was in a light blue tweed jacket. She smiled but retained the serious look on her face.

"He's in the side ward, I'll take you." she said in a cold matter of fact way.

"How is he?" asked Sophia nervously as she followed the nurse between the long row of beds, occupied by men who followed their women's progress with their eyes.

The nursing Sister didn't reply as she quietly opened the door of the side ward and gestured Sophia to enter. Her father lay motionless in the bed, his head heavily bandaged. His face was deathly pale. Sophia sat, trembling a little. She put her head close to his ear and gently said "" Father, it's Sophia."

There was no response.

Again, she whispered, a little louder, still no response.

Sophia sat by his bed with her thoughts for about an hour until she noticed two young male doctors and an older one doing their rounds calling at each bed. As they slowly drew closer, Sophia left the room, gently closing the door behind her and waited to be noticed. As the doctors reached the end of the ward, they turned and proceeded to call at the first bed on that side, ignoring her.

"Excuse me," said Sophia firmly.

One of the junior doctors turned saying softly, "Just a moment Miss, I'll tell Mr Malchard when he's finished with this patient."

Sophia could see the young doctor was nervous of the consultant so she simply smiled and nodded.

As the group moved on, the junior doctor spoke, "Excuse Mr Malchard, I think the young lady would like a word." he said gesturing towards Sophia.

The consultant approached.

"I'm Lord Hazlehurst's daughter, can we speak?"

Mr Malchard didn't show any sign that the title impressed him.

"As you can see, I'm on my rounds. If you can wait, I'll see you in my office when I've finished."

Sophia had observed that many of the patients in the ward looked quite ill and she had no wish to receive preferential treatment so she simply said "Thank you, I'll wait."

Returning to sit by her father she looked up occasionally to check the doctors progress up the ward. As soon as they left, Sophia squeezed her father's hand and walked swiftly after them. A hundred eyes silently tracked her until she left the ward. Emerging onto a broad corridor she was just in time to see a white coat turning the corner. Breaking into a run she managed to catch the group and stood at a respectful distance whilst they continued with their chatting. On concluding his talk with the junior doctors Mr Malchard beckoned Sophia to follow. He had retained a file under his arm and he spoke as he made his way along another corridor. "We'll talk in my office," was all he said as he marched at pace through another door and up a flight of stairs to yet another corridor but this was different with small offices on either side. Eventually he reached a door with a notice on the outside that said "Mr Malchard, Senior consultant Nuero Surgeon".

Sitting behind his desk, he opened a file studying it's contents. Lifting his head to face Sophia, his mood changed from a rather stern consultant to a softer father like figure. He motioned for Sophia to sit on the chair opposite.

"I'm sorry my dear but I'm afraid your father is seriously ill.. He was admitted last evening as an emergency. His doctor in Harley Street suspected a brain tumour. This was confirmed by X-Ray and we had to operate straight away in an attempt to save him."

The colour drained from Sophia's face as she listened in silence.

"The operation was only partially successful, we were able to remove a large part of the tumour but not all of it, it would have been too dangerous to have tried to remove it all. Your father is now in a coma and until he wakes, we are not able to say if there has been any further damage."

Sophia had never experienced death or near death in her family and she felt scared, more so as she had to face it alone.

"By damage do you mean that he might have brain damage?" she managed to ask at last.

"Yes, my dear, I'm afraid that this is a possibility."

"And the remaining part of the tumour. What can be done about that.?"

"As I said, it is too dangerous to remove, it has wound its way into the inner parts of the brain."

"I see," said Sophia with an air of resignation. "Thank you for being so candid."

Standing, Mr Malchard said. "You need to go home my dear, there is nothing you can do. we will let you know when he wakes."

CHAPTER 45

After work, as Rachel was preparing her evening meal for one, the telephone rang. It was Michael with the news about Sophia's father and that he could not now come and take her to see Andrew as arranged, he needed to be with Sophia in case of unwelcome news from the hospital.

"I understand son." she had said as she digested the news trying to untangle her feelings. On the one hand she tried to interpret her feelings towards his Lordship; was she glad or sorry that he was ill? She was no hypocrite so she couldn't feel too sorry or deny that she simply didn't like the man. Even now in his unconscious state, it seemed as though he was trying to scupper her plans to see Andrew, the man she wanted and would have to fight for. A smell of burning interrupted her thoughts, it was coming from the kitchen, her dinner was burning. "Oh hell." she shouted aloud as she grabbed the tea towel and ran to extinguish the flames on the frying pan. It was an hour later as she sat with a large glass of red wine and tried once again to process her thoughts. "I need to talk to someone." She uttered at last. There was only one person she could talk to, Peggy.

As she reached for the telephone it rang.

"I was just about to ring you; I need your advice."

"Before you start girl, I need to tell you something," stated Peggy excitedly.

"Oh, go on then."

"Well, Ralph has received some info on Marie and she is not as lovely as she makes out to be, she has a record."

"Your joking, a criminal record?"

"Yes, she did five years for fraud and embezzlement. She conned a boyfriend out of thousands and nearly conned him out of his house."

"Then, how on earth did she get the job at the hospital?"

"Good question. She probably forged her references."

"We must tell the authorities," said Rachel, "Which brings me onto the reason I wanted to speak to you.

Rachel explained about his Lordship and that Michael couldn't take her to see Andrew.

"Peggy's response was immediate, "I'll take you." she said, "but we must decide what we should do about Marie."

It had been a week since Sophia had been made aware of her father's illness. She had visited him every day, sitting by his bed for a couple of hours but there had been no change. Michael had taken a few days off work to support her and suggested she take a break so the pair drove to visit Michael's mother but she wasn't in. When he telephoned her work, they told him that she had also taken a couple of days off together with her friend Peggy and that they had gone to visit Andrew at his care home.

"I should have rung," said Michael, "It looks like we've had a wasted trip."

"Maybe not," said Sophia, "Whilst we are so near, let's go to father's house. Benson should be at home and perhaps he has heard something."

Sophia felt strange as she drove through the gates of the estate, along the avenue of sweet-smelling cedar trees and up to the house. Michael had mixed feelings, some pleasant about his first encounter with Sophia and the not so pleasant of his first meeting with his Lordship. Benson opened the great doors and smiled broadly as she saw Sophia.

"Wonderful to see you miss and you also Mr. Michael."

"No, I haven't heard anything from the hospital since he was first admitted," said Benson in answer to Sophia's question.

Sophia lifted the telephone in the hall and rang the London number.

As Michael stood rather uncomfortably by in the hall, Benson asked how hs mother was without revealing any details of their brief relationship.

"No change," said Sophia as she replaced the receiver and turned to face Benson. "Whilst I'm here are there any urgent matters that need my father's attention?"

"No Miss, everything is under control. Can I get you lunch?"

"Thank you, Benson, we'll be in the conservatory."

Michael couldn't help observe how easily Sophia took control and the natural way in which she spoke to the butler. "Well, she was born and brought up in this world, a world very different from his," he thought. "How would it be when they were married; she slipped in and out of his world very easily but he still found it uncomfortable in her world. "Be yourself," Sophia always said but it wasn't always that easy."

The conservatory was not how he had remembered it that day long ago when he had viewed it from the outside, but this was winter time and the French-windows were closed and the curtains partly drawn. The grand piano was still there with its stool tucked in beneath it. Portraits decorated the walls and his eyes were drawn to the beautiful lady dressed in a pale blue pastel dress. He had never seen anyone quite so beautiful. Sophia came up behind him and said softly, "Michael, let me introduce you to my mother."

"I thought it was you." replied Michael.

"Yes, everyone says that." And then looking directly at the portrait she said "Mother, this is Michael, my fiancé."

"It was in this room that I first saw you, playing the piano."

"Yes, I know," said Sophia, lifting the lid and pulling out the stool.

She then sat and proceeded to play saying, "This is what I was playing when I first saw you, Michael."

"Moonlight Sonata," said Michael, "I played the record that many times at university I wore it out."

"And what did you think about as you listened?" she asked.

"I think you know the answer to that that question Sophia."

"Come here Michael, "she said without missing a note.

Michael bent his head and they kissed a long loving kiss as Sophia continued to play.

There was a soft knock on the door as Benson entered with a silver tray holding a silver teapot, cups and saucers and a plate of cucumber sandwiches.

"Thank you, Benson." said Sophia.

As he turned to leave Sophia called after him. "Has there been any mail for me since I've been away?"

He thought for a moment and then said, "There have been a number of letters received, your father took charge of them."

"Including those with hand written envelopes?"

"Yes Miss."

"Do you remember any of them, what my father did with them?"

"I assumed he hand delivered them to you or forwarded them."

"Thank you, Benson." said Sophia with a smile and with that he left the room.

"Are you thinking your father destroyed my letters?" asked Michael.

"Yes Michael," she confirmed, her smile turning into a frown.

"M'n, these sandwiches are delicious", murmured Michael as he wondered silently what Sophia was going to do next.

As though she had read his thoughts, she stood and headed for the door.

"Where are you going?" he asked.

"To father's study," she replied firmly.

Hastily taking a further drink of tea Michael quickly followed her.

Making his way along the carpeted surfaces of the oak panelled corridor Michael saw light coming from an open doorway and entered. Sophia was sat behind an enormous mahogany desk. The light from the tall windows that occupied the back of the room shone on her golden hair. The two walls that faced each other were lined with bookcases that reached the ceiling. The wall facing the desk was occupied by portraits of his Lordship painted at various stages of his life. Perhaps he likes to look at himself whilst sat at his desk, thought Michael. Sophia seemed to be searching through the drawers of the desk.

"What are you looking for? "he asked.

Sophia held up a bunch of letters secured by an elastic band and said "These."

Sitting on the red leather chair opposite, Michael asked "My letters?"

Recognising one of the envelopes he stood and pulled it from the bunch. "Read this one," he said, handing it over.

Sophia opened it. It was a letter from Michael enclosing another in a yellow envelope with an Italian postmark. As she read it, Michael studied her face closely, it mirrored her feelings, it was from Lucia to Michael apologising for her actions in Lemoni. Its fragrant pages triggered in his mind the image of the beautiful Italian girl who almost cost him his beloved Sophia.

Sophia lifted her tear filled face and asked.

"Was she very beautiful Michael? She seems to have loved you very much."

Michael reached into his pocket for his handkerchief and gently wiped away her tears.

"Yes, she was beautiful," he said softly but you must know that I could never love anyone but you, you must know that," he said as he held her gently.

Michael B McLarnon

CHAPTER 46

The evening sky was illuminated by a full moon as Peggy wound her way through the narrow country roads. The air was crisp and the lights of the car lit the silvery surface of the tarmac ahead.

"Shouldn't be long now ducks," remarked Peggy.

"I'm getting nervous," replied Rachel, "Do you think we should have rung to say we were coming?"

"And give our friend time to escape?" replied Peggy, "No way, I'm looking forward to seeing her ace when we confront her."

Feeling excited with anticipation, Peggy increased speed hypnotising a baby rabbit that had ventured onto the road. The two women shrieked as Peggy slammed on the brakes and swerved to avoid the creature but then crashed into the hedgerows. As the two women struggled to free themselves from their seatbelts which had restrained them, a car sped by heading in the opposite direction.

"Are you alright girl?" asked Peggy

"I think so but my chest feels like it has been crushed."

"Lucky for us that we had the belts on, otherwise we would have been seriously hurt, "said Peggy breathlessly as she inhaled deeply.

"Also, I reckon that rabbit saved us from crashing head-on with that other car," added Rachel.

"They were really speeding whoever they were," concluded Peggy looking at the smoking bonnet of the car. Looks like we're walking the rest of the way girl."

Retrieving a pair of flat shoes from the boot of the car, Peggy inspected Rachel's shoes. "Good you've got sensible shoes; I wouldn't have got far with my heels."

The two proceeded to walk along the road, pulling up their coat collars and linking each other.

"What do we look like Rachel, two middle aged women walking along a country road in the middle of nowhere on Christmas Eve?"

"I wouldn't want to be anywhere else," replied Rachel softly, tightening her hold on her best friend's arm as an owl hooted loudly making them laugh out loud.

"Wouldn't you like to live out here in the countryside with its sights and smells, "asked Rachel

"It depends," replied Peggy.

"On what" asked her friend.

"On whether there were many shops around here that sold designer clothes."

Again, they laughed and held each other's arms as they walked on.

"Will Ralph be angry at what happened to the car? asked Rachel.

"Not when I tell him it was him driving, "replied Peggy.

"What do you mean Peggy, it was you driving,"

"It couldn't have been," said Peggy, "I've no licence or insurance, remember?"

Not for the first time, Rachel was stunned into silence.

"You can't do that, "replied Rachel.

Peggy was looking straight ahead. "Are those lights?" she asked pointing. "I hope so, I'm getting cold now."

Turning a bend in the road their destination came into view.

"Oh, it's beautiful," said Rachel completely forgetting the driving infringements.

The magnificent building was decorated with multi coloured Christmas lights as were the avenue of fir trees. A dusting of light snow lay on their branches. As the two approached the entrance the snow started to fall once more so as to complete the picture.

"Well, are we going to stand here all night or are you going to ring the bell? "asked Peggy

"I'm scared," replied Rachel. "What if Andrew still wants her over me?"

"Don't be ridiculous," retorted Peggy as she reached past and pressed the bell.

"What time is it?" asked Rachel.

A series of chimes from behind the door answered her question. It was nine o'clock. The snow had gathered momentum and swirled around the couple as they shivered in the porch. The door opened slowly and a young woman in a nurse's uniform and glitter in her hair answered. "Merry Christmas," she pronounced loudly and then, "Are you Carol Singers?"

"We could be,"replied Peggy quickly but then Rachel said "Actually we are here to see Andrew, Andrew Stuart. I'm Rachel Flynn and this is my friend Peggy"

"Oh, is he expecting you?" asked the nurse trying to put on a more professional voice.

Rachel was about to admit that no he wasn't but Peggy simply said "Yes."

"Oh, I wasn't told but I'll just see if he is in his room, he's not in the lounge area. We are having a celebration as it's Christmas Eve. Oh, please step in to the warmth." she said as she closed the door against the intruding snow filled wind.

As the nurse was about to head off, Rachel asked "Is Marie about?"

The nurse turned, a shocked look on her face. "I'm afraid I don't know." she said before hurrying off.

"She knows something, "said Peggy, "Did you see the look on her face when you mentioned Marie?"

Rachel and Peggy stood in the entrance hall waiting for the nurse to return. The sound of a piano playing Christmas Carols could be heard coming along the corridor and then singing voices joining in.

The nurse returned. "I'm afraid there has been an incident, Mr Stuart has retired for the night."

"What kind of incident?" asked Rachel anxiously.

"I'm afraid I can't say at the moment." replied the nurse nervously.

"I need to see him," said Rachel brushing past the nurse with Peggy close behind.

The pair headed for Andrew's room pursued by the protesting nurse.

Rachel pushed open Andrew's door scared of what she might find. It was empty, the bed had been made with the sheet neatly folded back. The curtains were closed. Peggy switched on the light and opened a wardrobe; it was occupied by Andrew's clothes. Rachel opened a drawer; it contained Andrew's undergarments and a fresh pair of pyjamas.

"Where is he? "Demanded Rachel.

The nurse was visibly shaken and pale. "I'll have to get Matron," she stammered before disappearing down the corridor.

"I thought Marie was the matron, "stated Peggy.

"No, she's Andrew's seeing assistant, arranges appointments and the like for his patients who are in need of counselling."

Rachel had met Matron before, she was a kind and softly spoken lady who had struck her as an efficient medical professional, she would know what was going on."

The nurse returned and nervously asked the pair to accompany her to matron's office.

"Hello again Rachel, nice to see you again." she said glancing at her companion.

"This is my friend Peggy. Now matron, what on earth is going on?"

"I'm sorry about the drama, the nurse didn't realise who you were. It would appear Andrew has left with his assistant Marie; it seems they are to be married."

"No, they can't." blurted out Rachel.

"Well, according to current gossip going around the common room that is what they intend to do. Is there any reason why they shouldn't?"

Peggy answered, "she's a fraudster, she's been in prison and we think she has befriended Andrew simply to get his money."

"Oh, my goodness, should I ring the police? Apparently, she and Andrew only left half an hour ago."

"Did Andrew say anything to you about getting married?" asked Rachel.

"Not that I can recall," answered Matron, "It came from Marie."

"In that case, I think that we should contact the police," stated Rachel, "We'll need to tell them the make of the car and its registration

CHAPTER 47

When Sophia and Michael leave for London, Nigel is left alone in the manor house contemplating his future. All other members of staff have long left unable to accept his Lordship's total lack of appreciation and poor pay. Nigel would also have left if it had not been for the hold his Lordship had over him, evidence of the hit and run incident in which a man had died. Nigel had approached his Lordship for help in the matter, he had admitted to it all, unaware that he had been recording his words on a tape recorder hidden inside his locked desk. This was his opportunity to find and destroy it.

The desk was locked, as he had expected. He had often witnessed his Lordship unlocking his desk with a key he took from his pocket. It was old iron key three inches or so in length so he thought that he must have retrieved it from somewhere in his study. He couldn't believe that he would walk around with it in his pocket all day, he was far too fussy about his appearance to tolerate a bulge in his jacket. But where could it be? In a book? there were hundreds in his study. On top of a shelf? Nigel spent the next hour searching through the books and then running his hand along the shelves without success. It was getting dark so he switched on the three standard lamps with their hand hunting scenes painted on the globes. After a further hour's search, he was about to give up for the evening and drew the long drapes across the windows. As he turned, his attention was drawn to a flaw on one of the fine paintings, now back lit on the lamp globe. He approached for a closer look. It was a key, a large key. Standing on a chair he retrieved it burning the back of his hand on the now hot light bulb. He let out a cry of pain mixed with a shout of triumph.

With his hands trembling Nigel inserted the key into the lock and turned it to the left. He heard the triple lock engaging and moving; success, the deep drawer opened revealing several thick files. Placing the first onto the desk labelled Italy, he looked inside. Several photographs spilled out showing Michael in a bed with a beautiful young woman who was not Sophia. Placing them back into the file, he placed the second folder on top, it was labelled Nigel. The third and last file was labelled Bank. He smiled and leaned back on the lush office chair. At the very bottom of the draw there was a spool of tape, no doubt containing the recording of his confession over the hit and run incident. Yes, now he was in charge. He would take his time examining the files and copying the papers that were of interest to him, but not tonight, tonight was to be a time of celebration and relaxation. Placing the files carefully back into the drawer, he locked it before placing the precious key into his pocket. Then opening the ornate drinks cabinet, he selected the cognac and a crystal brandy glass and then sitting in his Lordship's favourite leather chair, he poured himself a large drink and looking at the large portrait opposite, he raised his glass and said, Cheers your Lordship.

CHAPTER 48

Andrew is alarmed at Marie's driving and begs her to slow down. "Where are we going and why at night on a Christmas Eve."

"I'm sorry darlin, it's just that I'm so excited; there I'm slowing down. There's no need to worry, we'll be there soon."

"Where is that, Marie?"

"It's an adorable cottage on the edge of the forest. It's all ready for us. I'll soon have the fire roaring away and we'll be as snug as bugs on a rug. And on Monday we've an appointment at the registry office."

"Registry office, what on earth for?"

"Oh, darlin don't tease, you know what for, it's for our wedding."

"Now please listen to me Marie," said Andrew trying to firm up his voice, "As I said before, I'm very fond of you but I can't marry you."

"Oh, don't be silly," replied Marie, her voice becoming harder. "You have made it very clear over the past few months that you have feelings for me and anyway you owe me."

"I don't deny that you have done a wonderful job caring for me and I am very grateful but I said nothing about marriage."

"Let's face it Andrew," fired back Marie, "No one else is going to care for you, certainly not Rachel in the state you are in. And after you buying her a house, ungrateful bitch."

Andrew was now seriously worried. The car engine screamed as Marie accelerated" Who was this woman? this was not the lovely caring lady he had become so fond of. She sounded completely different and her lovely Scots accent had changed from velvety soft to that of a coarse hard, inner city street brawler.

"Please slow down Marie, I'm feeling frightened. Let's talk."

She didn't answer so Andrew decided not to say any more in case it drove her to even more extreme behaviour, maybe even violence or worse. After some more thought he decided to go along with her so as not to aggravate her even more and to wait until they were in company who could help. Being blind made him so very vulnerable.

"I'm sorry Marie, I do owe you, please forgive me, of course I want to marry you."

Immediately the car slowed and Marie's voice switched back seamlessly to her previous identity. "

"Of course, I forgive you darlin, it's going to be wonderful, just you and me." she said as she firmly gripped his hand.

Trying to relax, Andrew thoughts raced. He wasn't a psychiatrist but he felt pretty sure that she was suffering from Multiple Personality Disorder. He had never seen her like this before, he would have to play along and keep her calm, who knows what she might do.

CHAPTER 49

On her way to the hospital, Sophia recalled the words of Mr Malchard, the senior consultant surgeon. Brain tumour, coma, brain-damage. The ward sister had told her on the phone that there had been no change, her father was still unconscious, but she wanted to see him for herself. She needed to do this alone so had sent Michael home, he needed to get back to work. Entering the side ward Sophia hardly recognised the man who was her father. His face was contorted as though he was in pain and he looked much older than just a week ago. She sat next to his bed and held his hand and spoke.

"I'm sorry father that it has come to this. I wish things could have been different. I wish that you could have just enjoyed life without all the ambition. What was it all for? All the manoeuvrings and complications. Where you ever happy daddy? I wish things could have been different. In my happiness I have forgiven you and still hoped that you could have been happy for Michael and I, I wished that you'd have given me away as I had always dreamed. I'm leaving tonight for grannies to plan the wedding. I know Michael is not what you wanted for me but he is a good man and he loves me and I love him. I don't know if you ever knew what love was father but, in the end, that is all there is. God bless, I am praying for you." And then with a gentle squeeze of his hand she left.

Back at the Home for the Blind Rachel wakes from a fitful night.

"Happy Christmas," greets Peggy as she applies her make up in front of the mirror in Andrew's room.

"What", croaks Rachel, "What time is it, any news?"

"Quite a lot really, Ralph's hopping mad with me for crashing his car and it's still snowing outside. And oh, the police haven't found Marie yet but they're looking."

"I'd better ring Michael and update him on what is happening," stated Rachel, "I hope Andrew's alright; heaven knows what she's done to him."

"Well girl, the roads are blocked so there's not much we can do so we might as well enjoy Christmas Day here. Ralph said he would pick us up when the roads are clear but it won't be today so let's see if we can get some breakfast and enjoy the view, after all it's a lovely place, it's a pity most of the residents can't see it."

"I'll just ring Michael first" said Rachel sitting at Andrew's desk and looking through the window onto a winter wonderland where the snow was falling gently onto the fir trees that lined the avenue and a few coloured lights shone softly from their branches. After Rachel had finished on the phone, the two friends walked slowly along the carpeted floor towards the sound of chatter and laughter. As they entered the dining room matron met them and said they were welcome to stay and could take Andrew and Marie's place at table. No, there had been no further news from the police.

"This is heavenly," said Peggy looking around the room. The large Christmas Tree in the corner was adorned with lights and decorations and underneath a little mound of presents neatly wrapped in silver and gold with labels printed in Braille, there was a present for everyone. Each table was adorned by a red and gold table cloth and five residents were seated at each of the six tables. It seemed that they had been selected by a mixture of age groups, two elderly and two middle aged and a nurse or carer at each. The large windows showed that the snow was still falling. To complete the scene three large chandeliers lit the room and a log fire roared in the enormous grate. Matron joined Rachel and Peggy at their table and did her best to reassure them that everything would be alright. A Full English breakfast was served and Rachel found herself dreaming of a life here with Andrew. She would be his guide and his carer and if he still wanted her, his wife. She would make herself useful to the home by performing any tasks that would be asked of her, admin perhaps or even carer to residents as well as Andrew of course.

Peggy wakes her friend, "Rachel, you are miles away."

"Sorry, I was just dreaming."

"I wouldn't mind betting what about."

Rachel smiled back, "Oh nothing really, but I can see why Andrew was happy here."

The residents were finishing breakfast and the nurses and carers had started to give out the Christmas presents from under the tree. Once more Rachel and Peggy admired the way the nurses and carers looked after their charges, explaining what was inside their parcels and even describing the colours and patterns of the wrapping paper.

"Oh, feel this," said one the nurses as she held a soft woollen cardigan to the face of a resident and described it in great detail. On another table it was gloves, on another slippers, on another a scarf. The excited chatter was punctuated with the sound of Christmas Crackers being pulled and whoops of triumph by the winners of the small prizes inside. Peggy shared her cracker with Rachel saying, "C'mon girl we can't do anything about our situation so we might as well enjoy the day."

"Or maybe the week by the looks of weather" replied Rachel.

CHAPTER 50

When Tom returned to work on the Monday after he and Michael had been to the dance, he couldn't get Nancy out of his mind. Treading the long hospital corridors in the course of his work he discreetly searched for her. He knew she worked in the children's ward but on each of the occasions his job took him there was no sign. In the end he plucked up the courage to ask the ward sister if she still worked there. Sister Kate liked Tom, he was good with the children and had a gift for cheering them pulling funny faces and the like.

"Yes, she still works here but she has been on a course for the last two weeks but she'll be back on Monday." Noticing a slight blush on his face she asked mischievously, "Shall I tell her you asking for her?"

Blushing even more Tom replied, "No, that alright, thanks."

The weekend dragged. Tom had taken his two girls to the zoo but his thoughts were elsewhere, thinking over and over about what he would say to Nancy. Would he ask straight out if she would come out with him? No, he would have to prepare the ground a bit, talk about the music charts or the weather, or his children. No, she wouldn't be interested in his children so much, they would just sound like a responsibility which she could do without. And anyway, she was probably now going strong with the man he saw her with at the dance. He was good looking and likely had a really good job, like a doctor or something. What would she want with me, a porter with two kids?"

But then his thoughts were abrupted interrupted by his daughters, Charlotte and Daisy calling excitingly, "Daddy, daddy, come and see the lions."

Lying in bed that night, Tom's thoughts once again returned to Nancy. At last, he turned over with a final thought, "forget it, there's no way she will come out with me."

On Monday morning Tom had to drag himself out of bed; for the first time he wasn't looking forward to going to work, he had convinced himself that his heart's desire was beyond his reach. But Tom being Tom he soon cheered as he thought of the many blessings he had received since the day he had had his accident. Thanks to Michael's contact, Andrew, he was now back on his feet, had a job and two beautiful daughters. He had got his life back; his legs were getting stronger every day. As he pushed his trolley along, he started to whistle softly. Yes, he had a lot to be thankful for. Lunchtime came rapidly and sitting alone at a table in the canteen he enjoyed his sandwiches and a cup of tea. Feeling a hand on his shoulder, he turned, it was Nancy.

Smiling she said "Hello Tom, I hear you have asked about me."

CHAPTER 51

Meanwhile Marie had arrived at her hideaway and left the headlights on the car so that she could find her way to the front door and insert the key into the door. Returning, she wrapped a blanket around Andrew's legs to protect him from the cold which had intensified in the darkness.

"I won't be long darlin, the fire is made up: I just need to put a match to it and then I'll be back to get you in."

Andrew shivered under the thin blanket, partly from the cold but also from the fear he felt. He thought he had known Marie, but clearly he didn't, what else was she capable of?

Marie stood in the doorway looking into the blackness of the scene. Apart from the car there were no other lights to be seen. She had turned off the main road five miles back and driven along the now-covered dirt track to reach the isolated cottage. It was still snowing and the tyre tracks would soon be covered.

"No one will find us here," she thought, as she brought the luggage in and then returned for Andrew.

"Come on darlin we'll soon be sorted," she said as she guided her captive through the door and seated him on the couch in front of the now blazing fire. Taking a hip flask from her coat pocket she took a swig of the amber liquid before passing it to Andrew.

"Here, take a wee dram darlin while I get us something to eat."

Andrew tasted the whiskey and then gulped it down hoping it would calm him. The cushions on the couch were starting to warm up from his body heat and the fire and the whiskey warmed him and after a while he became drowsy and fell into an exhausted sleep.

The next day, Boxing-Day, was quiet. The snow still lay thick on the ground and it was cold, very cold. Marie turned away from the window and looked at Andrew, still fully clothed and asleep on the couch with a couple of blankets over him. She knelt by his side and whispered.

"Good morning darlin, I don't think we'll be going out today."

Andrew stirred and for a few moments he wondered where he was but then the dreadful reality dawned un him.

"Where am I Marie?" he asked.

"You're with me darlin," she said softly, "Everything is fine, I'll get you up shortly and get us some breakfast. The snow has stopped and with a bit of luck we'll be able to leave tomorrow."

Andrew shivered even though the fire in the grate was now taking hold. It was deadly quiet, there was no sound apart from the crackling of the wood in the fire. The only other sound was Marie humming in the kitchen. He shivered again as she broke into song, "We're getting married in the morning, ding-dong the bells are gonna chime...."

Trying to slow his thinking and not start screaming, he tried to formulate a plan. He would know when she got him into the Registry Office. Once the registrar commenced the service, he would announce that he was there under duress and ask for the police to be called. Yes, that's what he would do, no point in provoking her before then, there was no telling what she might do in her current mental state.

"Just waiting for the bacon to brown, "said Marie returning and looking through the window. The whole area as far as she could see was carpeted with snow and the tree branches of the forest were heavily burdened and hung low. It was a perfect Christmas scene and only a red breasted Robin stirred. "Oh Andrew, I wish you could see this darlin" she said before rushing towards the smell of burning bacon.

Andrew felt helpless. Marie had turned the radio on but the soothing music did nothing to calm him, then the announcer came on to read the 10 o'clock news which contained an appeal from the local police saying that they were looking for a couple in a black ford last seen on the road to Eastleigh on Christmas Eve. The registration was given and the public were asked to keep a lookout for the vehicle and to report it to the police immediately. Marie was still making breakfast and didn't hear it. She entered the room and placed a tray on Andrew's lap and asked if there was anything interesting on the news to which Andrew replied, "No, just reports of blocked roads due to the snow."

"Not to worry darlin, I'm sure we will be able to get through by Wednesday and keep our appointment at the Registry Office. Aren't you thrilled? We'll soon be married and no one will be able to separate us, ever."

"Yes dear, that will be wonderful," Andrew said meekly hoping that someone may have seen them and reported it to the police or that they would be intercepted on the way to Eastleigh. Fearing the police appeal might be repeated he asked Marie to turn the radio off as he had a headache.

CHAPTER 52

Rachel and Peggy tried to make themselves useful around the home as they waited for the weather to clear and for news of Andrew. Each time the telephone rang the pair jumped with alarm and expectation only to be disappointed. Peggy rang home and was relieved that Ralph seemed to be calmer and not as angry about the car. Theirs was a deep relationship, thought Rachel, one she hoped to have with Andrew, if she ever saw him again. The scene outside was very beautiful and under different circumstances she would be very happy being there, it was just the not knowing, would Andrew be O.K.? Would this mad woman harm him if she felt that the game was up. Still no news from the police, didn't they realise the danger Andrew was in?

"I'm sure they are doing their best," said a voice from behind her. It was the voice of her ever-faithful friend Peggy, "They are probably snowed in like us."

"I need to be doing something," said Rachel in reply, "I'll go and ask matron to put me to work, this waiting around is driving me mad."

The weather forecast had said that today would remain cold but that tomorrow it would be less so and that the thaw would start in the afternoon. This brought a feeling of both relief and fear, a relief that the police could resume their search but a fear of what they might find. Rachel tried to block her thoughts and carried on with the work she had been given. It was hardly work, she thought, talking to the residents and resolving their little worries like calling their relatives, a bit of fetching and carrying, and a bit of hoovering and dusting. Many of the residents had had important jobs before being afflicted by sight loss, one elderly gentleman had been private secretary to a government minister and another a Police Detective Superintendent who had lost his sight after having had acid thrown in his face by the vengeful wife of a London gangster. He was comparatively young at 57 but the one she felt for most, was a beautiful young woman, aged about 30,whose life had been turned upside down when she lost her sight completely overnight six months earlier. Matron had asked Rachel to befriend her because she was finding the sudden transition in her life very difficult to cope with. It seemed that her fiancé couldn't cope with the change and had broken off their engagement. Her widowed father had serious health issues and as he couldn't care for her, she ended up here. Rachel drew up a chair besides her in her room.

"Hello Nicola, I'm Rachel, I'm a friend of Andrew's."

Nicola's face brightened as she heard Andrew's name. "Is he here? she asked turning towards the voice, "he's such a lovely man."

She was pretty with brown hair and big wide eyes to match. Her voice was soft with a hint of a Welsh accent.

"No, he's not here at the moment but I'm expecting him soon, "replied Rachel optimistically, looking through the window.

"He's been such a help to me, "continued Nicola, "I don't know what I would have done without him, he's given me so much of his time, teaching me Braille but most of all he's just been my friend when I desperately needed one."

Rachel felt a pang of guilt, thinking that she had not been there for Andrew when he needed her the most. She continued her conversation with Nicola for the next hour telling her about her relationship with Andrew leading up to the time that he lost his sight.

"Andrew's blind?" asked Nicola at this point, "I had no idea, he never said."

"That doesn't surprise me," continued Rachel, "he's that kind of man."

"Marie is a very lucky lady, having a man like him."

"Yes," said Rachel, "a very lucky woman." She couldn't tell her what was really going on, this poor young woman had so much to cope with as it was.

"Do you know when he is to marry? I couldn't bare it if he left."

"Andrew won't be leaving," reassured Rachel. "But Marie will." she thought.

"Now let's get you in bed, "said Rachel tenderly "No one is leaving."

CHAPTER 53

Drawing the curtains in the front room of the cottage, Marie announced excitedly, "It's clearing Andrew, the snow is thawing quickly, we should be able to get away after lunch."

Andrew rubbed his eyes, which were watering from the smoke of the fire that hadn't quite yet provided any warmth to the room. He had spent his third night sleeping on the couch and his back ached.

"Oh, look at the state of you Andrew, all crumpled and untidy. We'll have to smarten you up, You, canna marry me in that state."

Holding both of Andrew's hands she tugged him to his feet, ignoring his cries of pain. An hour later she had Andrew installed in the car and inserted the ignition key. Turning the key, Marie screamed with frustration as the engine wined but failed to start. Anxious not to be stranded here, Andrew suggested she turn the key a little less aggressively. It worked. "Oh, you are clever darlin,"she said as she crunched the gears and started off down the narrow road that still had plenty of snow on it. Reaching the main road she was relieved to see it had been gritted and turned left towards the town.

"It won't be long now darlin, we'll soon be man and wife, "said Marie cheerfully but her mood changed quickly as she saw a blue light flashing in her rear-view mirror and heard the wailing sound of a police siren. Andrew heard the siren and Marie cursing in her natural rough Glaswegian accent and braced himself.

"What would this desperate mentally deranged woman do?" he thought before pleading with her to slow down. She ignored his pleas and accelerated even more. Marie skidded round a bend in the road and narrowly avoided crashing into a ditch. The police car continued to pursue her at speed along the long straight road. Up ahead she saw two police cars parked side on blocking the road. Undeterred Marie increased her speed even more. Fearing for their lives the officers quickly reversed, the one at the rear falling into a ditch. A split second later, screaming her defiance Marie crashed into the remaining police car sending it spinning into the opposite ditch but in the process overturning and skidding along the road on its roof before coming to a halt, its wheels still spinning. The police car that had been following slowed and stopped. The officers emerged to an eyrie silence before radioing for help and rushing to the aid of their colleagues. The wheels of Marie's upturned car had stopped spinning as two ambulances and a fire engine arrived. Smoke had begun to emerge from the engine as weak cries were heard from the interior.

CHAPTER 54

Monday 3rd July 1976, the dawn sun rays travelled rapidly across the land and through the window of Sophia's bedroom and onto her face. She felt the brightness on her eyelids and slowly opened them. This was her wedding day, the day she was, at last, to be joined with her beloved Michael. Opening her window, she allowed the sound of the bird chorus to sweep in and join with her in rejoicing her special day. Twirling in delight, she stepped barefoot onto her balcony and breathed in the sweet air and swept her gaze across the manicured lawns and flower beds filled with spring flowers. All the guests had arrived and were accommodated in Berkham Hall. Why weren't they up dancing in the gardens, didn't they realise this was her wedding day? Laughing at herself she opened her bedroom door and listened. There was no human sound, not a whisper. Of course, there wasn't, it was only 5a.m. It reminded her of Christmas morning when she was a child, all excited wondering if Santa Claus had been yet. Tip toeing along the gallery, Sophia looked down at the grand entrance hall where her mother and grandmother always had the Christmas Tree placed. There was no tree there today but there was a painting on an easel, which one could it be she asked herself. Skipping down the stairs barefooted, she stood facing the painting, it was her aged five being held by her mother. Sophia stood in almost a state of shock. How did this get here? Her father had commissioned it and it had always hung in the library at Hazelhurst Manor. Her nanna had always wanted to have the painting but her father had always refused. Nanna must have somehow got him to hand it over. No doubt she would find out how she did it today.

    Moving over the marble floor towards the great doors she opened one of them and stepped outside onto balustrade and looked over the gardens to the sparkling waters of the lake where she imagined herself as a small child holding the hand of her late mother. A swan in flight approached her and then veered and circled before landing graciously on the lake. A tear fell from her eye onto her cheek as she imagined the spirit of her mother had arrived in the form of this swan to be here with her on this most special of days. Smiling she turned to be met by the loving gaze of her grandmother, looking elegant even in her dressing gown.

"Good morning, Sophia," she said softly, "something told me you would be here my darling girl. Are you ready for the day?"

In reply Sophia hugged her and then the pair headed for the drawing room which was filled with the fragrance of fresh flowers. A young waitress was in the process of pouring fresh coffee at a small table by the side of the ornate fireplace.

"I thought you would appreciate a few moments of calm before the ceremonials," said grandmother sitting. "Also, I wanted to ask you a question my mother asked me the hour before I married your grandfather."

Both grandmother and granddaughter looked solemn. "I simply wanted to ask you if you are absolutely sure that you want to marry this man? I didn't get the chance to ask your mother the same question, your father gave her little choice in the matter. Their marriage was presented to me as a fate-a comply."

"Thank you, nan, for asking me the question, yes I am sure, he is a good and honourable man and I love him dearly and want to spend the rest of my life with him"

"Thank you, my daring, I knew of course, what your answer would be but I had to ask it. I am so happy for you, not least because I have become so very fond of Michael's mother, such a strong and wonderful woman, she reminds me of my own mother. I know you will be well loved and protected by her and Michael and I hope she finds her own happiness, with Andrew perhaps."

"That would make it all so perfect," agreed Sophia smiling.

The door opened and the maid announced to the pair that breakfast would be served in one hours' time in the Great Hall.

"Well, my dear, time to dress and meet your guests" her nanna said

Two days earlier, Rachel and Michael had travelled up together with Andrew and Laura in the Rolls. Peggy and Ralph travelled up in their own car. Lady Grace and Sophia had been busy making preparations for the arrival of their guests. Several rooms had been opened up and prepared. Lady Grace and Sophia had greeted everyone on the steps of the ancient hall. Caterers had been hired for the celebrations, Dorothy, Thomas and his wife Jane were honoured guests for the next few days. Later in the day another man arrived. He was elderly with a shock of white hair, casually but smartly dressed in black trousers, dark navy pullover and black jacket. Lady Grace welcomed him with a tender kiss and hug. She introduced him as Father Larry Costello, "My dearest friend and confessor." He would be saying Nuptial Mass and conducting the marriage ceremony in the chapel.

As the breakfast bell sounded Sophia and Lady Grace entered the dining room that was softly lit by three chandeliers. The assembled guests rose and applauded the two as they entered. Lady Grace seated herself next to Rachel and Sophia sat next to Andrew. The rest of the invited guests sat either side of the long, highly polished oak table. Tom's children who had arrived with him and his mother only the afternoon before, sat with Peggy and her husband.

"Where's daddy," asked one of the children. Sophia answered.

"Well children, your daddy is uncle Michael's best man and he is looking after him until later because he's not allowed to see us until the wedding."

"Why?" she asked.

Sophia was about to answer when the girls' grandmother said," It's tradition dear."

"What's trad...ition?" she stuttered, as everybody laughed.

"I'll explain later" replied her nan.

Outside the sun rose higher and shone on the gardens. The French windows were open and fragrant smells entered. The young girls, Charlotte and Daisy were allowed to leave the table and run onto the lawns, laughing and giggling as they went. Sophia could contain herself no longer and ran after the girls shouting to her guests, "Come on everyone, today is my wedding day come and play and dance with me."

A tear-filled Lady Grace looked on with Father Larry as all the guests leaped to their feet and joined the bride to be on the lawns, running, laughing and dancing. A lone swan looked on from the lake.

The wedding ceremony was scheduled for 11a.m and as the ancient mantel clock chimed 9 Lady Grace clapped her hands which brought everyone to standstill. "Ladies and gentlemen," she announced, "it is time to get ready. Please assemble at the chapel at 10.30."and then looking at Sophia and holding out her hand she said, "Are you ready my dear?"

Sophia stood and was led by her nan upstairs. Sophia expected to be escorted to her bedroom but was led instead further along the corridor to a room she assumed had been closed off. Lady Grace unlocked the door and pushed it open and gestured Sophia to enter. At first, she was blinded by the sunlight but immediately she detected the fragrance of her mother's perfume. As her eyes adjusted to the light she focused on the figure in the centre of the otherwise empty room. It was a manakin holding the most beautiful white wedding gown she had ever seen. It was both magnificent and simple. Silken lemon freesias had been sewn into the hem and modest neckline. The short sleeves were plain white with freesias bordering the cuffs. Sophia turned to face her nan.

"I thought you said I would wear my mother's wedding dress nan.

"This is your mothers wedding dress dear and mine before hers. The dress in your mothers wedding photographs was the one she wore for the ceremony after she was obliged to marry your father. She did try this one on the day before the wedding but she felt she couldn't wear it on the day because of the circumstances she found herself in. No, this is the dress she was meant to be married in and she told me that she wanted you to wear it on your wedding day.

Sophia took a step closer to the dress feeling the material and gently fingered the flowers. She then held it to her cheek hoping to feel her mother's presence. On a small table near the tall windows stood a bottle of champagne together with a dozen glasses. A gentle knock on the door prompted Lady Grace to say, "This will be your dressers my dear, are you ready?"

Sophia, still caressing the dress nodded.

Outside Michael and Tom arrived and went through to the breakfast room where Tom's mother was still trying to coral the children Charlotte and Daisy. "Look who I have found," said Tom as Nancy emerged from behind him. The children screamed with delight as they rushed to greet her. Tom's mother beamed thinking that this was the answer to her question "Would she come to the wedding and complete the family?"

After a few moments celebration the mantel clock struck the half hour which was the signal for Tom to say, "O.K. everyone, it's time. Mum and Sophie take children, Michael with me, we have less than an hour to get ready, we'll see you at the chapel. Tom's mum led the excited children and Sophie up the staircase to their dressing room two doors away from Sophia's. Tom and Michael made their way past the kitchens to their dressing room situated towards the back of the house. It had a door leading outside barely fifty yards from the chapel. It had been requisitioned for the day from the groundsman. Two suits hung on the picture rail, Tom's was a light grey and Michael's a dark blue with faint stripes.

"I was pleased to see Nancy" said Michael, "What did you say to persuade her to come?"

"I asked her to marry me," replied Tom, turning to Michael and smiling.

"What? just like that?" asked Michael, taking off Tommy Cooper with one of his gestures.

"No, like this, "replied Tom in a similar style.

Both lads laughed and then Tom continued, "Well at the time she hesitated, so I said she didn't have to give me an answer straight away and to take time to think about it. We have been seeing each other for a few months now and she loves the children and gets on well with my mother. So, I would like to think that by coming here she intends to say, yes."

"I'm really pleased for you mate, "said Michael.

"And what about you Michael, you've known each other for years now, do you still feel the same for Sophia as you did in the early days?"

"I think so, it's difficult to tell. To be honest I haven't really thought much about it. What I do know is that I was devastated that time when I thought I had lost her over the Italian affair that her father was behind." Michael brushed back his hair as he always did when serious. "What I do know, is that I'd never find anyone else like her and I know she loves me."

"You'll be very rich Michael, especially when she inherits all this," replied Tom holding out his arms wide."

"In a funny way that could be the only thing to get in the way. I've never had a lot, me and mum have had to strive hard for everything we have ever had. We've not been used to have had things handed to us on a plate."

"Maybe, you could start your own business; that would give you a purpose, maybe something close to you heart or Sophia's. Knowing that you have money behind you would comfort or encourage you. But that's for another day Michael, today is your wedding day. That reminds me, here I've got you these," finished Tom pushing a small thin box into his top pocket.

"What is it?" asked Michael.

"Oh, just something for the week end." replied Tom with a mischievous wink and then, "Come on we'd better be going."

The first floor of the house was buzzing with activity. Lady Grace seemed to float between the various dressing rooms inspecting and encouraging. The bridesmaid's room was chaotic, Charlotte and Daisy screaming with delight at the first sight of their elaborate dresses as the giant wardrobes were opened to reveal them in all their beauty. Powder blue material covered in prints of numerous spring flowers from neck to hem falling to the floor. Sussanne had arrived that from Switzerland joined the group. She had been invited to be chief bridesmaid and charmed the little ones with her enchanting French accent as well as Tom's mother and Nancy.

Tom and Michael walked the short distance to the chapel entrance. Flowers covered the archway and their fragrance blessed the two as they entered. Soft lighting lit the church dimly in contrast to the alter which was illuminated with many crystal lights and candles adorned the alter placed at either side of a golden crucifix. A figure in maroon vestments placed a large bible on the ovo and fingered the pages, finally leaving it open at the required page. Several Coats of arms decorated the ancient walls above framed Stations of the Cross. At the end of each row of pews a bouquet of flowers had been hung.

"Wow, "said Tom as he escorted Michael up the isle to their places. Fr. Larry introduced himself saying that he would be conducting the service. Addressing Michael, he looked directly into his eyes and spoke. "Today, Michael," he said in his soft Irish accent, "You will be joining a very illustrious family. I have known Lady Grace for many years and Sophia all of her life. I baptised her hear in this very church. Hearing a commotion behind him, Michael turned to see a troop of about twenty young children in school uniform enter all chattering excitedly. A female figure clapped her hands to gain their attention and then said, "Now choir, say good morning to Fr Larry."

"Good morning, Fr Larry," they said slowly in unison.

"Good morning children," he replied, "Are you all in good voice?"

"They are Father," answered the teacher. "We have been practicing all week for this special day. Now children follow me please." Opening an arched door at the rear of the church she beckoned the children to climb the stone steps up to the balcony. A few moments later she started up the organ and played a few notes.

Michael and Tom looked up at the small angelic faces peering over the balcony at them. Then, the guests stated to enter and take their places. Tom glanced at his watch and felt for the wedding ring in his waistcoat pocket.

"Not long now Michael, are you ready for this?"

Michael who had turned rather pale looked at his friend and said quietly, "Thank you Tom for being here with me. It has been a long time coming. Yes, I'm ready."

Michael's mother, Rachel closely linking Andrew, kissed her son tenderly. Michael had noticed a sparkling ring on his mother's left hand and took Andrew's hand and shook it vigorously. Laura took her place in the pew next to her father and smiled. In the pew behind sat Peggy and her husband Ralph together with Benson and Tom's mother and Nancy. On the other side, the front pew was reserved for Lady Grace and behind sat all the permanent staff dressed in all their finery.

Meanwhile Lady Grace emerged from the grand entrance of the house into the spring sunshine, holding Sophia's hand. On the lawns a few yards from them sat a lone, magnificent swan looking directly at them. Sophia smiled and curtsied low, a small tear in her eye. Sussanne did similarly and the young bridesmaids Daisy and Charlotte tried to copy. And then the cortège proceeded, accompanied by a chorus of birdsong from the hedges bordering the paved walkway. As the group neared the entrance to the chapel a young boy who had been keeping watch disappeared into the church and immediately, the organ that had been playing the prelude Jesu, Joy of Man's Desiring struck up with Wagner's Bridal chorus from Lohengrin. Michael stole a look and gasped at the sheer beauty of it all. The children, Daisy and Charlotte entered first, closely followed by Sussanne wearing an elegant, plain pale blue morning dress. Sophia followed wearing her blindingly white billowing dress. The simple neckline was bordered with lemon freesias. On her head, she wore a crown of fresh spring flowers atop of her flowing golden hair. In her hands she carried a Boquete made up of symbolic flowers, the rosemary representing remembrance, the myrtle an ancient symbol of a happy marriage. the sweet peas a favourite and the flower of her birth month. Close behind, Lady Grace, dressed in a light lilac suit with matching shoes and fascinator pinned on her grey, slightly curled hair. As the procession reached the alter, Sussanne guided Daisy and Charlotte to the side leaving Lady Grace and Sophia standing at the side of Michael and Tom. As the organ stopped playing a smiling Father Larry stepped forward to face the couple. Lady Grace kissed her granddaughter on the cheek before stepping to the side. Michael stared at his bride in awe and Sophia stared back at Michael, the man she loved, with a gracious smile that only she could give.

    And so, the couple were married by Father Larry in a solemn yet joyful ceremony and the two left the church to Beethoven's Ode to Joy to start the rest of their lives as man and wife. Their original plan, formed years earlier

Michael B McLarnon

was to honeymoon at Lake Garda but because of what happened there they switched to Lake Maggiore.

the end

Michael B McLarnon

About The Author

Michael Trelissic, real name Michael Barry McLarnon was born during the deep winter of 1946; a few months after the war in Europe had ended.

Brought up in the industrial north of England by his widowed mother and his beloved grandmother his childhood was a happy one. After the death of his father when only six months old, his mother worked long hours as a paint sprayer in a firm of cabinet makers situated at the far end of the town. As a young boy he would often wait at the bus stop for her return. She would bring him waste offcuts of wood which his imagination turned into model bridges, castles and the like. He invented the first marble run in the mid 1950's, so much more intricate than the plastic versions you see today. He was devastated by the death of his mother at the young age of 55 from heart disease, no doubt brought on by the many years of exposure to lead paints and cigarette smoke. She and his grandmother, who had died a few years earlier, left him a legacy of unconditional love by which principal he has tried to live his life. Some of this is reflected in his latest novel, Sophia. As a child his playgrounds were the chemical dumps and contaminated fields which he shared with his best friend Rod and which his imagination had transformed into the much fabled green and pleasant lands of England.

Michael B McLarnon

Now, at the age of 77, macular degeneration is badly affecting his ability to see and therefore to write, but he continues as best he can.

His other publications include:
Tales of the Titanic
Heron
Fairy Tales for the Cynic

Printed in Great Britain
by Amazon